W9-CHB-542

SWITCHBACK

SWITCH BACK

DANIKA STONE

Swoon READS
New York

A Swoon Reads Book
An imprint of Feiwel and Friends and Macmillan Publishing Group, LLC
175 Fifth Avenue, New York, NY 10010

Library of Congress Control Number: 2018955610
ISBN 9781250221650 (hardcover) / ISBN 9781250221667 (ebook)

Book design by Aimee Fleck
Emoji designed by Freepik from Flaticon

First edition, 2019

10 9 8 7 6 5 4 3 2 1

swoonreads.com

FOR JEAN,

WHO KNEW WHAT THIS BOOK

COULD BE BEFORE I DID.

Janelle Holland, 10th Grade PE Teacher
Sir Alexander Galt High School
Lethbridge, Alberta

Dear Parents and Guardians,

On Thursday and Friday, October 17 and 18, the PE 10 class of Sir Alexander Galt High School will participate in an overnight class field trip to Waterton Lakes National Park. This field trip is a required portion of the outdoor ed curriculum and will involve two day hikes and an overnight tenting experience.

NOTE: Students cannot pass the class without it.

Students should arrive on campus Thursday at 7:30 a.m. with their equipment packed and ready. (See attached list.) The class will leave the school by bus at 8:00 a.m. and head to Waterton Park, arriving at Red Rock Canyon at 10:00 a.m. Students will hike the Snowshoe Trail, have a bagged lunch en route near Avion Ridge, and will reach Twin Lakes campground by nightfall where dinner will be provided. The following morning, students will eat breakfast before hiking the Blakiston Trail side of the loop back to Red Rock Canyon, again having lunch on the trail. Both of Friday's meals are provided. Snacks are not. The bus will return to Lethbridge and drop the class off at the school at 10:00 p.m. Friday.

A total of three teachers will act as class escorts to ensure the safety of the entire class during this field trip. These are: Mr. Karl Perkins, Mr. Ron Barry, and myself. Tents, sleeping bags, and the main meals will be provided, but students should bring a bagged lunch for Thursday and any snacks they might want. Please note: PHONES AND TABLETS ARE NOT PERMITTED. (If your child would like to take photos, they will need to bring a camera.)

Please sign the consent form and have your child return it to the school office before Thursday. If you have any concerns, feel free to contact me directly.

Sincerely,

Ms. Janelle Holland, BSc, BEd
Physical Education Department
Sir Alexander Galt High School

PROLOGUE

"Certainty of death. Small chance of success. What are we waiting for?"

GIMLI, *THE LORD OF THE RINGS: RETURN OF THE KING*

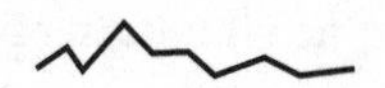

ASH HAD ONLY just dropped his sword, surveying the remains of the battle, when the elf at his side spoke.

"Look there," Valeria panted. "The Dark Lord has sent another wave."

"Another?!"

She pointed with the tip of her sword. "From the north."

Ash turned. One final squadron of orcs poured over the hills in a wave of inarticulate screams and blood-splashed armor. He took position. "I'll just have to stop them, then."

"The other fighters are heading to the gates," she said. "We should go."

"No."

"You'll die here, Ash."

"The orcs can *try* to kill me."

“They’ll succeed. Even the old gods couldn’t hold back so many.” She laughed grimly. “Nor the new.”

He glanced over at her—auburn haired and defiant—and he forced a hard smile. “Then I’ll die, but you don’t need to. Go on, then, Vale. Follow the others.”

“Mmm . . .” She wiped the bloody sword on the side of her pant leg. “I think I’ll stay.”

The orcs grew closer, the dark smudge growing.

He felt, more than saw, the elf take her place at his side. Ash knew there was no way two fighters—even good ones—could stop an onslaught like this. The elf was young. Inexperienced. It pained him that she’d die here.

His fingers rolled over the sword’s hilt. “We need to stop them before they reach the gate. They’ll take the castle otherwise.”

Valeria nodded. “There are twelve,” she said. “But none on chargers. That’s a bit of luck.”

“Mmph. Not enough luck.” Ash lifted his battered shield, sword arm shaking. He widened his stance. Though he was a born fighter, he was tired. Today’s campaign had sapped him. Foot by foot, the orcs clamored and wailed, broadswords lifted as they surged up the hill. Twelve against two. An impossible number.

“Ready . . . ready . . . ,” Ash muttered.

Orcs, like ogres, were by nature impulsive, and most of them came straight toward the two fighters. But partway up the hill, four fanned out. *They’ll head around the side*, he thought. *Flank us as we fight.*

Ash’s gaze flicked to the elf at his side, and his heart twisted. She was here because of him. "I really think you ought to go," he said. "I can hold them off."

"Liar."

"Fine. I could hold them till you reached the gate."

She laughed. "It wouldn't be long enough. You'd still die. And so would I. And they would reach the gate . . . and the others. And the campaign would end."

The first orcs were nearly to the top now. Ash could see their blackened teeth and yellow eyes. He could almost smell the dung clinging to the riders' boots, the blood that soiled their tunics.

"Then we stay and die," he said.

She nodded. "Together."

Ash's pulse surged as adrenaline took hold. The first orc reached them, and he slammed his sword through its chest, jerking it out a split second later. The elf at his side attacked the second. He gritted his teeth and readied for the third.

And so the end begins . . .

Ash looked away from the faces on the computer's screen and grinned. Far away in California, the Dungeon Master, Brian, continued to talk the remainder of the group through their campaign. With Ash and Vale dead (at least until someone could retrieve their bodies and use a spell to revive them), they were free to take a break.

Ash flicked his long black hair out of his eyes. "That was fricking awesome!"

"It'd be *more* awesome if they hadn't destroyed us," Vale said with a tired laugh. "But you were right. That *was* pretty fun."

"See? I *knew* you'd like D&D!"

"Well . . . I think I'd like it more if I didn't die on my first adventure."

"Pfft! That's part of the learning curve. You've gotta level up somehow, right?"

She laughed and tossed the borrowed twenty-sided die onto the couch cushion. "Guess so."

"Besides, we held them back long enough to save the rest of the team." Ash pointed to the computer screen where four separate players talked through the battle. "Marco and Jutta are still going. And Rhys here? He's got the gate closed. They're moving away to—"

"You almost sound like you're *glad* that we died."

"Not glad, no." A tangle of hair fell back into his eyes, and he tucked it behind one ear. "But happy it turned out." Grinning, he glanced back to the videoconference where his teammates across the world braved onward, Vale and Ash's sacrifices giving them the opportunity to carry on the larger campaign. Brian's voice boomed forward: "*With the gate closed, the orcs are finally repelled . . .*"

"We did what we had to do," Ash said.

When Vale didn't answer, he turned back around. She had her coat on and was unplugging her phone from the charger.

"Wait. You *can't* be going home already!" he said. "I want you to get to know the rest of the group." Ash knew if he could just get Vale to stick through another couple of hours, he could persuade her to start gaming again—a goal he'd had forever. "Come on, Vale. The campaign just started!"

"Started?" She giggled. "We've been playing for hours."

"Yeah, but—"

"I've got to go, Ash."

"Just another hour. One more." He nodded to the basement. Vale had seemed *happy* when they'd been playing together. (Happier than he'd seen her in ages.) And though they hadn't gamed together since middle school, he *knew* that she'd love it once she started again. Ash waggled his eyebrows. "I bet Rhys is already making a plan to revive us."

"Ash . . ."

"You watch, we'll be back in no time."

"Sorry, I would, but I really can't."

"Why not?"

"Because it's like . . ." She glanced at her phone. "Ten thirty."

"Exactly. Ten thirty. And you're sixteen, not eight."

She stuck out her tongue. "But it's Wednesday night."

"So what?" Ash stood from the couch. Side by side, the two friends were almost comically mismatched. Ash's head brushed the basement's low ceiling; Vale barely reached his shoulder.

"We have to be at the school *extra* early tomorrow. The bus leaves at eight; we need to be there at seven thirty."

Ash stared at her, confused.

"The trip to the mountains," she said. "Remember . . . ?"

Ash grimaced. "Ugh . . . right. The hiking trip." He'd forgotten, but now that Vale had brought it back up, he felt a weight settle on his shoulders.

"I've got to finish organizing my backpack." Vale headed for the basement stairs. "You ready to go?"

"Um . . ."

Vale shook her head. "Ash, have you even *started* packing yet?"

He grinned. "Uh . . . kind of . . . ?"

"Good. Because tomorrow's not a joke." She reached the top of the stairs and headed to the front door. Ash followed, waiting as she toed on her running shoes. "Two days in the mountains is going to be tough."

"It shouldn't be that bad, should it?"

"Well . . ."

"C'mon, Vale. You hike all the time. You seem to like it well enough."

Vale zipped her jacket before she looked up. She wasn't smiling anymore. "Hiking and outback camping are *not* the same thing," she said, then pulled open the front door. "Holland's arranging meals for us, but make sure you pack enough snacks for yourself, okay? It's going to be a long couple days."

He grinned. "Snacks. Got it."

"Good." She stepped out into the night and smiled. Behind her the streetlights twinkled, the early autumn air just starting to cool. "And don't forget to pack extra clothes. It's going to be cold, especially at night. Bring a hat."

"Uh-huh. Will do."

"You'll need some first aid stuff too. Band-Aids and all that."

"Got it."

"We meet at the school at seven thir—"

"I know, Mom. I know." He laughed.

"See you then. And don't forget what I said about supplies."

"Supplies. Right."

She jogged down the steps, pausing one last second. "Ash . . . you're not going to ditch on me, right?"

He rolled his eyes.

"Aaaash . . ." she groaned, drawing his name out to twice its length.

"You *like* hiking, Vale. I'm hardly the mountaineering type."

"Don't you *dare*." She pointed at him. "I will *kill* you if you skip out tomorrow."

He laughed louder.

"Seriously," Vale said. "I'll literally walk to your house and wake you up if you're not waiting for the bus at seven thirty."

"Yeah, and that doesn't sound crazy at all." He snorted.

"I played your game with you, didn't I?"

Ash smiled. "Yeah, you did."

"And I died *terribly*!"

"So?"

"So you owe me one."

He laughed. "Are you fricking *blackmailing* me to do this dumb hike with you?"

Vale let out an angry huff. "Seriously, Ash, just . . . just be there."

"Will you promise to be part of another campaign if I say yes?"

She shot him a dirty look.

"Kidding!" he laughed. "I'll be there. Relax."

"Good." Vale sighed and shook her head. "G'night, Ash."

"'Night, Vale. Text when you make it home."

"Got it." She waved once and headed down the street.

Ash watched until she reached the corner before he pulled the door closed. He frowned. Ash *hated* the outdoors. He had no idea what food to bring along, never mind first aid supplies. And if they were supposed to *sleep* outside, then shouldn't he bring a pillow? Or a sleeping bag? Wasn't there a letter that went through all that? He sighed, weighing the idea of skipping out. Guilt nipped at him the moment it crossed his mind. Vale *had* come over and played Dungeons & Dragons tonight . . . the first game she'd played in years. That meant something. He grinned. *Now if I can only persuade her to get back into video games too, we'll be—*

A triumphant shout from several of the other players echoed forward.

Hearing it, Ash turned in surprise. "What the . . . ?"

Rhys's voice echoed up from the basement. "*Awesome!*" he said. "*I cast a regeneration spell. Are Ash and Vale still around?*"

"Hold up! I'm still here!"

Ash sprinted back down the basement stairs, ready to rejoin the ongoing battle, Vale's good advice already forgotten.

His team needed him!

CHAPTER ONE

"There are two kinds of evil people in this world. Those who do evil stuff and those who see evil stuff being done and don't try to stop it."

JANIS IAN, *MEAN GIRLS*

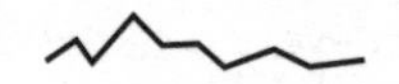

VALE STARED AT the clock, waiting for the alarm to ring.

6:25 a.m.

Dread filled her limbs, the stress that had built over the past few weeks a physical ache. Today was the "outback adventure" to Waterton Lakes National Park. The digital characters flickered and she winced.

6:26 a.m.

Is it too late to claim I got the plague?

It wasn't that Vale *hated* hiking. Quite the opposite, in fact. She loved camping with her family and exploring Lethbridge's river bottom on weekends. She had at least ten nature books sitting on her bedroom dresser. No, Vale's dread stemmed from her classmates.

Barring Ashton Hamid, her best friend since kindergarten, no one in her class even spoke to her. Vale hadn't clicked with *anyone* in the past month and a half since school began, making tenth grade twice as unpleasant as ninth had been. Two days with her PE classmates meant two days of snide remarks. Two days of rude comments. *Two days of hell.*

She opened one eye to check the clock's readout.

6:27 a.m.

Vale pulled the pillow over her face and groaned. *Why is phys ed a course requirement for a high school diploma? I'll NEVER use it again!* Vale had an A average in every other class she was in, but in PE she was fighting to hold on to a B minus. Only Ash, with a dismal C, had a worse grade. "*My epic gaming skills make up for my complete lack of athletic abilities*," he'd once told her. She wished she shared his attitude.

The sound of distant music filtered past her pillow. Vale's mother was downstairs in the kitchen, the radio tuned to a retro nineties station as she sang along to the songs of her youth. From the bathroom at the end of the hall a blow-dryer roared to life. One of Vale's older sisters had started her morning routine. Vale's phone buzzed on her dresser, and she reached out, fumbling blindly. She opened one eye.

On-screen, a text from Ash glowed.

> OMGGGG Can't find the
> checklist. HELP ME VALE!!!

Another text buzzed through before she'd finished reading the first.

WHY doesn't Holland have it on the website?!? WHAT YEAR IS SHE LIVING IN?!!! ☹ ☹ ☹ ☹ ☹ ☹ ☹ ☹
☹ ☹ ☹ ☹ ☹ ☹ ☹ ☹ ☹
☹ ☹ ☹ ☹ ☹ ☹ ☹ ☹

Vale giggled. Ash was in freak-out mode. (Again.) She put her thumb to the screen to type in a reply.

Relax. Sending you the list now. You can handle this. ☺

No! Nooooooo! NOOOOOOOOOOOOOOOOOOOOOO! I CAN'T!

Yes, Ash. You can.

I WILL DIE IN THE WOODS. 😬 😬 😬

No you won't.

I WILL! I haven't even started packing yet!

WHAT???! But I TOLD you to pack when I left! 😠

😮 I got distracted by the campaign.

Then you need to START.

BUT VAAAAAAAAAALLLLE! I don't WANT
to go! 😫 😫 😫 😫 😫 😫 😫 😫 😫
😫 😫 😫 😫 😫 😫 😫 😫 😫 😫 😫
😫 😫 😫 😫 😫 😫 😫 😫 😫 😫

Stop texting and PACK.

With a sigh, she set the phone back down. She glanced at the clock just as the digits flickered.

6:30 a.m.

A pop song blared to life on the clock radio. Vale grumbled as her cat, Mr. Bananas, yawned and stretched, then launched himself from the bed. Mr. Bananas jiggled open the unlatched door and padded down the hall, tail twitching.

Vale groped for the snooze button. "Not today, Satan. Not today."

For five more minutes, she stayed under the covers until a new text buzzed through. *Ash again.*

😧 I'm going to try the sick angle on my mom.

Vale took a hissing breath, her thumbs blurring over the screen.

Don't you DARE! You promised
you were coming! 😣 😣 😣

Vale added a second reply.

BFFs don't ditch BFFs on field trips, do they? ☺ NOW GET PACKING.

With a smirk, Vale sent it off, but this time Ash didn't answer. She stared at the phone's screen for several long seconds. Her smile faded. *What if he ditches after all?* The thought left her struggling to breathe. Ash's attendance track record was less than stellar, and while Vale had many online friends, only one person was there at school each day—*Ash*—and she'd just yelled at him. *What if his mom lets him stay home?*

The bedroom door swung open. "Rise and shine, sleepyhead," her mother said in a cheery voice. A second later, Vale felt Mr. Bananas jump back up onto the bed and walk up her legs. "You've got to get moving, Vale. It's your Waterton adventure. Remember?"

Vale groaned and pulled the covers over her head. "Like I could forget."

Her mother came around the side of the bed, and Vale felt the mattress dip as she sat down. The cat began to purr. "Valeria," her mother said gently. "You're worrying about nothing."

"It's not the hiking that worries me. It's the people." Vale tugged the blankets off her face. "The kids in my class hate me."

"They don't hate you."

"They do."

"Then hang out with Ashton. He's coming along, right?"

She and Ash had been friends forever. He didn't mind that Vale was at the bottom of the high school pecking order, and she never minded that he was a full-time gamer with questionable hygiene. They clicked when no one else did. *But Ash wasn't the only one coming on the trip . . .*

Vale glanced at her phone's screen. *No answer yet.* "Yes," she said with a sigh. "As far as I *know*, he's still coming, but—"

"Stick it out and you'll be fine. It's only two days of—"

"Pure and utter torture. Boys harassing me. Making fun of each and every—"

"There are three chaperones going. Three," her mother interrupted. "If you have an issue with those kids again, just tell someone."

"It's not that simple."

"It is. Teachers are paid to deal with things like that." Her mother frowned. "Honestly, I think you're being overly sensitive."

Vale wanted to argue, but she knew it was useless. Her mother saw high school troubles through the rosy-hued glasses of someone who'd been popular. Vale's mother was a onetime cheerleader and homecoming queen; she'd married her high school sweetheart. Truth was, Vale's mother had *no idea* what actual high school was like. She might as well have grown up in a television sitcom!

"I bet Mike teases because he's got a crush on you. If you paid him a little attention—"

"Mom, STOP!" This was *another* thing Vale's mother never understood: Vale was aro-ace, both aromantic and asexual. She'd told her parents she just wasn't interested in dating any number of times . . . But they never seemed to get it. To them, Vale's sexuality was a "phase" that they were certain she would one day outgrow. Their obliviousness was a raw spot for Vale. "That's *not* why Mike bugs me," she said. "He's a jerk. He always has been. Same with his friends."

"Then stick with Ash."

"I will," Vale said, "but there are only so many times I can listen to a recap of *Outer Realm Annihilation* without falling into a coma."

Her mother broke into a peal of laughter so bright and happy that for a moment Vale could see why everyone loved her so much. Her mother was full of joy. If Vale had been in high school in 1999, *she* would have idolized Debra too.

"Don't sound so grumpy, Vale." Her mother tousled the top of her daughter's hair. "You'll love it once you're out there." She turned back in the doorway. "And if Mike teases you, try *talking* to him, sweetheart. You never know where it'll—"

"Nope," Vale said. *This* was the sort of willful ignorance that frustrated her: The suggestion that she'd fall for a guy if she'd just give him a chance to prove himself. "That's not going to happen, Mom."

"Oh, Vale, come on. You'll have a *great* time with your class."

"I highly doubt that."

Her mother sighed and closed the door.

It was 7:15 when Vale arrived at the school parking lot. With all the excitement of someone on their way to the electric chair, she joined the line of students on the sidewalk. She scanned the crowd, and her smile disappeared. Ash was late . . . *really late*. Perhaps he *had* persuaded his mother he was sick after all. Panic flared—sharp-edged and fluttering—within her chest. That would mean having no one to buffer her from Mike and Brodie's harassment.

Vale pulled out her phone. Seeing nothing waiting on-screen from Ash, her frown deepened.

She typed in a quick text.

You packed yet? I'm already at school. 😮

She hit send and waited. *Nothing happened.* Ash was either off his phone (a scientific impossibility) or not answering his texts. The uneasy feeling in her chest grew. *What if he skips out?*

Suddenly her phone buzzed, and Vale scrambled to check it. A message from Bella waited on-screen.

Just posted my latest aro-ace vlog,
if you want to take a peek!

Vale and Bella had met online two years earlier, when Vale had sought out an online community for support. Bella, living in another city, had been one of the first people Vale had clicked with. Their friendship had kept Vale afloat through her torturous middle school years, and on any other day of the week, Bella and Vale texted almost as much as Vale and Ash did. Today, Bella's support wasn't going to cut it.

Vale tapped in a one-handed reply, then hit send.

Can't look at it today, B. The highlight
of the high school PE program is
about to begin. ☹ ☹ ☹

For twenty seconds there was nothing and then . . .

Wait. You're heading off today??? 😮 😮 😮
I thought your trip was tomorrow!

Nope. Just about to leave. ☹

Sorry! That sucks.

You KNOW it. Forecast says rain. Maybe
even snow. (I have a coat and scarf though.)

Before Bella could reply, Ms. Holland, their physical education teacher, strode out of the school. Vale's thumbs blurred over the screen.

Ugh. HELLand just got here.

Okay. Ping me when you're back.
Have an AMAZING time, V! ☺

Doubtful.

Your friend Ash is coming
along with you, right?

Scowling, Vale typed in a quick answer.

Supposedly-but he's not here yet. 😑

Yikes! What happened???

Looks like he ditched. I'm flying solo.

Sorry Vale! That sucks. 😮

SRSLY. Got to go. The phone
police are on the way.

Vale hit send and slid the phone deep into her jacket pocket as the teacher neared. Around her, other students did the same. Ms. Holland carried a large purple Tupperware container under one muscled arm.

"You know the routine," she said. "Phones out. Put them in the box." A chorus of moans filled the early morning air.

Inside Vale's pocket, her phone buzzed as a new text arrived, but she didn't take it out to check.

"Vale?" Ms. Holland said. "Your phone."

"What if something happens on the trip, and I need to contact my parents?" Vale asked.

"There won't be any reception where we're hiking. Your phone's dead weight."

"What if I want to take a picture?"

"The permission letter expressly said 'no phones.' You want pictures? You should have brought a camera."

"But Ms. Holland—"

"No exceptions."

"But *why?*"

"Because *last time* I led a group on an 'outback adventure,' a student lost her phone in the woods and we wasted four hours looking for it. Didn't reach the buses until dark." Ms. Holland shook the purple container. "Best bet is to leave them here. You can have your phone back when we return tomorrow."

"Fine." With a resigned sigh, Vale dropped her phone into the box.

She stepped out of line just as a rusted orange Honda with a mismatched blue door came to a squealing stop on the street. A disheveled-looking teen tumbled out of the driver's seat. "WAIT!" Ash shouted. "Wait for me!" He grabbed a hastily filled backpack with clothing hanging half out of it, slammed the door with his knee, then sprinted forward, cell phone held aloft.

The tension in Vale's chest released, and a wide grin broke across her face. *Ash came after all!*

If Ashton Hamid had a Patronus, it was an overgrown Great Dane. He was all long arms and knobby-kneed legs, bony elbows and size-sixteen feet. The resemblance extended to his face too. His brown eyes seemed perennially tired, punctuated by drooping lids and sloping black brows. Chin-length hair flopped over his eyes and behind his ears. His clothes—bought to fit his six-and-a-half-foot frame—always looked three sizes too big.

"Woo-hoo! I made it!" Ash shouted as he ran toward the class. "Ms. Holland! MS. HOLLAND! I'm—"

Halfway across the parking lot, he tripped over his untied laces and his bag tumbled to the ground, spewing clothing across the pavement. Kids laughed. (Whether it was intentional or not, he often played the role of comic relief for the class.) Ash grinned as he grabbed his pack off the ground and jammed a dropped sweatshirt and socks back inside, then half jogged, half skipped to Vale's side. Laughter filled the air.

"Nice entrance," she said. "You might get a standing ovation next time."

He did a stage bow. "It's all in the timing."

"Timing, hmm?" She giggled. "I thought it was untied laces."

"They're my signature, you know. Pure class."

Vale laughed "Classy is *not* the word that came to mind. It looks more like you—"

Her words were cut off by a grating voice. "Hashbrown! You made it. Thought we were gonna have to leave without you!"

Vale flinched. *Mike.* On the first day of ninth grade, Ash had dropped a plate full of hash browns in the middle of the school's cafeteria. Mike spent a solid month harassing Ash about the incident and his teasing had spawned a nickname: Hashbrown. It stuck.

Ash turned and grinned. "Hey, man! Good to see ya."

"Figured you were skipping out!"

"Nah . . . just late as usual," Ash said. "You know how it is."

"Not as much as YOU do," Mike said, punching Ash's shoulder.

Ash took a ninja pose, and the kids around him giggled. "What can I say?" he said. "Slacking's a skill. One I have honed through my many years of practice."

"A skill, huh?" Mike snorted.

"Absolutely. Let me teach you my ways, young grasshopper."

Mike cackled as Vale rolled her eyes.

Ash had the gift of laughter. Everyone he met was his friend, even those hardened students who seemed to revel in torturing others. Ash seemed immune. He went along with Mike's teasing—turning the barbs into self-effacing jokes. Even though Vale *knew* Mike was trolling Ash, she admired that the stupid comments never bothered him. She wished she had the ability to do the same.

"Brodie, Ethan, and me already claimed the back seats in the bus," Mike said. "Good view of the girls in the class." He waggled his eyebrows. "You joining us?"

Ash's gaze flicked to Vale almost too fast to see. "Nah, I'm good," he said with a grin. "Gotta grab a few *Z*s before we hit the trail."

"Well, if you're planning to sleep, ain't nothing better than hanging with Valley Girl," Mike snorted. "She's a certified sleep aide."

"Go away, Mike," Vale said coldly.

He laughed. "Or what? You gonna lecture me to death?"

She shot him a dirty look. "I could start now, if you'd like."

Ash's head wobbled, and he held out his arms like a sleepwalker. "I'm feeling sleepy . . . so sleepy . . . ," he droned.

Vale glared. "Not funny, Ash." She *hated* when he went along with the teasing.

"Yeah, Hashbrown! That's how it is!" Mike punched his shoulder. "So you gonna hang out with me and the boys or what? Come on. It's gonna be great!"

"Nah, I'm good, man." Ash dipped his chin. "I'm not kidding about having a nap."

"Your loss, buddy!"

Ash turned back to Vale as Mike headed off to his group of

friends. For a moment, Vale considered telling Ash that she didn't appreciate the joke at her expense, but he was grinning, so she set it aside. Ash *did* hang out with her. *That's what matters, isn't it?*

"So what did I miss?" Ash asked.

"Not much. Holland's got her box and—"

"There you are, Ashton." Ms. Holland stepped away from the other students toward the two of them.

"Hey, Ms. H! Thanks for waiting for me."

"You're late," she said. "The bus is already loaded. Five more minutes and we would've been gone."

"Sorry," he said, hoisting his pack onto his shoulder. "I forgot my phone in the house and had to double back. Didn't Vale tell you?"

Vale opened her mouth to answer, but Ms. Holland was faster. She held out the purple container. "Well, I'm glad you found it, Ashton. Now in it goes . . ." With a sigh, Ash dropped the phone in.

The teacher turned around, balancing the plastic box on her hip as she shouted directions to the rest of the group. "We've got everyone on our list. Time to get on board! We need to get moving, people. It's an hour and a half to Waterton and a half hour after that until we reach the trailhead . . ."

Vale watched as Mike Reynolds crept up behind Ms. Holland, reached past her arm into the open box, and snatched his phone back out with the ease of a practiced pickpocket. Vale opened her mouth to say something, but stopped when he shoved the phone down the front of his shorts into his crotch. She looked away. No way was she telling Holland to look *there*!

A moment later, Vale, Ash, and twenty-three other students were aboard. The first five rows were already full, but Vale guided them toward the sixth. She wanted to be as far away from Mike and his group as she could be. "Can't believe you didn't tell Holland I was going to be late," Ash said as they reached a pair of open seats. "You're supposed to be my responsibility champion."

Vale shoved her backpack under the seat in front of her. "I *am* your responsibility champion. I told you to pack."

"You did, but Holland almost left without me!"

"Sorry about that," Vale said. "Gotta say, I can't believe you were actually late getting here. You live like *three blocks* from the school."

"Hey now. I made it. Didn't I?"

She laughed. "It's pretty lazy to drive, you know."

"Lazy?!" Ash's brows disappeared under his hair. He looked like a Muppet when he was trying to be earnest. "I couldn't let you do the survival-in-the-woods thing alone, could I?"

She side-eyed him. "I thought you were going to ditch."

"Mom wasn't buying the whole appendicitis thing. Wanted me to go to the doctor's office."

"That's the trouble with having a mom who's a nurse." Vale snorted. "Honestly, though? I'd rather spend the day at the doctor's office, and I *hate* the doctor."

"You know what the gamer said when the doctor told him he was terminal?"

"No idea. What?"

"He said: 'Cool story, bruh. But how many lives do I have left?'"

Vale laughed and sat down next to the window while Ash settled in beside her. She peeked over the back of her seat. Mike Reynolds had tossed his pack onto the back seat to stake his claim, but he stood, blocking the aisle, as he talked to a group of girls. Vale rolled her eyes and turned back around.

Ms. Holland shouted: "Seats everyone!" and the bus started.

Vale tried to get comfortable while Ash slumped lower and lower. Soon his long legs were jammed against the back of the seat in front of him, one foot sticking into the aisle. He crossed his arms on his chest, and his lids fluttered closed. Vale kept her gaze on the road as the bus left the city and veered south. In the distance, vaulting peaks appeared, their white-painted tops glittering in the morning sunshine. *Waterton Park.* It was beautiful and remote, one of the most untouched places in North America. For the first time since Vale had woken, a swell of excitement rose inside her. A wide smile spread across her lips.

Ash bumped her knee with his. "What's up?"

"What d'you mean?"

"You're grinning at, like, *nothing*."

Her smile faded. "No, I'm not."

"You are!" He sat up. "Wait. Are you actually *excited* about this dumbass trip?"

"Well, I'm not sure I'd say excited, exactly, but—"

"You ARE!"

She giggled. "I guess I am—at least a little bit—now that I'm not hiking alone anymore."

"I wouldn't *actually* ditch you. You know that, right?"

"Uh . . . Sure, Ash."

"No, really. I wouldn't." He yawned. "I'd at least try to get *you* to skip out too."

Vale smiled despite the anxious flutters inside her chest. "Skipping school's more your thing than mine," she said.

"Desperate times call for desper—" A yawn overtook Ash's words, and he wiped tears from the sides of his eyes. "Measures."

"You okay?"

"Yeah. Just hope I can stay awake on the trail." He smothered another yawn under his hand. "Had a pretty late night."

"More Dungeons & Dragons?"

"Until about midnight, yeah. When we finished up, I switched to *Death Raiders*; played that until a little after three. There was this team from Sweden working against the four of us. We got into the second level in the lab, but then we got ambushed by zombies. Had to fight 'em for almost an hour. The attack—" He yawned again. "Turned out all right, but I need a nap. Can't keep my eyes open." He glanced over the back of the seats to the rows that stretched out behind them. Three back, there was a pair open. "You mind if I move so I can lie down?"

"Go for it, Ash."

"Cool, cool." He gave her a wide grin as he tucked his jacket under his arm. "Wake me up when we get there. A'right? I don't want Holland forgetting me in the bus for two days."

Vale snorted. "You got it."

Ash headed down the aisle as she turned back to the window. The mountaintops were shining with a dusting of new snow, the late-autumn day bright and cloudless. Vale smiled.

Maybe it'll be all right after all.

CHAPTER TWO

"I have a bad feeling about this mission."

MATT KOWALSKI, *GRAVITY*

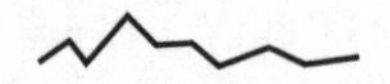

AN HOUR LATER, Vale was regretting the decision to let Ash go to sleep. She'd been the butt of several jokes in the short time since he had switched seats. If Ms. Holland heard, she didn't care. She was up at the front next to the driver, leaving the students in the *Lord of the Flies* no-man's-land of teen bullying.

In the last fifteen minutes, the bus had moved from rolling foothills to the majesty of the Rockies. Golden waves of autumn grass interspersed thickets of yellow-leaved birch, the green splash of pine trees appearing in knots farther up the slopes. On either side of the road, purple mountains with snow-dusted peaks held court, the bus and the looping road dwarfed by their presence. Vale didn't have time to appreciate it.

With her best friend asleep three rows behind her, there was no one to divert the bullies' attention or to distract Vale from her torment. She cast a frustrated look over her shoulder. On the other side of the aisle, Ash's long legs dangled out over the edge of the seat, snores rising and falling with the steadiness of a poorly tuned band saw. It was a scientific truth as undeniable as gravity: *Ashton Hamid could sleep anywhere.* With a sigh, Vale turned back around. Outside the glass, the jagged edge of the Rocky Mountains ran past; she watched the dip and rise of peaks rather than look at her classmates.

Ten more weeks, she thought, *and I'll never have to take another phys ed class in my life. Ten. More. Weeks.*

If Ash was awake, it would have been different. Their friendship kept the tormentors at bay. But with him asleep, Vale became a target. Ms. Holland's class was all jocks and popular kids—

"It's true, isn't it?" a boy behind her said, jarring her from her thoughts.

Vale glanced back, and her heart sank. *Mike.* He'd switched seats at least five times since they left the school, and sometime in the last few minutes, he'd taken position directly behind her. "What's true?" she asked.

"You sent a naked picture of yourself to Brodie Wilson."

"No!"

"Liar," Mike said. "I saw the pic. Definitely you."

"It wasn't. I'd never—"

"You must want him *bad* to share . . ." He eyed her up and down. "That."

Vale glared. She didn't see the appeal of hooking up. It didn't interest her and never had. "Seriously, Mike. I didn't send Brodie anything. I don't even know his number."

"That's what *you* say . . ." Mike took out his phone and pulled up a photo app, scrolling through. "But the pic sure looks like you to me." He turned the screen to show a half-naked girl—her face hidden by a fall of all-too-familiar red hair—as she leaned over to tug up a pair of gym shorts.

Vale's breath caught. Blood rushed in her ears. *Oh my God, that's ME!*

She stared at the image, aghast. The blue panties and emoji-printed socks were easily recognizable, and the striped sports bra was the same one she was wearing now! The realization hit her like a slap. *One of the girls must have snapped a pic when I was in the changing room, then sent it to Brodie!*

Vale turned to stare out the window. "That's *not* me," she said in a hollow voice. *Just ignore him. Deal with it later. Mike feeds off attention. He's just a jerk who likes to bully kids who—*

Mike tugged the sleeve of her shirt, and it slid down an inch, revealing the edge of her striped bra. "Well, well . . . Looky here!"

She jerked away from him, pulling her shirt back over the strap. "Seriously, Mike. Leave me *alone*."

He cackled. "You gonna deny that picture now?"

"I *never* sent it."

"Liar."

Vale's hands rolled into fists, her short nails scoring her palms. "Just . . . go . . . *away*."

Mike clambered halfway over the back of Vale's seat, his face appearing in her peripheral vision. "Go away? I'm only trying to help you."

Vale didn't answer. If she'd had her phone with her, she'd take it out—do *anything* other than sit here, pretending to be mute—but today she had no escape. Her gaze flicked back down the aisle. *Why aren't you AWAKE, Ash?*

A foot bumped the back of her seat. "Yo, Valley Girl. I'm still talking to you."

Vale didn't answer. She could barely breathe!

"It'd be a shame if that photo got around. I mean with you being all hot and bothered for Bro—"

"I'm not!" she snapped. "And I *didn't* send that!" Physical attraction, the urge to make out with, or date, someone—*anyone!*—were things that had never appealed to her. She didn't want sex. She didn't even want to hold hands. Truth was, Vale had exactly *zero interest* in Brodie, but she was *not* going to try to explain that to his best friend.

Mike grinned. "O-ho! Valley Girl's got a temper! I just want to talk to—"

"Conversation requires two participants," she said. "As far as I can see, you're full of it, like always. So why don't you head on back with the rest of the stoners? Leave me alone."

Mike's laughter faded. For a second it seemed like he was going to leave, and then a dark smile crossed his face. He leaned back and shouted over his shoulder. "Yo, BRODIE!" he bellowed. "C'mere a sec!"

"What'd you say, Mikey?" a voice on the far side of the bus answered.

Vale flinched. It was Brodie Wilson, the most popular boy in the school. Vale avoided him at all costs. While it was true he had an aesthetic quality to him that Vale could appreciate in the same way she could recognize a pretty sunset or an interesting flower, he had a mean side that Vale knew all too well.

Mike reached for the sleeve of Vale's shirt again. "I want to show you something!"

"Mike, stop." Vale jerked away. "You delete that photo, or I'll tell Holland you took your phone out of her box."

"I didn't!"

"I *saw* you."

His eyes narrowed. "Yeah? Well, I'll just tell Holland I forgot to hand it in. You think she's gonna remember?" He waggled the phone at her, the half-naked image dancing before Vale's eyes. "You really want the teacher to see what you sent to—"

"I DIDN'T send it!" Vale's voice broke. She wanted Mike to leave her alone. Wanted off this bus. Most of all, she wanted the picture gone! But it felt like *anything* was going to make the situation worse. "You've *got* to delete that picture."

"Not a chance. Yo, BRODIE!" Mike shouted a second time. "C'mere!"

Brodie stood up. "What?"

"I want to show you—"

"Mr. REYNOLDS!" Ms. Holland barked. "You get back to your SEAT! This bus is moving! And you too, Brodie! SIT DOWN, both of you!"

Ash's snores paused, and he scrabbled upright. "I'm up, Mom! I'm up!" The students on either side of him broke into peals of laughter as Ash blinked weary eyes. "Wh-what happened . . . ?" The laughter rose.

Ms. Holland stood and pointed to Mike and Brodie. "To your SEATS! Both of you!"

"You got it, Holland," Mike said. Laughing, he jogged down the aisle to the last row and threw himself into the seat. Vale shot a pleading look toward Ash, but—half asleep—he didn't notice. At the back of the bus, Mike handed the phone to Brodie, who hooted in laughter. Brodie handed it to the boy next to him, and the hoots grew louder. Vale slid down until the top of her head was well below the back of the seat. Tears prickled her eyes.

Ten more weeks, then I'll never have to see these jerks again.

Ash wasn't athletic at the best of times; sleep deprivation made it worse. Struggling up the steady incline, Ash discovered just what a poor hiker he was.

"Y-you go on ahead, Vale," he panted. "I'll catch up."

"Nah," Vale said, smiling. "I'm good right here." She glanced over her shoulder at the teacher who'd plodded three steps behind them the entire morning. "A team always hikes at the speed of the slowest hiker, right, Mr. Perkins?"

The man grumbled rather than answered.

"Seriously, Ash," Vale said. "We're in no rush."

Ash looked up. "Hey! Is that . . . ?"

"The lunch spot!"

"We've got to hike *farther*?" he groaned.

"This is the halfway point," Vale said. "But at least now we're caught up to the rest of the class."

The teens had gathered in an open clearing. Behind them, the banded lines of Avion Ridge formed a ragged edge between sky and ground, a rock wall looming above the trees. Ash shivered. The hikers stood in shadow here, the warmth of the day gone.

"It's colder than I expected it to be," he said.

"Wish I'd brought mitts," Vale said. "I bet we'll have frost tonight."

Ash frowned and zipped his jacket up over his sweatshirt. "It's still hot back in Lethbridge. I . . . didn't expect this."

Vale shrugged. "Yeah. But the weather's always a bit tricky in the mountains in the fall."

Ash glanced down at his runners: slick-bottomed Keds that had never seen anything but pavement until today. "You think we should've brought winter boots?"

"I, uh . . . hope not." She tightened her grip on the shoulder straps of her pack. "Before we eat, we should let Holland know we're here."

"God, I'm starving," Ash moaned.

"Then you're in luck. This is the lunch spot." She nodded to the far side of the clearing. "C'mon. Holland's standing over there by the trees."

They headed across the meadow, passing groups of students eating lunch. A mottled bird that looked like a cross between a chicken and a pheasant burst from the undergrowth. Ash watched it flutter into the trees, then land in the bushes.

"What in the world . . . ?"

Vale followed his gaze to where the bird waddled through the undergrowth. "It's a spruce grouse."

Ash stared into the trees. A few steps away from the meadow, the light dropped by half. "What did you call it again?"

"Spruce grouse is the official name, though they're sometimes called prairie chickens or fool hens."

Ash chuckled. "Fool hens, huh?"

"Yeah. People think they're kind of dumb—the way they let other animals get close to them. They're pretty mellow."

Ash watched it as it faded back into the autumn foliage, the plumage a match to the brown and orange leaves. "How do you know all this stuff?"

"I don't know," she said. "I read things, I guess."

"I know *that*, but where'd you learn the stuff about birds?"

"I've got a couple books on wildlife. Books on the woods, and on camping, and survival, and . . ." Vale shrugged. "I just read a lot of stuff. Okay?"

Ash grinned. "Pretty cool."

"Most people think it's lame," she said with a snort. "But . . . I kind of like it."

"Nah. It's good, Vale. It is."

"Thanks." She smiled. "Now we better hurry up and tell Holland we're here."

They jogged across the clearing. The movement gave a much-needed rush of warmth to Ash's limbs. He had the sudden wish that he'd actually packed when Vale had asked him to, but there was no way to fix it now. He was here. *Stuck.*

Their teacher looked up as the two of them arrived. "Ashton and Vale," she said. "There you are."

Ash slid his pack to the ground. "Sorry, Ms. Holland. I'm not a fast hiker."

"Try to keep up for the second half," she said. "You don't want to get lost. You too, Vale."

"We're going faster than I'm used to." She glanced at Ash. "And Ash here hasn't *ever* gone hiking."

Ash felt a wave of relief, quickly chased by guilt. No matter the situation, Vale *always* covered for him. *But I couldn't even tell Mike and the guys to leave her alone.*

Ms. Holland frowned. "Then both of you should stay near the front. That way you can set the pace and Mr. Perkins doesn't have to wait for you."

Ash glanced over his shoulder. Mr. Perkins's job was to bring up the rear of the group so no one got lost. He'd walked three steps behind Ash and Vale the entire time, irritated by their slow pace. "*We're on a schedule*," Perkins had told them. "*The conditions are good right now, but weather can change fast . . . It gets dark early in the mountains.*"

"I'll try to go faster on the next leg," Vale said. "Promise."

"Good," Ms. Holland said. "Those clouds on the horizon look like rain."

Ash dug through his pack as Ms. Holland and Vale chatted about the changing weather. He pulled out a half liter of Mountain Dew and a crumpled bag of Doritos. Seeing them, Ms. Holland shook her head. "Is that your lunch?"

"Uh . . . yeah," Ash said, scrambling for a lie. "I've got a high metabolism. Figured I should go with high-energy food."

"You certainly have *that*." She nodded to Vale's backpack. "You'd better eat something too, Vale. Everyone else has already started."

"Right."

Vale pulled out her lunch bag while Ash munched on chips. He scanned the open field. This lunch area wasn't a camp per se, just a small clearing in the valley. It had no picnic tables or anything to sit on. On the far side, Mike and his group climbed trees, having finished their lunch long before Ash and Vale had arrived. Ash cast wary glances their way. If the bus ride had been any indication, Mike was in a mood today, Vale (as always) his favorite target.

Just stay over on your side, Ash thought. *We'll stay here. No troubles.*

He turned away from the trio to find Vale still standing. She chewed her sandwich as she stared out at the rocky cliffs to the north. Seeing her expression, Ash frowned. *She looks worried. I wonder why . . .*

"Want to sit down?" he offered. Ash leaned back in the long grass, the contents of his untidy bag spread across the ground. He pushed a pair of shorts that had fallen out of his backpack to the side. "There's lots of room here, and the grass is pretty soft."

Vale gave a weak smile. "Yeah, Ash. Thanks."

She sat down next to him, legs neatly crossed, while Ash shoved handfuls of Doritos into his mouth. Weary and hungry, neither spoke. It reminded Ash of their years in elementary school, when the lunch tables at school had been so tightly packed that Ash and Vale had never had a place to sit. Frustrated with the end of the benches, they'd made a pact. *Eat lunch as fast as possible, then go outside before anyone else finished.* The jungle gym on the edge of the field had been their refuge; they'd claimed the bird's nest on top every single day when the weather was good. Ash poured the last of the chips into his open mouth, then washed them down with soda.

Even then, the two of them had been on the outside.

Ash had just finished chugging his Mountain Dew when Ms. Holland ordered the class to tidy up. "C'mon, everyone!" she shouted. "We've got to hike that far again before nightfall. No time to waste."

Ash groaned. His legs ached, and the thought of going *farther* left him wanting to scream. "Is she fricking kidding me?"

"I don't think so."

"But I can't keep walking! I'm gonna die out here. I'm gonna—"

"Shhh!" Vale said through a bite of sandwich. "Whining's not going to help." She pulled out the second half of her sandwich and stood up. "Ms. Holland . . . ?"

"Yes, Vale?"

"Ash and I haven't finished eating. We're not rested."

Ms. Holland lifted her gaze to the sky. "Then you two had better hurry up. We've got to go."

Ash groaned. "It's not fair!" He threw an arm over his eyes. "Why me?"

"Why *all* of us?" Vale said. "And you should pick up your clothes, Ash. Everyone's tidying up."

"Ugh . . . fine." He gathered his scattered clothes from the ground, frowning as he did a slow circle. "Have you seen my socks?"

"Over there," Vale said, pointing. "By those bushes."

"Thanks."

"There's a pair of shorts on the other side too. Hurry, Ash. We've got to get going."

"Right, right. I know . . ." He frowned. "Wait. Where are the shorts again?"

Vale pointed a second time. "Over there."

"Got it." He shoved the shorts in and tried to zip his pack closed. The zipper caught. "Ugh! I can't—" He tugged harder. "I—I can't get this—" He jerked another time. "Zipper's caught—"

"It's too full." Vale shook her head. "Hold on. I'll help you reorganize."

"Thanks."

While Vale pulled out his clothes and refolded them, Ms. Holland rushed from group to group. "Hurry up, everyone!" she called. "Pick up your garbage. Put it in a sealed plastic bag in your pack so it doesn't attract animals. The wind's picked up, and the weather's starting to change. Let's GO!"

Ash raised his eyes. Above Avion Ridge, a line of dark clouds hovered; an icy breeze blew down over the trees. He shivered.

"There. All done," Vale said.

"Thanks!"

"No problem. But we need to start hiking." She pulled her knit hat out of her bag and zipped her jacket up to her throat. Ash wished that he'd brought a hat. His ears burned as he followed her toward the trail that led into the western forest. In the center of the meadow, Mr. Perkins stood, doing a head count.

"Vale and Ash. Twenty-three . . . twenty-four," he muttered, checking off his list. "Get walking. Try to keep up this time."

"You got it." Ash nodded and tucked his head down.

Vale stuck out her tongue, but, busy with his attendance list, Perkins didn't see.

Ash and Vale were almost out of the meadow when Vale suddenly stopped. "Oh, you bastards," she hissed.

Ash looked up. "What's that?"

"There." Vale pointed across to the trees. In the forest off to the side of the meadow—out of the hawkish gaze of Ms. Holland and

Mr. Perkins—Mike, Brodie, and the others appeared. Ash *knew* what Vale had seen: The mound of garbage that danced in the wind at their feet.

Vale veered off the trail, straight toward them. "Hey!" she shouted. "You need to pick that up!"

Mike turned. "What'd you say?"

Vale stomped toward him. "I *said* you need to pick up that garbage."

"What garbage d'you mean?" Brodie sneered. "'Cause the only trash I see is YOU, Valley Girl."

Ash flinched. He wanted to intervene, but all his jokes had escaped him. "Vale, I don't think—"

Vale jabbed her finger toward the wrappers spinning in circles. "THAT garbage! This is a national park. You can't just leave garbage like that," she snapped. "Animals will eat it. They might DIE!"

"Well, you'd better not *eat it*, then, pig!" Mike barked. Brodie and Ethan howled with laughter.

Ash could see tears prickling Vale's lower lids, and the urge to defend her rose like the tide. He fought it down. "Just ignore those jerks," he said quietly.

The other boys turned to go, but Vale yelled after them. "Wait! You need to come back and clean that up!"

Brodie flicked her the finger. "You two better hurry! Perkins ain't waiting for ya!"

Ash's gaze moved through the trees to the meadow. Perkins stood with his back to them. With the howling wind, he hadn't heard a thing.

"I'm gonna tell Ms. Holland about this, you know!" Vale shouted.

"Ooooooh! I'm so scared." Mike turned to Ash. "C'mon, Hashbrown. Let's head out before Holland flips."

"All good, man!" Ash said with a wave and a guilty smile. "I'll catch up with you in a bit."

"Your loss, Hashbrown!" In seconds, Mike, Brodie, and the others were bounding across the field, leaving Vale and Ash behind in the forest.

"Jerks!" Vale grumbled.

"Let it go. They're not worth it."

"But it's their mess!"

"Yeah, well. We can get it. And then tell Holland about it afterward." Ash stumbled around the clearing, picking up the scattered garbage as the wind abruptly rose, a small tornado of wrappers rising up and scattering farther into the trees, out of sight of the trail.

Vale rushed to grab the wrappers. "Thanks for helping with this, Ash. Seriously. Thanks."

He smiled. "That's what friends do, right? It'll just take a sec."

It took a while before the two of them caught the last piece of garbage. Ash jammed it into a plastic bag. "Here, Vale. Give me the rest. I'll carry it." She handed it to him, and he shoved it into his coat pocket. "See? Easy-peasy." Ash pulled out his phone, checking for messages.

"You . . . you brought your phone." Vale gasped.

"Yeah. So what?"

"But Ms. Holland—"

"Has my brother's busted iPod in her box." His face broke into a wide grin. "I texted you about it this morning."

"I . . . I didn't see your text."

"Well, now you know." Ash winked. "I spent half the drive out playing *Into the Abyss*."

"I thought you were sleeping."

"I was . . . for the first part of the drive." He shoved the phone back into his pocket, pulled on his pack, and headed out of the trees toward the trail. His feet slowed as they reached the tree line. The trail that led to the Twin Lakes Backcountry campground was bare. In the fifteen minutes they'd taken to pick up the garbage, they'd become completely separated from the larger group. Even Mr. Perkins was gone.

"Whoa," Ash muttered. "Where is everyone?"

"They—they're gone." Vale stared out at the open field. Her face went white except for two bright spots of color on her cheeks. If Ash didn't know better, he'd think she was going to cry. She spun on her heel. "Perkins wasn't supposed to leave until everyone was accounted for," she said in a high-pitched voice. "That was the rule. He *wasn't* supposed to leave us. We aren't on the list!"

"But he'd already counted us."

"He *what*?"

"Right before we went into the trees, he counted us. I heard him."

Vale stared out across the crumpled grass of the meadow. "Oh my God . . . they left us behind!"

"They can't have gone far. We'll catch up with 'em." Ash tightened his grip on his pack's shoulder straps, picking up his pace as he headed down the trail. Vale bolted after him.

"Wait for me!"

He slowed as Vale jogged to his side. "You okay?"

"I'm fine," she said. "But we need to stay together. There are dangerous animals in the mountains."

"Like what . . . ?" He snickered. "Fool hens?"

"Wolves and cougars and bears and—"

"Bears . . . ?" Ash gasped.

"Uh-huh, bears." Vale took her place at his side. "So, um . . . let's stick together. Okay?"

Ash nodded and pulled out his phone, then tucked his earbuds into his ears. "You got it. Just lead the way."

For a long time they hiked in silence, the faint sounds of music echoing through the earbuds the only interruption. Vale couldn't identify any of the songs, but they were all epic orchestral themes, as if the video games that Ash played had become the soundtrack to his life. Worried, Vale kept her eyes on the trail.

An hour after they'd left the clearing, a heavy layer of fog filled the valley like a moist blanket. The trees grew into amorphous shapes, mountains gone.

Ash stopped dead in his tracks. He stared into the forest with wide eyes. "Whoa! D'you see that?"

Vale jerked to a stop. "What? Where?"

"There in the trees." He pointed into the forest where the rainy undergrowth grew thick with a veil of gray-white mist. "The haze."

"What about it?"

"Looks like game lag. But like . . . *real lag*. Real-life lag." Ash grinned at her, his brown eyes sparkling. "Like the forest is supposed to be there, but it's not totally loaded by the computer yet."

"That's going to be trouble."

"Why?"

Vale nodded to where Ash *knew* the mountaintops should be, but were no longer visible, caught in an otherworldly lag. "It means we can't *see* the mountains."

"So?"

"So we can't see where we are going anymore."

Ash frowned. "Er . . . yeah."

"C'mon. Let's keep walking."

They'd gone a few feet when Ash bumped her shoulder. "Hey, Vale. I got a joke for you."

She smiled. "Okay."

"What do you do when the world champion of *Scrolls of the Illuminati* knocks on your door?"

"I . . ." Vale giggled. "I have no idea."

"You say, 'Well done, sir!' then pay the man for the pizza!"

Ash cracked up at his own joke, and a moment later, Vale began to laugh too. For a few seconds, it felt like everything was normal again.

"Good one, Ash." Vale's smile faded away. "Now we *really* should hurry. We need to catch up."

On they walked.

An hour after the mountaintops disappeared, the first flecks of moisture dotted their jackets and it began to drizzle. Ash pulled out his earbuds and tucked them into his pocket. He blew on his hands. "You don't happen to have an umbrella, do you?"

"Sorry. Never thought to bring one."

"Me neither." Ash pursed his lips. "How long until we get there?"

"Not sure."

Ash squinted at the misty cloud bank that covered the sky from horizon to horizon. "Should I try to give someone a call?"

"Will Ms. Holland even *have* a phone with her? She's pretty fixated on not bringing devices along."

"Don't know about Holland, but Mr. Perkins sure does."

"*You* have Mr. Perkins's number?" She snorted. "You two buddies or something?"

"No!" He laughed. "But his son, Josh, plays on the same *Death Raiders* squad as I do. I got his phone number last year back when the group of us did a three-night endurance tourney, battling squads from each of the main action levels. Josh didn't want to be interrupted while—"

"Ash." Vale lifted her hand. "Can you pause the story a minute?"

"Huh?" He blinked as if he'd been on a different channel and had just switched back to Vale. "Sorry. Had a bit of a 404 there." Ash grinned and pulled out his phone. "Gotta text Perkins." He thumb-typed in a quick message. After a few seconds, he swore.

"What's wrong?"

"Text messages aren't sending."

"Can you call him?"

There was the low boom of thunder, and Ash looked up in surprise. His face was splattered with heavy droplets of rain. With a swear, he jogged away, taking shelter under a tree. He lifted his phone, hoping and praying for reception bars.

Nothing.

"You shouldn't be standing there," Vale called. "If there's lightning, you could get hit."

He looked up to see her waiting out in the rain. "I'll take my chances." He glanced back down. There was a single band. With a grin, Ash dialed his phone, then held it to his ear. After a few seconds he glared at the screen.

The band was gone.

Ash let out a blast of swearing. *No fricking reception out here!* They were in the middle of the mountains, so it wasn't a surprise—Ms. Holland had said as much—but it worried Ash. He didn't know what to do if he didn't have his phone!

Lightning arced across the sky, and with that the storm clouds opened up entirely. This wasn't the end of a passing storm; it was the beginning of one. Waves of rain fell in silvery sheets. He heard Vale mutter something, and Ash looked over at her from the relative safety of the tree.

"You should get out of the rain," Ash said. "I know Holland said not to stand under trees, but it's not like we can walk up to Walmart and buy a raincoat or—"

There was another crack of lightning followed almost simultaneously by the roar of thunder. Ash flinched. (But he was still alive a moment later.)

"That's it!" Vale laughed.

"What's it?"

"Raincoats. You can use anything plastic to make one." She dropped down to her knees, pulled out a black bag and shook it out. "I've got trash bags."

Ash tucked his phone deep into his pocket as Vale rustled through her pack. "What're you doing?"

Vale tore open a hole at the bottom and a smaller one on either side. "I'm making a rain slicker," she said.

"Out of a garbage bag . . . ?"

"Uh-huh. You want one?"

"Sure, I guess."

A minute later they both wore black garbage bags. It didn't prevent the rain from hitting their faces, but the difference to their bodies was noticeable.

Ash gave her a crooked smile. "Good idea, Vale."

"You say it like you're surprised."

"No, I mean yes. I mean . . . I knew you were . . . *woodsy* and all that. But this is some MacGyver-level thinking."

Vale laughed. "Thanks. That's a compliment, I think."

"It is! This is way cool, Vale! We're totally saving HP this way."

Vale smiled despite herself. "Uh . . . thanks, Ash." She straightened her pack and turned back to the trail. "Now we'd better catch up with the others."

"Twin Lakes should be straight ahead. Right?"

"I think so."

"Then let's keep walking."

Janelle Holland had rarely been in such a bad mood, but today *everything* was pushing her buttons. The bus ride had been awful. She'd spent half of it trying to quell her nausea, the other half dealing with Mike Reynolds and his goonies. More than once, a mantra had risen in her mind: *I don't get paid enough for this crap.*

It was only when the Twin Lakes campground finally appeared—campfires flickering in the distance—that the angry voice inside her quieted. She lifted the checklist from her backpack, scanning through the items. The paper was immediately soaked, her handwritten notes blurring. Around her, kids scattered into the trees.

Janelle looked up. "Go to Mr. Perkins!" she shouted. "Go check in!"

Half the students obediently made their way to Karl's side; the others milled around the smoky fires and the tents that circled them. Janelle gritted her teeth. Outback camping was fun when it was warm and dry, so of course tonight it was raining.

It's going to be a long night.

"Angela!" she shouted. "Trey! Maya! Get over to Mr. Perkins and sign in."

"Britt told Perkins I was there," Maya said. "He already knows."

"You go over yourself," Janelle snapped.

"But Ms. Holland—"

"Do it right now, Maya, or I'm going to make everyone line up again and—"

An ear-splitting shriek filled the air, and Janelle's hand jerked to the bear spray at her side. Another scream rang through the forest. A second later, a sobbing girl—Eden Sanderson—and her best friend came through the screen of trees. Eden had one sleeve of her coat off, the girl's face white with terror.

"What's wrong?" Janelle said, jogging to the girls' side, the student checklist forgotten. "What happened?"

Eden tried to answer, but her voice was hitched with sobs. Janelle turned to the teen next to her. "Drea. Tell me what happened!"

"There's a spider on her," Drea said. "It won't come off!"

Janelle's heart sank as she looked down at Eden's arm. Sure enough, the bug was firmly attached, eight legs tucked under itself, its face securely attached as its abdomen ballooned with blood.

"It's not a spider," she said grimly. "It's a tick."

"A tick?!" Eden shrieked.

"Relax," Janelle said. "I'll get it off, and we'll save it for testing when we get back to Lethbridge." A group of students gathered around her in macabre interest. "Back up," she snapped. "Go check in with Mr. Perkins!"

"I can't find him," one student said.

"Me neither," another added.

Janelle looked up. Students milled around the campground, Karl Perkins nowhere to be seen. Beyond the tents, the fog was so dense it looked like they were on the coast of British Columbia where Janelle had grown up. Rain fell in sheets, the temperature dropping. *If it keeps up, we're going to have snow too.* Over at the far side of the fire, the third instructor crouched, his hands held out to the flames.

Frustration rose inside Janelle. "Mr. Barry!" she shouted. "I need a med kit over here. Hurry!" She looked down at the tick embedded in the girl's skin. "Of all the days . . ."

Counting students would have to wait until later.

CHAPTER THREE

"I'm not gonna lose you too."

CHIEF RAY GAINES, *SAN ANDREAS*

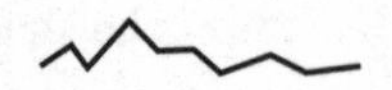

ASHTON HAMID *HATED* HIKING. He hated the woods. Hated the whole insistence on "real-life experiences" and "survival" and "nature" in general. He took another step, wincing as the blister on his heel throbbed. *THIS is why I prefer VR!* The trees grew close together here, and the trail on which he and Vale hiked wove between them like a ribbon. He squinted into the forest. If Vale wasn't leading, he'd have no idea where to go. The trail was little more than a muddy path.

At least one of us knows what she's doing.

With Vale's auburn hair pulled back into a sensible ponytail and her cheeks flushed with color, she looked younger than sixteen, the spray of freckles over her nose as clear as it had been in kindergarten.

Vale caught his eye. "What are you staring at?"

Ash blinked. "Wait . . . What?"

"You're staring, Ash. What's up?" She wiped a string of hair away from her cheek. "Do I have something on my face?"

"I . . . no. It's nothing."

"If it's a booger, Ash, just say it." She rubbed vigorously from chin to forehead. "I can hardly feel my nose."

He snorted happily. "It's *not*. I would've taken a picture if it was."

Vale giggled. "Jerk."

"Takes one to know one." He turned back to the muddy trail, his laughter fading. "Just hoping we reach the campground soon."

"God . . . Me too."

With the weather as bad as it was, Ash knew he and Vale wouldn't arrive until nightfall. There'd be no time for hanging out and telling stories. No time for a campfire. *We might not even get supper!* Ash's stomach growled in protest. He hunched his shoulders and walked faster.

Up ahead the forest thickened. In the past few hours, the rain had grown heavy and rivulets now crisscrossed the trail. Ash jumped across. A moment later, Vale splashed through the puddle.

"Can you wait a sec?" she said. "I . . . I need a break."

He glanced back. Vale had fallen ten steps behind him and had one hand pressed to her side, her face tight with pain.

Ash's stomach dropped. "Geez! You okay, Vale?" He took two splashing steps back to her side. "Did you hurt yourself? Pull a muscle?"

"No, I—"

"Is your back sore? You need me to carry your bag or piggyback you or—"

"No, Ash," she said with a tired laugh. "I'm fine."

"But—"

"I've just got a stitch in my side. I need a break."

Ash let out a relieved sigh. "That I can do."

While they rested, he searched for landmarks. The mountains they'd walked into were gone, a hazy gray ceiling of storm clouds in their place. It gave him the unsettling feeling of being caught inside a box. Ash turned and looked back the other direction. His attention caught on the forked top of a pine tree, and he frowned. *What in the world . . . ? That looks like the same tree we passed fifteen minutes ago.* It felt for a moment like he was in a poorly designed game and had just come across a repeating landscape. His gaze dropped down to the part of the path they'd just passed. His stomach churned uneasily. The trail was a faded smudge, the line of it almost too faint to follow in the gathering darkness, but there was a small outcrop of rocks in the trees that *also* looked familiar.

His attention jumped back to the pronged top of the branches. "What the . . . ?"

"Something wrong?"

Ash nodded to the forked tree. "Does that tree over there look familiar to you?"

"Which one?"

"That tree. The one there with the split top. I . . . I think that I might have seen that one before."

"Like, another tree, on another hike?"

"I *don't* hike, Vale," he said with a snort. "No, I mean, like, today."

"But . . . we didn't come this way before."

"You sure?"

"We're walking straight. Following the path to Twin Lakes. We're . . ." Vale scanned the trees. Her eyes came to rest on the rocky outcrop, and the blood drained from her face.

"What?"

She caught his eyes. "*Did* we come this way before?"

"I dunno."

"But you pointed out the tree."

Ash's heart began to pound, palms growing sweaty. "I'm the one asking *you*, Vale. So, do you recognize it or not?"

"I . . . no. I don't think I've seen it before."

"But are you *sure*?"

"Not sure, no. But I . . ." Vale chewed her lip. "I don't think so . . . ?"

Long seconds passed. Ash peered up at the forked treetop again. *Maybe that's just how those trees grow. How would I know? I'm no expert.* He looked back to Vale, staring out at the forest. The trail waited, growing muddier by the second. "Well, if you didn't see it before," he said, "then it probably just looks weird, right?"

Vale nodded. "Yeah."

"You good to go now?"

Vale tugged the knit hat lower and pulled the strings on her jacket's hood to tighten it around her chin. "As ready as I'll ever be."

"Good. 'Cause I'm starving and I don't have any chips left."

Vale laughed tiredly. "Priorities."

"You *know* it."

And they walked again.

It had taken Janelle Holland almost an hour before she realized anything was wrong. Once she'd removed the tick from Eden's arm, she'd rechecked the class list. That's when she discovered neither Ash nor Vale were on it. Confused, she'd been about to do another head count when Owen Roast had come running toward her.

"Ms. Holland!" he shouted. "Ms. Holland, I got something on my legs!"

Janelle shoved the list back in her pocket. "What happened now?"

"I was in the woods," he said, gesturing to the angry red welts that crisscrossed his bare calves, "and I must have stepped in something. It itches like crazy."

She crouched at his side, inspecting the raised skin. "Stinging nettles," she sighed. "Hold on. I'll find you the Benadryl."

"But it stings!"

"I've got some antibiotic cream too." Owen reached down, but Janelle grabbed his hand before he could touch the skin. "And *stop* scratching it, Owen."

"A'right."

Five minutes later, she had the boy patched up and she tried, yet again, to confirm the class list. "Karl!" she shouted. "Can you double-check on the students? I still haven't seen Ash and Vale since we arrived."

"Pretty sure they're here," he said. "I had them on my list at lunch."

"But have you seen them since?"

"Uh . . . I don't think so." He frowned. "I'll find them."

"Thanks."

There were a myriad of challenges that came with controlling a group of teenagers. One by one, Janelle worked through them, frustrated by the worsening weather. The fires were piled high with wood, but it was cold all the same, and the students were unhappy. *Herding cats*, she thought as Karl Perkins walked up to her. *Get one going the right direction and the rest scatter.*

Janelle frowned as he reached her side. "You locate Vale and Ash yet?" she asked.

Karl shook his head. "No, not yet."

"But—"

"I talked to Mike Reynolds, though."

Janelle's jaw clenched. If Reynolds was involved, there was bound to be drama. It was hardwired into the boy's DNA. "And what did Mike say?"

"He says that the last time he saw Vale and Ash, they were picking up garbage at the meadow."

Janelle blinked. "But that was back at lunchtime."

"Yeah, it was."

"That can't be when we lost them."

Karl dropped his gaze to stare at his feet. "I . . . I think it was."

The fear Janelle had been fighting for the past hour surged with his words. "But you were bringing up the rear of the group," she said. "There's no *way* those kids could have stayed behind if—"

Karl looked up. "I didn't check the trees. I . . . I'm sorry."

Janelle felt the ground beneath her shift, fear hitting her with the strength of a truck. *How did I let this happen?* "You didn't check?!"

"They were on the list; I figured they were already in line."

"But you were supposed to check the *trees*, Karl!"

"Sorry, Janelle. I was the last person in line, and I followed the main group out. I assumed that we had everyone on the list . . ." He winced. "I should have checked the tree line, but I thought we were all together."

"So did I."

"So, what do we do now?"

Panic pulsed beneath Janelle's skin. *Oh my God, oh my God, oh my God!* With shaking fingers, she pulled a flashlight from her pocket. "You stay here," she said. "I'm going back to look for them."

"But it's almost nightfall."

Janelle headed toward the trail. "It is."

"You'll be hiking in the dark!" he shouted.

"Uh-huh."

"There are bears out here, Janelle. It's not safe!"

She glanced back. "I know. But we've got two kids out there too."

For another hour, Vale and Ash walked, damp cold leaching into their bones. They shouted for help, but no one answered. Vale was beyond tired. Her feet moved on instinct, her mind circling a fear she was only now starting to name. *It's my fault we fell behind. I was the one who'd insisted on picking up the garbage. I made us late.*

Exhausted, Vale stumbled on numbed feet. Ash caught hold of her arm, steadying her before she hit the ground. They stood in an unfamiliar forest, the trail a charcoal line that ran away into the darkness on either side of the two of them.

"We got to keep moving," Ash panted.

"I—I just need a minute."

"What's wrong?"

"M-my feet," Vale said. "They're freezing. C-can hardly feel my toes. We should stop."

"Stop for *what*? There's nothing here! There's just trees and rain and—"

"I think we should wait for someone to find us."

"What?"

Vale cringed. "I—I don't know where we are anymore, Ash. No one came when we called for help."

"So that's it, then!" He kicked at a rock on the trail, and it skittered into the grass. "We're LOST in the mountains! Well, that's just fricking great!"

Vale winced. "Someone will find us. We can't be *that* off track. Right?"

Ash tucked his hands under his armpits. "How would I know? I've never even *hiked* here before!"

"Neither have I, but we were halfway to Twin Lakes when we stopped for lunch. That was a good four hours ago or more. We *should* be close . . . I think."

"You *think*? Why don't you KNOW?"

"Because I haven't hiked here before. So don't yell at *me* about it." Vale turned away from him, blinking back tears. "We missed the trail somehow," she whispered. "We've been walking for hours. We're obviously too far away for them to hear us, and we're on a trail, but not the *right* one."

"There's a couple places where the path forks off into the woods a ways back," Ash said, "but no signposts. I've got to be honest. I'm not even sure we're following an *actual* trail anymore. I think this might be a . . ."

"A game trail?" Vale offered.

"Yeah, exactly. I think we somehow got onto a game trail. So can we go back the way we came? Follow our tracks until we find the right trail again?"

"Not right now, Ash. It's too dark."

"So what? We just stay here?"

"For now."

"But where *are* we?"

Vale's heart pounded as she lifted her eyes to the foggy forest that surrounded them. It was like an image from a movie. Swirls of mist wove around their feet, and dark branches reached out with skeletal fingers. The silence filled her with dread.

"I have no idea."

Janelle's heart was in her throat as she hiked the trail, the beam of light flashing up over the muddy path in front of her. *Karl counted the kids*, her mind chanted. *He HAD Vale and Ash on his list!* Her foot slipped, and she caught herself before she fell. With a grunt, she stepped back onto the path. Her legs ached, the hike already taking its toll. *They must have wandered off sometime after Avion Ridge. Unless they DID go back to the trees. Oh God! What if they—*

In the forest beside the trail, something moved.

With a yelp, Janelle swung the flashlight toward it, her left hand jerking to the bear spray on her belt. Through the misty forest, silent brown ghosts flowed past, a herd of deer on the move.

"Jesus," she panted.

The deer had walked up without her even hearing them approaching. *Thank God it wasn't a bear.* The light wobbled. Janelle looked down at her hands, surprised to find them shaking. Her fingers tightened around the flashlight, and she took a deep breath, forcing the terror away. *Ash and Vale are out here. If they didn't bring flashlights, they'll be hiking in the dark.*

With that thought, she turned back to the rapidly disintegrating trail to walk once more.

Ahead of her, the forest thickened. With the rain growing heavier, the difference between the trail on which she hiked and the game trails that wove back and forth across it was growing harder to discern. Twice she found herself in ankle-thick mud. When she checked her position, she found she'd lost the path. Using the flashlight as her guide, she backed up to the main trail, reoriented herself, and then kept walking.

The clouds lowered; the rain came. Together, they leached away the last light of the day, leaving her walking in the dark. Somewhere deep in the forest, an animal roared. With shaking hands, she unhooked the bear spray and flicked off the safety clip.

That was no deer . . .

A layer of fear had grown around Ash in the last minutes. This wasn't a game. It was real. And that meant that he didn't have any do-overs, no way to escape if things got bad. Not the way he could in a game. The worry that had dogged him ever since Vale had admitted she didn't know where they were grew with each icy splatter.

No effing WAY! This CAN'T be happening to us!

Standing at the top of a hill, Ash pulled out his phone and shielded it from the rain. *Come on, baby. Just one bar of reception!* He watched the corner of the screen, but nothing appeared. Swearing, he shoved it deep in his pocket.

Lacking reception, he was no better off than someone with no phone at all. Ash brought his hands to his mouth and blew on them. *Even if I got reception, what could I tell Mr. Perkins? That I'm lost in a forest? That there are trees everywhere?* Barring the small hill on which he stood, there were no landmarks anymore. The clouds formed a gray ceiling that dropped closer to the ground with each passing hour, fog filling the space in between the trees. He and Vale were alone. They were lost. And the weather was getting colder. Ash shivered as he carefully picked his way down the steep hill, his eyes on Vale, waiting for him at the bottom.

She huddled on the ground next to a large pine tree, a scrubby pile of brush beside her. Every so often, a narrow beam of light bounced through the fog like a lightsaber. *Vale brought a flashlight.* In the darkness, Ash tripped on a root, then caught himself with cold-numbed hands against a nearby tree.

The light swung upward as Vale jerked in surprise. "Oh, it's just you."

"You expecting someone else?"

"It's not that, it's . . ." She pointed the small flashlight toward the darkness behind him. "I thought I heard something moving in the trees a minute ago." She gave him a weak smile. "Glad you're back."

"I'd be happier if I had some good news."

Vale's smile disappeared in a heartbeat. "No phone reception up on the top of the hill either?"

"Nope. We can try getting to higher ground tomorrow." He patted his pocket under the plastic bag. "Turned it off to save the battery. It's already down to twenty-three percent."

"It was worth a try. Thanks, Ash."

"No worries."

"We should stay together now, though."

"I didn't go far," he said. "I could see you the whole time."

"I know but . . ." Vale glanced up at the trees. Flecks of sleet now slanted through the rain, drawing a faint white line along one side of the tree trunks. "There *was* something in the trees. I just don't know what."

Ash grimaced. "This is *not* the time for ghost stories, Vale."

"It's not a ghost story. I really *did* hear something. It was over in the trees and—"

"Look, I live for zombie games. You are *not* going to freak me out, my friend. So don't even try."

"I'm *not* trying to freak you out," she said. "I really heard something."

The corner of Ash's mouth twitched. "Know why I'm so good at zombie games?"

"No idea."

"Dead-ication."

Vale let out a tired laugh.

Ash glanced at the trees, then back. "Seriously, though. It looks pretty empty to me."

"Hopefully . . ."

"Definitely." He crouched down beside her. The brush he'd seen wasn't brush at all, but a number of pine branches. "What're you doing?"

Vale reached up to the tree next to her and selected one of the dead boughs. Evergreens this large often had dried lower branches that no longer got adequate sunlight. Vale grabbed hold—it was still attached, but the dried wood was brittle. She twisted the branch until it came loose from the trunk, then tore it off with a sharp jerk. "We need a shelter," Vale said. "I'm making one." Ash stared at her. "You remember what Mr. Perkins said about hypothermia, right?" she said.

"Uh . . ." Ash laughed. "Might've been taking a nap. You mind giving me a refresher?"

"Most people die of exposure long before they die of hunger or thirst." She pointed at the trees that surrounded them. "I figure if we're stuck here, we ought to get something built to hunker down in, at least until the storm passes."

"Build something like *what*? We don't have tents."

"Well, if there was a cave or something, we could use that, but—" She let out a bitter laugh. "That's *not* an option, so we've got to make something ourselves."

"But we don't have any tools."

"Don't need them." Vale pointed to the lower branches of the nearby trees. "Go grab me a bunch of those pine boughs, would you?"

"What for?"

"Just grab the pine boughs. I'll explain as we build."

Ash put his hands against his thighs and pushed himself back up. "You got it."

Cold and aching, he stumbled through the knot of trees, grabbing and pulling at the branches. For a long time he worked in silence. The rain eased up for a few short minutes, then renewed twofold. Water trickled down the side of his collar, soaking the jacket beneath the garbage bag. Ash began to shiver.

"Hurry, please!" Vale shouted, pulling him from his thoughts.

Ash looked up. "What's that?"

"I said *hurry*! The weather's getting worse."

Ash snapped off another branch, struggling to make his hands work. His fingers felt wooden. "Going as fast as I can."

"Go FASTER!"

Ash frowned and glanced over his shoulder. *Hold your horses, Vale.* Around the forest, the sounds of wind grew into a howl as the autumn storm took control of the valley. Sleet blinded him, but still he worked. His hands grew numb, his body racked by shivering as he dragged the pile of branches back to Vale.

"Get more," she said, not even looking up.

Ash headed back into the trees. His stomach let out a growl, and he groaned. *What I wouldn't give for a burger!* He was hungry enough he felt sick, but he didn't stop. The weight on his shoulders grew heavier by the second. They were lost. They were alone. They were in the Rocky Mountains—farther away from civilization than Ash had ever been in his entire life. *And I'm so hungry!*

Lightheaded, Ash grabbed at a nearby bough, wincing as the needles cut into the palm of his hand. "Ouch!" he yelped.

"You okay?" Vale called, her voice made thready from the distance between them.

"Fine. Just a splinter."

He stared down at his palm. A single green needle jabbed through the calloused skin, a berry of blood at its base. He took a breath and released it, his panic fading. *Well, this is just GREAT.* With the edge of his thumbnail he dug the ragged skin away, tugged out the pine needle and flicked it aside.

He glanced back through the trees. Vale was moving the branches into separate piles, organizing them by size. He still wasn't sure what she was planning as a shelter, but it looked like she might be—

"Ash? You there?"

"Yeah!"

"Hurry, please! I need some more branches."

Ash grabbed one last branch and tore it from the tree. "Hold on a sec!" he called. "I've got a bunch more."

He hoisted the newly torn boughs up under his arm and dragged them back the way he'd come. Flecks of snow swirled in the air along with the sleet, freezing his hands until they felt like stumps at the ends of his arms. *Night's coming.* With the light gone, he could barely see Vale hunched in the shadows. He stumbled, almost dumping the branches directly onto her head.

Vale yelped. "I—I didn't hear you coming!" She looked into the darkness, then back at him. "I . . . Were you standing there long?"

"Just got here. The wind's picked up pretty good," he said, then nodded to the branches under his arm. "This enough to work with?"

"Yeah, I think so." Vale stood and wiped her hands on the sides of her jeans, then reached for the branches. She carried them to a nearby tree and dropped them into the pile. "Now it's just a matter of putting it together. You take this side. I'll take the other."

Ash stared at her. Vale seemed to have everything under control, and he had *no idea* what she meant by "you take this side." He cleared his throat. "I, um . . . I don't mean to sound dumb, but what are we doing?"

"See the bottom of the tree? Those lower branches?" Vale pointed to a pine tree with boughs that fanned the ground. "That's going to be our base."

"Base for . . . ?"

"For the *shelter*, Ash. I know staying overnight is not ideal, but it's going to start snowing soon!"

Ash's gaze flicked to the trees in the distance and the shadows of clouds that obscured the mountain peaks. The snow *had* started. It was already sticking to the upper branches. They needed some kind of shelter, and fast. As he realized this, the uneasy feeling tightened into a knot of fear. He looked back to find Vale waiting.

"So we're building a lean-to with the rest of the branches?" he said.

"Exactly." She grabbed several boughs, pressing them against the existing fan of branches. "I've already got the first layer done. We just need to get enough on top that it's semiwaterproof."

"Shouldn't we have a fire or something to stay warm? I don't know about you, but I'm soaked."

"A fire would be awesome, but I didn't bring any matches." Her eyebrows rose. "Oh my God, Ash! Did you bring some?"

"Nope." He swore under his breath. "But we've got to make a fire somehow."

"No, we don't."

He shook his head. Almost *every* survival game he played had a scenario like this. *Wood plus friction equals fire, right?* "Hey! I know what to do!"

"What's that?"

"We rub two sticks togeth—"

"It doesn't work the way it does in the movies," she interrupted. "Everything is *wet*, Ash. It'll take too long."

"But if we don't have a fire—"

"Just trust me on this."

"But—"

"Shelter's the first priority," she said. "Hypothermia is the *real* danger. If we don't get warm—"

"But we don't have a fire!" he snapped. "Without a fire, we won't be *able* to stay warm. And if we can't stay warm, we're screwed!"

Vale stared at him for a long moment. She had that look on her face, the one she got so often when she was about to argue with him. Instead she nodded. "I agree about the fire," she said. "And we *will* try to build one. We will, Ash. But let's worry about fire once we've got a shelter done, okay?"

Ash glared into the forest. In any game, he'd know *exactly* what to do, but here he was out of his depth. He was angry . . . scared. *What the heck are we doing?*

"Ash, listen. I . . ." Vale winced. "I can't feel my feet anymore. My hands are numb. I'll help you with the fire. *Promise!* But we've got to get out of the rain first."

Ash looked up. The sky was dropping fat white flakes onto them. A shudder ran through his body. *We're already wet. Add snow and we're really gonna be in trouble.* He looked back to Vale. "I don't know what to do," he said. "I . . . I'm no good at this kind of thing."

"Shelter first. Then we figure out the rest."

"Right. So what do I do with the branches?"

"Just weave them in," she said, showing him. "One over the other."

"Got it." Ash jammed the next layer of branches above the ones Vale had woven into the existing frame, shivers running through him. "Here. Let me take some of that." He grabbed another handful just as Vale touched his arm.

"Thanks," she said.

Throat aching, he nodded rather than answer.

For a long time, the friends worked side by side. The sleet was a constant presence, beating down upon their heads in needles of cold. Ash's ears burned, his body pushed to the limits. Across from him, the hood on Vale's jacket turned white, frost blurring the edge where it met her knit cap. The flashlight's beam barely made it past the flakes and eventually she tucked it into her pocket. Around them, the ground was covered with a thin layer of snow, more building by the minute.

Hypothermia.

The thought ignited a terrified fervor within him. Ash rushed from tree to tree, stripping the branches and piling them on top. The action pushed meager warmth into his limbs, but it wasn't enough. Shivers rocked his body. Snow coated the branches almost as fast as he added them to the shelter, creating a dark cave under the lowest boughs. When he came back the last time, a hand darted out and caught his leg.

He yelped.

"Get in," Vale said. "It's pretty dry inside."

"J-just a few m-more—"

"No. Come in." She pulled at the pant leg of his rain-drenched jeans. "You're soaked, Ash. You don't even have a hat. You need to warm up."

"I d-didn't think I'd need a hat," he snapped. "C-coming h-here wasn't even my idea! I hate the outdoors! I hate hiking! I—I—" His voice broke. The dark forest, swirling with fresh snow, blurred through a veil of angry tears.

"It's okay," Vale said gently. "Just come inside. It's warmer here." She gestured for him, then backed into the shelter. "I've got a scarf. You can wrap it around your ears. It's in the bottom of my pack." She disappeared into the shadows. "I'll find it for you. You sit down."

He wobbled in place, exhaustion hitting him. He staggered down to his knees and crawled inside the hut. Vale had hung a small glow stick onto a branch above her head, and it cast a sickly green light.

"You brought a light stick," he said.

She glanced up from her bag. "Uh . . . yeah. I brought two of them, actually. And the flashlight." She pulled a ribbon of fabric from the opening of the pack. "Here's the scarf."

"Th-thanks." Ash wrapped it over his head like his grandmother did. He knew he probably looked silly, but he didn't care. For the first time in hours, his head was warm. "That's better. My ears were half-frozen."

"Sorry, I should have offered it sooner. I was just working on something." Vale looked down in front of her, and Ash followed her gaze. She had a pile of twigs and leaves and two sticks. *No fire.* "I . . . I can't seem to get this going," she said.

"You want me to try?"

"Sure."

Vale handed him the sticks, and Ash tried to get the rhythm, but his hands were numb and he kept slipping. After twenty minutes of frustration, he shoved them aside.

"Th-this is stupid!" he said through chattering teeth.

"The wood is wet, Ash."

"B-but it should work! Wood plus friction equals fire. It *always* equals fire!" He made an angry sound and tossed the sticks aside. "S-so d-dumb!"

An awkward silence drew out between them. He could hear Vale's teeth chattering, but she wasn't arguing with him. She'd known what to do. She hadn't panicked. She was the only reason they were alive at all. Realizing it, Ash felt terrible. Vale was right. The wood was wet. *Everything was wet.* He would have wasted their chances if he'd tried to start a fire rather than make a shelter. He wrapped his arms around his knees, the garbage bag crinkling. Vale had given him *that* too. She was the one with the supplies. Not him. He'd packed whatever was on hand this morning. Nothing had been planned. The light sticks and flashlight were hers; the shelter, her idea.

A wave of frustration rose inside Ash. He wanted to yell—*keep yelling*—until he felt better, but Vale was here. He couldn't do that to her, not after everything she'd done for them. He crossed his arms on his chest and put his chin to his knees.

"Sorry," he grumbled. "For not listening to you. I . . . I've never done anything like this before."

Vale looked up, her face so pale he could count her freckles. "It's fine."

"No," he said. "It's not. I was upset. I should have listened. I—I—" He gave a short laugh. "I'm *hangry*, all right? I'm fricking starving here."

Vale reached for her backpack. "I already ate my granola bar, but I've got some gorp, if you want."

"Some *what*?"

"Gorp: granola, oats, raisins, and peanuts. It's an old-fashioned name for trail mix." She laughed tiredly. "There are chocolate chips in it too, though. So . . . maybe it's supposed to be gorpc?"

"Gorp, huh? You're a real outdoors person. That's pretty awesome."

"Not really. I just . . ." Vale sighed. "I like to be prepared."

"I tell you, Vale. *This* is why you'd be great to have on a D&D campaign."

"You can stop bringing it up. I'm *not* joining your group, Ash."

"You say that, but I really think you should. Look at how last night's campaign went!"

Vale laughed and shook her head. "It was terrible! I died in my first battle."

"So? I've died in like a thousand of them."

Vale giggled.

"Look, in a campaign you just have to learn to go with what happens," he said. "You roll the die and you take your chances." He shrugged. "But there's strategy too. And you're always prepared, Vale.

You keep your wits about you when things go down." He paused, hoping that his next suggestion sounded more casual than he meant it. "I, uh . . . I know you said you weren't going to game anymore, but I'd take you back anytime if you wanted to."

Vale groaned. "I'm just not into video games."

"You used to love them!"

"Used to." She sighed. "That was like . . . three years ago."

"Two. And it was *awesome*!"

"Hardly, I—"

"We were a *great* team! The two of us used to take on *everyone*."

Vale frowned. "Yeah, but . . . we weren't the only ones playing."

A long uncomfortable silence followed her words. Ash knew Vale was remembering the harassment that had started among the other squads and had spread to the entire gaming community where they played. Many of those gamers were now gone, but Vale had never returned.

"No," Ash said quietly. "But it was still nice when we were playing together. Just me and you."

Vale smiled sadly. "Yeah, it was."

"Last night you stayed with me when everyone else left. We faced the orcs together."

"And we died." She smiled again. "But thanks. I . . . I get what you're saying." She reached into her pack and pulled out a bag full of trail mix. "Here. You have it. I already ate my granola bar, so I'm good. You need something to eat too."

Ash took the plastic baggie. He wanted to shovel it with his hands, dump fistfuls into his mouth, and fill the pit in his stomach in seconds. Instead, he said: "Are you sure, Vale? I mean, this is your food. Your supplies."

"It's fine, Ash. Just eat."

Tears filled his eyes, and he blinked them away. "Thanks," he said. "I . . . I appreciate it."

He grabbed a handful and shoved it into his mouth. It wasn't enough, but it was *something*, and for that Ash was grateful.

CHAPTER FOUR

"I can't lie to you about your chances, but . . . you have my sympathies."

ASH, *ALIEN*

IT TOOK ASH a good half hour before he stopped shivering. Strangely, it was the arrival of the snow that caused the change. Outside the open entrance to the shelter, a blanket of white covered the landscape, transforming it into shades of blue and gray. He felt as if they'd been transported into a different realm. *Another level in the game.* Autumn was abruptly gone, winter in its place. The weight of snow filled the gaps in the interwoven branches, sealing out the rain and pressing down on the boughs above their heads. Minute by minute, the entrance grew smaller. What had started as a large half C—big enough for a teen to crawl through—narrowed into a sloppy circle the size of a dog door, then a half-moon the size of a football. The temperature inside the crude hut slowly rose.

Still, the snow fell.

The iciness of the air under the pine boughs faded. The clouds from Ash's breath disappeared, and his limbs relaxed. He wasn't *warm* exactly, but he wasn't freezing any longer. The hollow where he and Vale huddled under the tree reminded him of the doghouse his aunt and uncle had built for their huskies. As a little boy, Ash had been obsessed with his iPad, but on one weekend visit, he'd forgotten to bring the charger. When the iPad had finally lost power, young Ash had gone outside to play while his mother had coffee with her sister. Bored with building snowmen, Ash had crawled inside the wooden structure next to the porch to play with the dogs. Eventually, he'd cozied up to one of the huskies and fallen fast asleep. Despite the icy winter conditions, the interior of the doghouse was snug and warm. Ash had been woken hours later by the shouts of his panicked mother, and he'd crawled out, completely fine after several hours outside in subzero conditions.

The lean-to smells a lot better than the doghouse did, Ash thought with a smirk. Everything under the tree branches was pine scented, like Christmas trees or winter sledding. Under that sharp smell was a faint odor, something flowery and soft. *Vale's shampoo.* He glanced over at her. In the watery green light, she could have been a statue. Her head was tucked down to her knees, her whole body curled in on itself as she waited out the storm. It made his heart twist to see her.

He and Vale had been friends forever (or at least as far back into *forever* as kindergarten felt). In the high school social strata, theirs was an unexpected companionship. Ash was everyone's friend while Vale was almost no one's. At lunch, they sat together, and after school occasionally studied together. The rest of Vale's friends were online, though even *those* were limited. It hadn't always been that way. In middle school, Ash and Vale had *both* been gamers, but that had ended with a months-long bout of harassment. It wasn't just online. At school, the bullying had only grown worse.

Vale wasn't unattractive, but she didn't preen the way other students did. She didn't have a boyfriend or girlfriend, just one close friend: Ash. Her lack of a clique made her a target for bullies. So did the fact that she stood up to them.

The same guilt that had risen inside Ash while they were walking in the woods returned. In PE class, Vale was an easy target. Whenever Ash saw the bullying happening, he joked and diverted the attention, but he never actually spoke up for her. If he did, Ash knew *he'd* be on the outside too.

Another thought flickered to life: *Does that make me as bad as the rest of them?*

Ash's gaze returned to his friend. Vale had her hands tucked under her armpits and her nose pressed down into the collar of her coat. An uneasy feeling prickled Ash's conscience. *We would have frozen out here if it wasn't for her.* The thought carried a tendril of shame. Vale had seemed completely in control when she'd taken over making a camp—giving directions like she was a teacher or something. She reminded Ash of his cousin Salma. She was in a medical program these days, "*kicking ass and taking names*," as she put it.

That was the kind of girl Vale Shumway was: *in charge.*

While Ash had been raging about the snow, she'd seen what needed to be done . . . and she'd done it. His gaze dropped down to the small pile of kindling scattered between them. *I would've died trying to get that stupid fire going. There's no way I would've made the night. I'd be outside, in the snow, freezing my butt off. But Vale knew. She KNEW.*

The guilt strangled him.

Ash cleared his throat. "Hey, Vale?"

Vale glanced up. "Uh-huh?"

"You look cold."

She closed her eyes again. "Th-that's because I *am* c-cold."

He opened his mouth to make a joke, then closed it again. *She DOES look cold!* "So . . . if you're cold, move over here. We can huddle together."

Vale didn't answer.

"Vale . . . ?"

One eye opened. "What?"

Ash sighed. "C'mon and sit over here. It'll be warmer."

"T-too t-tired," she mumbled. "D-don't want to move." She turned her face to the side, avoiding his gaze. "J-just want t-to sleep."

"All right," he said. "Have it your way."

Ash waited, but she didn't look up. He wanted to help her, but didn't know how. He owed her one. Vale was obviously colder than he was. *She gave me her scarf, and her food*, he thought guiltily. *And she reminded me to pack last night, but I never did.* After a long moment, he pushed the kindling out of his way and slid over so he was next to her.

Vale glanced up again. "Wh-what're you doing?"

"You look cold," Ash said. "And I . . . I think we should sit together." She didn't move, so Ash slid closer. "I . . . I'm going to put my arm over your shoulders, okay?" He laughed nervously. "Nothing weird. I'm just—" He coughed. "Seriously. I'm not trying anything. I just—You look cold. All right? It's gonna be a long night. It'll be better if you're not freezing the whole time."

When Vale didn't respond, he moved in until they sat side by side. It was as close as Ash sat when he was at the movies with a girl, ready to slide his arm over the back of the seat so he could make a move. This *wasn't* how friends sat. (Not even best friends.) At that thought, his face began to burn, but he forced his embarrassment aside. *She's just cold—way colder than I am—and she'll get colder still if I don't help.* Ash slid his arm cautiously around Vale's back, setting it across her shoulders, softly at first, then more solidly. He let out a slow breath.

Two minutes in and it felt like he'd defused a bomb.

With them touching, he could tell how cold she was. Shivers ran through her, passing from her body to his in small tremors. He leaned in closer so that they were pressed together from hip to shoulder. He rubbed her back. The shivering continued. The sound of Vale's teeth chattering put him on edge. It struck him that she hadn't *stopped* shivering since the rain had begun.

"Give me your hands," Ash said.

When Vale didn't respond, he squeezed her shoulder. "Hey. You hear me, Vale? I want to check your hands."

She looked up, confused. "Wha . . . ?" She sounded like she'd been sleeping and he'd just woken her.

"You're still cold," he said. "Give me your hands. I'll warm them up."

"O-okay." Vale unwrapped herself with the slow, plodding motions of a drunk. She wobbled, then placed her hands in his. "H-here."

"Sheesh! They're like ice, Vale."

She didn't answer.

Ash held her fingers tightly in his, but no amount of rubbing would dispel the chill that had leached into her body. He frowned. That feeling he'd had before—when he'd realized the seriousness of the situation they were in—was back, only now it was focused on someone else. Bits and pieces of Perkins's talk from the class filtered into his mind, heightening his fear. "*Shivering is one of the first signs. It's the body trying to warm itself up . . . then there's the slurred speech. Confusion . . . People have difficulty thinking. They're drowsy. Eventually they lose consciousness . . . they often don't wake up.*"

"Vale, we've got to warm you up," Ash said in a sharp voice.

"B-but I thought . . . ?"

"Take off your coat. We need to get your core temperature up."

She blinked in confusion. "B-b-but I'm cold," she said. "I d-don't want t-to take m-my c-c-coat—"

"I need to warm you up," he said—hating how high pitched and frightened his voice sounded. "I need the wet layer *off.* Come here."

"I d-don't think—"

"Look, Vale, I don't have time to argue about this!" Ash reached out, touching the zipper of her jacket. "If you'll—"

"N-no!"

Ash jerked his hand back. "Sorry, I just—"

"L-leave me ALONE!"

With a huff, Ash put his chin down to his knees. "Fine, then!" Ash snapped. "Be that way." He couldn't very well *force* Vale to let him help her. Not when she was freaking out. Outside the shelter, the wind howled, snow piling higher as the storm continued.

“F-fine!” she said. “I w-will!”

He closed his eyes, dozing for a few minutes, then jerked awake once more. The temperature was steady, his body almost comfortably warm. He yawned and looked over at Vale. In the pale glow of the light stick, she was a statue. A nervous twinge filled his chest. She looked like she was wearing lipstick. He leaned closer.

My God! Her lips are fricking blue.

Ash reached out and touched her cheek. He jerked his hand back, heart pounding. Vale’s flesh felt like bacon straight out of the fridge. A sudden terror shouted at him for attention. *She’s too cold!*

Vale wasn’t just cold, she was hypothermic.

“Vale?”

She didn’t answer.

“Vale! I . . . I need to warm you up.”

She mumbled something, but otherwise didn’t move.

Ash moved closer. “Vale!” he snapped. “I *need* you to take your jacket off NOW!” He reached out for her zipper, half expecting her to slap his hand away. Vale’s head lolled sideways. He unzipped her coat. She mumbled, but didn’t open her eyes. The panic rose inside him. “Oh God . . . Oh God . . .”

Vale’s got hypothermia for sure!

Ash’s stress had jumped three levels in the past minute and a half. “Got to get these wet layers off,” he said. “We’ve *got* to!” He reached for the collar of Vale’s coat, easing it down her arms. She mumbled and wobbled in place. “Hold on,” he said, fighting with the second sleeve. “I just need to—”

It was at *that* moment that the Vale he knew seemed to return. She blinked in confusion, then shrieked. "S-S-STOP!" She struggled blindly, whacking Ash in the side of the face with her icy palm.

"Ouch!" He staggered back, smacking his head on the shelter's bowed roof. A shower of sifted snow dropped onto both their heads.

"B-back o-off!" Vale pulled her hand back again.

"Vale, STOP!"

"Y-you c-c-can't just DO that!" she snapped.

"But you're freezing!" Ash reached for her sleeve, ducking as she swung drunkenly to stop him. More snow fluttered down. "Vale, just stop! STOP, PLEASE!"

Vale glared at him, her breaths coming in sharp pants. Her skin was unnaturally white, lips purple blue, eyelids drooping. As she lowered her arms, she wobbled in place.

"I s-said t-to l-leave m-me—"

"No!" Ash said, voice cracking. "You've got hypothermia. You honestly do! And you're gonna die out here otherwise. And I—I can't—" A worried sob bubbled from his throat. This, here, was Vale's tone . . . *her words* from hours earlier. He added more gently: "Just trust me. Okay? I need to warm you up." He reached out hesitantly. "Once your wet clothes are off—"

"N-NO!" Vale said through chattering teeth. "W-why are y-you t-t-trying to undress me?"

Ash let out a frustrated groan. "Because if you get the wet layers OFF, then you can warm up!" He dropped his hand to his side. "Listen, we can cuddle and—"

"I-I'm n-not c-comfortable with that."

"Why not?"

"I-it's w-weird," Vale said. "I d-don't like you that w-way."

Ash frowned. Years before, at a middle school dance, he'd tried to kiss Vale. That impulsive peck had *not* gone well. Ash wondered if *that* memory (and the awkwardness that followed) was bothering Vale now. "Well, I don't like *you* that way either."

"B-but—"

"I *know* it's awkward, and I'm sorry. But your lips are *blue*. You're cold and getting colder." He let out a hiss. "*Please* just trust me on this. Perkins warned us about this. Hypothermia kills people. *You KNOW that!*"

"So j-just for warmth?"

"Just warmth," he said. "Nothing else. I swear to you."

"F-fine."

"Let's get off the wet layers," he said.

Ash slid off the plastic bag that covered his clothes and laid it on the ground, then did the same with the one Vale wore. Her jacket—unlike his—was soaked through with water. He carefully guided her arms out of the sleeves, and undid his own jacket. Next, he helped her out of her long-sleeved shirt, but left her tank alone. He pulled off his own tee. Ash was surprised at the warmth of the lean-to, but it wasn't enough to help Vale. In the open air, wearing little more than a T-shirt and damp jeans, her shivering grew more intense.

"I'm gonna lie down," Ash said, wishing that Vale was anyone else in the entire world. His brother Leo even! She was his friend, but nothing else. And that made this situation feel weird. "You lie down in front of me. Back to front."

Vale's eyes widened until there was a line of white around the edges. "B-b-but—"

"I'm not *trying* anything, Vale," Ash said. "Promise! Just . . . just lie down." He winced. "Please."

"F-f-fine. J-just don't g-get the wrong i-i-idea."

"I won't."

"N-no kissing! N-nothing like that."

"I promise."

Vale crawled forward on hands and knees. She stumbled, head-butted Ash, then fell onto her side next to him. "S-s-so c-cold," she said through chattering teeth. "C-c-can't feel my hands or feet."

Ash undid her hiking boots and set them aside, then pulled her into the cradle of his arms. She was soaked through, and touching her limbs felt like holding cold clay. Even moving her was a struggle. Finally, he pulled her into a small ball, and laid the two jackets over both of them. Ash's teeth chattered for a few minutes, then stopped. Vale's continued.

He tightened his arms around her torso. "You're gonna be fine, Vale. We just need to warm you up."

Barring their footwear, they were covered in every piece of clothing the two of them had been wearing, only they were together under all the layers, rather than separate. Vale lay back against his chest, her breathing coming in shallow pants, teeth chattering a staccato beat that never stopped. After a time, he felt her relax against him, though her shivers continued. Wave after wave ran through her.

"How're you feeling now?" Ash asked.

For a few seconds she didn't speak and then: "B-b-better."

Ash pulled her tighter against him. Her back was against his front, his taller body an outline of her own. For the first time since he'd taken hold of her hands, a small flame of warmth grew between them. It was only in one spot at first—the center of Vale's back and Ash's bare stomach—but half an hour later, it had moved to include his entire chest and the places where Ash's arms wrapped Vale's crossed arms. It struck him that she was no longer shivering.

Ash lifted his head. "You still doing okay there?"

"Guess so. I mean . . . given the situation."

"I know it's awkward—"

"That's an understatement," she said.

"Sorry about that."

She sat for a moment longer, then sighed. "I . . . I don't like you, Ash. I mean, I *like* you—as a friend, I mean—but not . . ." Her words faded uneasily.

"I know."

"You . . . you do?"

"I don't like you that way either." He laughed. "But it's better than freezing to death. Right?"

Vale seemed to be on the verge of saying something else, but then she shook her head. "Yeah, it is." She was quiet for a few heartbeats. "Thanks. Sorry for arguing about taking off my coat."

"Just so you know, I wasn't gonna try something."

"Good."

"We're friends, Vale. That's it. I mean, I don't think of you like that. You're not like other girls."

Vale turned slightly in his arms. "I'm *exactly* like other girls. And just so you know, that's an awful thing to say."

"Sorry, I didn't mean it that way—I only meant—" Ash groaned.

"That's *not* how it was supposed to come out. It was supposed to be a compliment."

"It's *not* a compliment. You should *never* say that to another girl. Seriously, Ash. It's a rude thing to say. It's like saying there's something *wrong* with being like everyone else."

"Uh . . . yeah. I got that part."

There was a long uncomfortable moment, the only sound the howl of the wind in the trees. "Look," Ash said. "I just meant to say I wasn't trying to make a move on you or anything. I . . . I just wanted to warm you up. Not that someone *couldn't* think of you that way. I'm sure lots of people have crushed on you. But I didn't assume you felt like that for me, or anything. I mean, if you did—or *do* . . . well, that's cool and all. I just, I—I—"

Vale turned over the rest of the way. "Ash, I'm aro-ace."

He stared into the shadows, wishing he could see her face clearly. He wondered what he could read from her expression. Ace meant asexual. He'd read that online somewhere. Aro he wasn't actually sure. He thought it might have something to do with—

"So are you going to say anything?" Vale asked.

"Am I supposed to?"

She laughed tiredly. "I don't know, Ash. Some people just get . . . weird about it."

"Oh." Ash took a slow breath and let it out again. He'd occasionally wondered about Vale's sexual orientation. (She'd never dated anyone in all the years they'd been friends.) But he thought it was more to do with being shy. Ash cleared his throat. "So if you're ace, then—"

"I'm aro-ace; asexual *and* aromantic."

"Right. Aro-ace. So you just . . . don't like anyone? Guys or girls?"

"I like them as friends—at least nice ones, like you and Bella—but I don't feel romantic toward them. I don't feel any urge to make out, or have sex or, well, to do anything *but* be friends."

"I never knew that."

"You never asked."

Ash chuckled. "Guess not."

Vale sighed and settled closer. "I actually enjoy being *close* to people. I just don't want them to confuse cuddling with something else."

"Got it."

There was a long quiet moment, and then Vale spoke again. "If you tell *anyone* in our class about my sexuality, I swear to God, Ash Hamid, I'll hunt you down and kill you myself."

Ash smiled. "I wouldn't do that. It's not my business to tell anyone."

"Good."

"And you're welcome for saving you from dying of hypothermia."

He felt, more than heard, Vale giggle. "Well, I'm the one who thought of the shelter, so let's call it even."

He grinned. "I guess that's fair."

For a long time, neither spoke. Minute by minute, the growing spot of warmth spread all the way down to where her socked feet were tucked between his calves. Ash grew sleepy, the warmth of the makeshift tent and the heat of their bodies growing warmer by the minute, drawing him into a sleep born of exhaustion and terror. He was hovering on the edge when Vale rolled over. He jerked awake, but she only burrowed deeper, her cold nose—like a dog's snout, he thought sleepily—pressing against the hollow under his chin. He tightened his hands around her back and closed his eyes.

"Thanks, Ash," Vale murmured. "For real, just . . . thanks."

"No problem."

And in the darkness of the lean-to, the snowstorm raging outside, the two friends slept.

Janelle Holland had been up for nearly twenty hours, but as she reached the bus and used the wireless to call the Waterton police station, exhaustion was the last thing on her mind.

"There are kids lost *where*?" the officer on the handheld asked.

"Lost on the trail between Twin Lakes and Red Rock," she said as she glanced up at the sky. It was a black, moonless night, every bit of light sucked away by the storm clouds overhead. *Ash and Vale won't be able to see unless they brought flashlights!* "They're out there somewhere. I . . . I can't find them. And it's starting to snow."

The handheld crackled with static. "I'll call the warden station, and we'll have a team out in half an hour. When they get there—"

"I'm not waiting," Janelle interrupted. "I'm going to hike back again."

"But—"

"Those kids are lost out there. They're—" Her voice caught and broke. "They're not dressed for this weather. I need to *find* them."

"Do you have a flashlight at least?" the officer said. "Don't need another person getting lost while stumbling around in the dark."

Janelle wiped away a tear. "Yes, I've got a flashlight."

"Bear spray? This is the worst time of year to run into a grizzly."

"Yes," she sniffed. "Bear spray too." Somewhere in the dark forest, an animal howled and she turned. "I-I've got to get going, Officer. I'm sorry."

"The searchers will be there soon. I think you should wait for—"

Janelle clicked off the wireless and set it back into the bus. She grabbed a handful of fresh batteries from the glove box, tucked them into her pocket, and then headed back to the trail for the second time that day. There was no choice; she needed to keep going. No time to stop. No time for fear.

Their parents trusted me with those kids.

The forest closed in around her. Wind howled, sleet stinging her face and hands. She squinted into the sky. *It's already snowing at the higher elevations.*

Janelle had been in a state of near-constant panic since the moment she'd realized she'd lost two of her students. Janelle could almost understand Ash getting lost—the boy had difficulty following clear directions at the best of times—but Vale was a rule-follower to a T. The girl never let any infraction go without an argument. In the dark woods, something moved and a sliver of fear ran the length of Janelle's spine. *What if they ran into a bear?* It was autumn. They were hiking in a remote location. Janelle winced. It was all too possible.

She reached Twin Lakes (for the second time that day) just after four in the morning. By then, it was snowing in earnest. A heavy layer of flakes painted everything like frothy white icing. The moon had reappeared, but it left the landscape transformed. Karl waited outside the tent, tending the fires.

He jogged toward her as she stepped from the shadows. "Did you find them?" he called. "Are Vale and Ash—?"

"Not found yet." She swore. "So they didn't show up here?" she asked, already knowing the answer.

Karl shook his head. "No. Not here." He winced. "I walked back a ways on the trail and called for them for a long time. No luck."

Wobbling on her feet, Janelle turned away. "I'm going to run the trail one more time."

"Again?"

"Yes," she said grimly. "*Again*. If they're out there, I need to find them." And in seconds, she was hiking again.

Snow fell. Cold spread through her bones, making her hands ache and her feet feel like stumps made of ice. The trail she'd taken was barely visible now, and Janelle struggled to find her way, finally making it back to the meadow below Avion Ridge in the dark hour before dawn.

"Hello!" a woman shouted.

Janelle stumbled and almost fell. *Vale?*

"Hellooo!" the voice called again. "Vale! Ash!"

Janelle's shoulders slumped. *It's the searchers, of course* . . . She lifted her hand, waving wearily. "It's Janelle," she shouted. "Janelle Holland, the teacher."

Bobbing lights appeared in the trees, and a group of searchers wearing headlamps came toward her. They were dressed more for the weather than she was. A brief flare of intense frustration rose in her chest, strangling her. *I should have canceled the trip when the weather started to turn!* But Janelle had taught for more than fifteen years. This trip had been done that many times. There'd never once been an issue.

There was now.

As the searchers reached her side, Janelle paused, her legs wobbly. "I—I just came back from Twin Lakes," she choked. "N-not there, as f-far as I can see."

One of the searchers—a warden, by his uniform—nodded. "You need to head back to town. We'll take it from here."

"But I need to—"

"Go to town. The police need your help," the warden said. "They'll be starting a helicopter search in the morning."

Janelle nodded. "Okay, then. I . . . Okay." In her exhausted state, *nothing* made sense. "I'll walk back."

The warden—an older man with graying hair—put a hand on her shoulder. "You can tell the parents we're doing everything we can to find their children."

Janelle fought back the urge to scream. "Thanks. I'll tell them that."

The searchers moved on, and Janelle was once again alone in the forest.

Reaching Red Rock Canyon, she took the school bus and drove to town. There, she stopped at the Waterton police station, where they were already in a state of high alert. Constable Jordan Wyatt had contacted the Lethbridge police. They'd brought in the park's rescue team several hours ago.

The people I met on the trail, she thought.

"The searchers are combing the woods on the Snowshoe Trail from Red Rock Canyon all the way to Twin Lakes," Constable Wyatt said. "They'll extend the search to the area beyond the trail tomorrow morning. The Lethbridge police have contacted the parents of the students . . . They'll be here soon."

"Soon," Janelle repeated.

Wyatt nodded. "In the next hour."

Janelle looked down at her hiking boots, rain sodden and flecked with grime, snow clinging in pills to the laces. *Oh my God*, her mind screamed. *What do I tell them?* She took a slow breath and looked up.

"Thanks for calling them," she said in a hollow voice.

"No problem." He smiled, though it was sad. "Don't worry yet, Ms. Holland."

"When *should* I worry?"

His expression grew serious. "Worry if we can't find them in the next few hours."

Janelle's gaze moved to the window. Outside, streaks of pink lit the eastern sky. Vale and Ash were lost. The Shumways and Mrs. Hamid were on their way. She rubbed her temples. She'd lost their children, and they were going to want answers.

The sky had lightened from sooty black to dark gray when Ash awoke. He was warm and relaxed, Vale's body a soft shape in front of him, her hair brushing his nose. He sighed and shifted, then froze. With the arrival of dawn, something *else* had arrived.

His mind sent out a plea of sheer terror. *Oh my God, body, now is NOT THE TIME TO GET AN ERECTION!*

For a few seconds, Ash took slow breaths, focusing on anything *other* than Vale pressed against him. He thought about his mother's house, his brother's stinky runners, even his math class. Nothing helped! With Vale's butt pushed up against his groin, there was no way *not* to react.

Panicked, Ash eased himself away from Vale. She'd barely allowed him to help her warm up. A morning boner would make the situation infinitely more precarious. He slid as far away as he could get and pulled his jacket on atop his damp clothes. Oblivious to Ash's worry, Vale slept on. Her eyes were closed, and the slow rise and fall of her breathing rustled the coat that covered her.

Thank God she's a sound sleeper!

But now that he was awake, Ash had a *new* problem to deal with. His body worked like clockwork. Fifteen minutes after he awoke, each and every day, he was in the washroom. And on any day *other* than today, he'd be sitting on the toilet with the music blasting, ready to enjoy what Ash's grandfather euphemistically called a "morning constitutional." Ash's gut churned, and he stifled a groan. Vale sighed in her sleep, and he clambered out of the lean-to into the icy predawn, worried he'd wake her.

Around him, the woods where they'd stopped for the night were covered in a heavy layer of snow. There was just enough light to see the faint shape of the shelter. Around him, pine boughs hung low under a heavy blanket of snow. If his stomach hadn't been churning, Ash would have been amazed at the sight. As it was, he caught himself against a tree, wincing until the stomach cramp passed. His body didn't know his schedule had changed, and that was a problem. He scanned the darkness for someplace that would function as the bathroom he needed. No use denying it: He had to take a dump . . . and he needed to do it NOW.

Intestines in knots, Ash stumbled farther and farther into the forest. He scanned the trees. *Got to watch for animals.* But nature was calling, and that meant he needed to be far enough away that he could have some privacy. With the fresh layer of snow on the ground, his tracks were a clear path back to the lean-to where he'd slept most of the night; he hoped that Vale would be smart enough not to follow him.

In desperation, he sprinted to a knot of trees with a lush screen of bushes around their base. He crouched, then froze. A shiver ran up his spine. Somewhere in the distance, a branch broke. *Probably just the weight of the snow*, his mind chattered. Some of the branches hung all the way to the ground. Another branch broke on the other side of the forest, and he spun, heart thudding. *But what if it's NOT the snow? What if it's an animal?*

He nervously scanned the woods as far as he could see. *All clear.* Seeing nothing except for a few curious birds in the trees, Ash dropped his trousers and crouched.

"Ugh!"

When he leaned over, his pants pooled around his ankles, making it impossible for him to relieve himself without soiling them. He swore and pulled them up to his knees; he crouched again, holding them in place with one hand. Ash wobbled. It was an awkward position, but it got them out of the way. Pants at his knees, he hobbled over to a nearby tree and caught hold of it with one hand. Balanced like this, he could keep from falling over, could hold his pants out of the way, *and* he could answer the call of nature.

"There we go . . ."

A minute later, Ash sighed in relief. He felt a hundred times better; all he needed now was—

"Oh, crap!"

He had no toilet paper.

"This is NOT funny!" Ash grumbled.

Ash duck-waddled away from the steaming pile of excrement (careful not to step in it) and over to a nearby bush. He reached out for a handful of leaves, then froze. *What if they're poison ivy?* Ash knew nothing about real-life camping. His experience was limited to the "camping" of online games where he'd occasionally hole up to avoid getting killed. When it came to nature, Ash was oblivious. He spent 95 percent of his time indoors (and at least half of *that* in his mom's basement playing games). The leaves could be anything at all. Ash just didn't have the knowledge.

"No fricking way!"

For several seconds, Ash crouched, undecided. It was the aching in his thighs (and the stink in the air) that made the decision for him. He tightened his grip on the handful of leaves and—with a silent prayer—wiped himself clean. When his pants were back up, he checked the bottom of his boots, then stepped away from the mess. Lacking running water, he used a snowball of sloppy, wet slush to wash his hands, then dried them on the sides of his pants.

He followed his footsteps back toward the shelter, nodding happily to himself. *First challenge down.* With his morning constitutional complete, even finding their way back to the trail felt doable. *Now we just need to figure out where—*

In the shadows of the tall trees, an animal moved.

Vale woke, heart pounding. Her eyes opened in the darkness of the shelter as she struggled to make sense of the strange sound that had woken her. *What in the world was that?* Whatever she'd heard was nearby, but groggy from sleep, she couldn't put a finger on its origin. *Maybe it was just a dream. I could have—*

"Maaa-a-a-am!"

The plaintive crying appeared a second time. It was high pitched, like a baby, or perhaps a child, calling for its mother. Confused, Vale pushed herself up on one elbow. It was almost pitch black inside the lean-to—the light stick having faded into a dull green—but beyond the darkness, a circle of predawn gloom appeared.

"Did you hear that, Ash?" she whispered. "Something outside in the . . ." She turned and her words faded as she caught sight of the bare patch behind her. She sat motionless, fear filling her like the cold that had spread through her limbs last night. "Ash?!"

He was gone.

Outside the shelter, something moved through the forest. The footsteps sounded like a person walking at a distance, or perhaps a dog moving through the snow. "*Maaa-a-a-am!*" the voice cried again.

"What the . . . ?" Fighting panic, Vale struggled to pull on her coat, then crawled to the open entrance of the shelter. Her breath released as she stuck her head out the door. "Oh thank God," she muttered.

A line of footprints headed away from the shelter into the nearby woods. Though it was barely light enough to see yet, Vale suspected Ash had gone to relieve himself. Her eyes widened as she took in the scene beyond the shelter. In the hours since they'd fallen asleep, the seasons had changed. Outside the narrow opening was a winter wonderland; a heavy layer of snow covered every tree, bush, and mountain peak.

"Maaa-a-a-am!"

A branch broke and Vale jerked. From the far side of the forest, a flicker of movement drew her attention. A small shadow appeared, then another . . . and another. They came forward, appearing by degrees.

"*Maaa-a-a-am!*" the smallest called.

Vale grinned. *It's just a deer.*

The fawn was half-grown. A yearling, at most, the spotted marking of babyhood no longer on its flanks. Around it, other, adult deer walked wraithlike through the trees, moving nervously away from the lean-to.

"*Maaa-a-a-am!*" the fawn cried again.

Vale watched, breath held, as the fawn passed directly in front of the opening of the hut. The deer held one leg up, its crooked three-legged walk causing her smile to falter. *It can hardly keep up with the others.* Vale leaned farther out the open doorway, her gaze following the herd as they moved deeper into the trees, and the single fawn, trailing behind. She held her breath. Vale had never been this close to a wild animal before. She wished that Ash was here to see it too.

The fawn stumbled, then glanced back over its shoulder. Its gaze paused anxiously on the shelter, then lifted.

Vale smiled.

"Maaa-a—"

Everything happened at once: The branches directly above the lean-to shifted with a suddenness that shocked Vale into silence; a scream—like a woman's voice melded with the roar of a lion, loud and near—broke through the wooded glade. Snow pellets smacked

Vale's face. The snow a few feet beyond the shelter exploded as a large golden animal—*a cougar!*—dropped from the trees straight above the lean-to and pounced on the fawn. Blood sprayed the snow as the cougar shook the fawn, breaking its neck.

She stared in horror as the cougar loped away from the shelter, dragging the fawn. Its dead eyes stared back at Vale. The rest of the herd bounded away in long graceful jumps, disappearing into the shadows of the tall trees.

Perhaps ten seconds had passed.

From the other side of the clearing, a new shadow appeared, tall and ungainly. *Ash.* "Vale?" he called. "What was—?"

"Shhh . . . !" Vale hissed. "Get back here. Fast!"

Ash jogged toward her. "What was that sound? I thought I heard—" He staggered to a stop at the exact point where the cougar had dropped. The snow was smeared red with blood. "What the hell?"

"Hurry, Ash!" she snapped. "You need to get back inside!"

"But what—?"

"Get in here! There's a cougar in the woods. It just killed a deer." She swallowed against a dry throat. "There could be another one."

Ash struggled into the shelter, smacking his head on the roof as he did. The pine boughs and snow felt like a flimsy protection, but it was all they had.

"You saw a *cougar*?" he whispered. "Like . . . *here*? In the woods?"

"Yes. It killed a deer. We've got to be quiet."

Ash's eyes widened. "Should we try to run?"

Vale shook her head. "Too risky. There could be more than one cougar out there." She winced. "We'd never see it coming if it came after us."

Ash shuddered. "I'll grab the flashlight."

"Good idea."

Vale huddled at Ash's side, her heart in her throat. Somewhere nearby, the scream of a cougar broke through the glade. *Another cougar out hunting.* Vale put her chin to her knees, but she couldn't bring herself to lie down. Not with the cougars outside in the forest. Not with them being lost.

She closed her eyes, fighting the urge to cry. *We're lost because of me.* Far in the distance, a third cougar roared, and then the forest was silent once more. Vale rubbed away her tears, while next to her, Ash stared up at the branches above their heads.

Side by side, they waited for the light.

CHAPTER FIVE

"Okay, Jim. I've got some bad news."

MARK, *28 DAYS LATER*

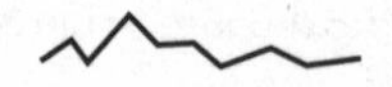

VALE JERKED AWAKE with an angry ache in her gut. *So hungry.* She rolled over, squinting as a band of sunlight slashed across her vision. At some time in the hours since the cougar attack, she'd fallen asleep. Momentarily blinded, she was greeted by a glittering world. Snow shone with brilliance that hurt. The hollow of the entrance had been pushed open from the inside, a human-sized shape in its place, and beyond it, the day shone silver blue, the bounce of sunshine on snow dazzling.

"Ash . . . ? You out there?"

She got no answer.

Vale's stomach growled, and she sat up groggily. Outside the open door of the shelter, Ash was nowhere to be seen, though a new line of tracks led off into the trees, heading the opposite direction from the night before. She shivered as the coat she'd been sleeping under slid down to expose her bare arms. It wasn't as cold in the pine bough hut as it had been last night, but it was still below freezing. Her fingertips were icy, and the hair that had pulled free of her ponytail clung to her face in stringy tendrils.

Vale tugged her jacket on and zipped it up to her chin, wincing as the damp fabric clung to her chilled skin. It felt like she'd pulled her clothes out of the dryer half an hour too soon. She crawled outside and stretched her back. The forest was calm and quiet, the only sound a few birds in the trees.

"Ash . . . ?" she called warily.

Still nothing.

A sliver of fear rose up Vale's spine. *What if he took off on me? What if I'm stuck here alone?* She followed Ash's footprints away from the hut for twenty feet, stumbling to a stop as she came across a series of tracks carefully laid out in the snow. The letters spelled out the word *PEE*. From the tail of the last *E*, the trail of footprints continued on into the forest.

A giggle bubbled from Vale's throat. She cupped her hand to her mouth, shouting: "You, uh . . . You doing okay out there?"

"Other than freezing my balls off and accidentally peeing on my shoe?" Ash said, his voice echoing in the distance. "Yeah. Totally fine. Best day of my life. Thanks."

Vale laughed. "Um . . . okay, then. TMI much?"

"You *asked*, Vale."

With a snort, she walked back to the camp, climbed into the lean-to to get her pack, and dug through it in search of supplies.

The food she'd brought was completely gone, an empty plastic bag and a bit of garbage in its place. Vale's stomach rumbled in protest. She'd think about that later. *Food*, Vale thought, *is a last-priority item*. The average person could live up to three months on body fat alone. It would be unpleasant, but not impossible, to last until they were found by rescuers . . . and that was the goal.

Be found.

Vale shook out her pack onto the black garbage bag, sorting through the items on the plastic that had formed the vapor barrier on which she'd slept. She had:

A change of clothes including one tank top, a fresh pair of panties, and walking shorts.

A safety kit that included eight Band-Aids, four antiseptic wipes, one small tube of antibiotic ointment, a small roll of medical tape, four pieces of gauze, and six blister-sealed acetaminophen tablets.

The kit also included one foil emergency blanket. Vale gasped as she saw it. *This could have been useful last night!* She'd entirely forgotten it was in the kit.

Two extra pairs of socks. Vale pulled those on immediately and put her damp pair in the backpack.

A small palm-sized flashlight that ran on a single AA battery.

Three empty black garbage bags (including the two they'd worn as rain slickers, then slept on).

One empty Ziploc baggie filled with crumbs of trail mix from the day before. Vale took a moment and licked out the bottom of the bag. It only made her hunger worse.

A twenty-ounce metal water canteen, mostly empty.

Six tampons and three heavy-flow sanitary pads (brought along at the insistence of her mother even though Vale's period wasn't due until next week).

A small compass—completely useless because she didn't know which direction they needed to go.

And one large Ziploc bag full of wrappers and an empty juice box.

Vale stared at the pile of supplies for a long time. This was it. This was what she had to survive with. It had felt like more than she'd ever need when she'd packed it under her father's watchful gaze, but now it seemed useless. Obvious things—like a handheld radio—were missing, useless items—like the sanitary pads—in their place. Her heart sank as she looked down at the pile.

"Matches," she murmured. "I should have brought matches."

Janelle Holland, Debra and Brad Shumway, and Ashton Hamid's mother, Zara, sat in the Waterton police headquarters office across from Constable Jordan Wyatt, the officer handling the missing persons' case. They'd been here for an hour, but it felt like ten times that.

Janelle stared down at her hands, willing herself not to cry. (The effort was harder than it seemed.) She'd broken down a few minutes ago, and as she stared into the grief-stricken faces of the Shumways and Mrs. Hamid, her body threatened to do it again.

"I'm sorry," Janelle said for the tenth (or perhaps twentieth) time. "I truly don't understand *how* Vale and Ash got separated from the rest of the group. They were accounted for at the lunch site, but—"

"If they were accounted for," Mr. Shumway interrupted, "I don't see *how* you lost them. There were three instructors, weren't there? *How?*"

"Yes, but it was foggy as we neared the campsite," Janelle said. "We were walking in the rain and—"

"But there's only one trail," Mr. Shumway said, pointing to the map on the office wall. "If there were other trails, I could understand it, but it's a straight run from Avion Ridge to—"

"Actually," Constable Wyatt said, "there *are* other trails."

"Stupid, stupid . . . ," Vale muttered. "They're the obvious thing to bring."

"What's that?"

Vale turned in surprise to see Ash crouched near the entrance to the shelter. His face was flushed like he'd been running, his dark hair tufted up on one side. She grinned. Somehow having a friend here made the whole lost-in-the-woods scenario feel less daunting.

"Nothing," she said. "Just wishing I'd brought along some matches. It would've changed *everything*."

"Yeah, well, beggars can't be choosers." Ash crawled through the doorway to join her inside.

"What's *that* mean?"

"It means we've got trouble."

Vale's breath caught. "We do?"

Ash sat down heavily on the ground next to her, the top of his head bumping the branches and dislodging a handful of snow that sprinkled down onto the two of them. Vale wiped it away from her neck and shivered. It had stopped snowing, but it was still unpleasantly cold.

"The trail's gone," Ash said. "The snow covered everything." He poked at the pile of supplies laid out on the garbage bag rather than look at Vale. "I took a bit of a walk, tried to find where we came in last night, but I couldn't."

"But the trail *can't* be gone."

"I've been out there searching since dawn."

"But that—" A painful lump caught in Vale's throat. "That doesn't make any sense. It can't be!"

"It can't be, but it *is*." Ash looked up, and for a split second, Vale could see the fear in his eyes. "I walked back and forth trying to locate the trail we came in on. There's lots of trails, lots of paths . . ."

"Game trails," Vale said quietly.

". . . but nothing I can see clearly. I just—I *think* I know the point where we came into the valley, but it was cloudy last night. So I can't be sure."

"So, the trail's gone," Vale said. "And we're lost. We've got to figure this out." She pointed to Ash's backpack. "Show me what you've got."

Ash frowned. "What I've got?"

"What supplies did you bring?"

Ash gave her a sheepish smile. "Nothing much. Sorry."

"Let me be the judge of that, okay?" Vale said. "Pour it out."

Ash grabbed his pack and started to unzip it, then stopped. He reached into his coat pocket. "Cell phone." He set it in the pile of equipment. "Though it'd be better if it was charged."

"And if we had reception." Vale sighed. "Even the hill wasn't high enough. The valley walls must be blocking it."

"Maybe." Ash's brows lifted. "Hey! We could climb one of the mountains. See if we could get reception!"

"You think we could? The peaks here are pretty high."

"We don't have to go all the way to the top. Just high enough to get reception."

"I don't know," Vale said. "I mean, I don't have any climbing equipment, and neither do you."

"But we could try to get a *little* higher at least."

"All right. That's a plan for later," she said. "What else do you have in the bag?"

Ash took the pieces out one by one. He had:

One bandanna.

An empty Mountain Dew bottle.

A long-sleeved thermal sweatshirt.

One large Ziploc full of Mike's lunch garbage.

A twenty-seven-ounce plastic water bottle, half-full.

Three sticks of Juicy Fruit gum, still in their wrappers.

"You've got foil!" Vale gasped.

"What?"

"The gum," she said, grabbing hold of it. "You've got foil! That's it! This will work!"

Ash stared at her. "What'll work?"

"If you have a battery"—she grabbed the small flashlight and popped open the battery case—"and you've got foil or steel wool or *something* conductive, then you have a spark." She laughed. "We've got fire!"

Ash stared at her for several seconds, and then a smile broke across his face. "Fire? Are you kidding me?"

"Nope. Not kidding. Foil and a battery make a crude lighter." She lifted her hand for a high five, and Ash smacked her palm. "We've got fire."

"Better yet, we've got an RTS!"

"A real-time strategy?" Vale snorted.

"You *know* it!" He made a whooping sound. "We're ready to deal with this crap situation!"

Vale giggled. "Uh . . . yeah. But the only problem is that it wears down the battery pretty fast, so we can't use the flashlight as a flashlight anymore. It's important the battery stays charged."

"Fair enough. So no flashlight." He grinned. "Hey! I've got a joke for you. How many gamers does it take to screw in a light bulb?"

Vale smiled. "I don't know."

"I dunno either. They're still rolling initiative to see who makes the first attempt."

Vale groaned.

"So we've got a lighter now," Ash said, pointing to their inventory. "That's cool!"

"It is, but we need to ration out the gum wrappers. They'll burn once we use them, so we've only got three total." Vale grinned. "We're going to get out of this mess one way or another, but if we're stuck here another night, at least we'll be warm."

"Awesome!" Ash clambered up and knocked his head on the ceiling again. More snow rained down on them.

Vale brushed it off her hair. "Ash? I'm not trying to bug you or anything, but could you be more careful? I don't know about you, but I'm all out of dry clothes."

"What? Oh, right." He crawled out of the shelter. "Sorry, Vale."

"It's fine. We've just got to stay dry if we can." Her smile faded. "And we've got to get out of the cougar's territory before it hunts again." She shivered. "It was in the tree above us last night. Don't know where it is now."

"We need to get out of here."

"Agreed."

Vale shook the snow off her head and gathered up the supplies. She carefully picked up the silver-wrapped gum and inspected it. "Praise God for too much TV," she said, then glanced out the open entrance. Ash was staring up at the mountain range that surrounded them.

Vale crawled out of the hut to join him. "So we use your phone to get a message out, then make a fire to stay warm while we wait."

"Sounds good to me. I want to go home."

"Me too."

Vale smiled. *Maybe this would turn out all right after all.*

The valley was a dish. On each side, mountain peaks rose like sharp white teeth, the fresh layer of snow spreading as far as the eye could see. In the trees, narrow paths wove like ribbons through the forest. Vale's stomach growled, and she took another swig of water to silence it. As unimportant as her hunger was, it made today ten times harder. Her limbs were weak, each step a struggle. And she wasn't the *only* hungry thing in the area.

Wild animals live here too.

As Ash had said, there were game trails *everywhere*, and with the passing of the deer in the early morning hours through their camp, there was no hint of which trail was the one they'd wandered in on. The wintery scene was one of stark beauty, but it held a sliver of fear. There was no hiding from the truth: They were well and truly lost.

None of the landscape that surrounded them was familiar to Vale. And try as she might, she could no longer tell which side of the valley they'd come in on. With all the hiking in the dark, she'd gotten completely turned around. Plus, there'd been the blood splatters in the snow, far too close to where they'd spent the night, and the large padded prints that crisscrossed through the woods. *Cougars.* The truth dampened Vale's earlier enthusiasm for walking back to civilization. The forest where they hiked was cougar territory.

"I think we should head up to that ridge," Ash said as they emerged from the forest into a wide clearing.

Vale followed the line of his finger to a ragged edge of rock that crossed the horizon. "Which one?"

"That one over there. See?"

"It has a lot of snow on it. Don't you think?"

"Well, yeah," he said. "But it's got an open path along the ridge *and* it's in the sunshine."

She gave a short laugh. "What does sunshine have to do with anything?"

"Side quest," he said, grinning. "You know how in a game, you don't know where to go, but then something lights up, and it's a sign." He pointed to the ridge. "That's our side quest!"

She stared for several long seconds as Ash's grin slowly faded.

"You don't want to go?"

"No. I just . . ." She pulled out her compass. "Hold on a sec. Let me check something."

The ridge was on the south side of the valley, at one of the lower points. Given that the Snowshoe Trail they'd originally come in on was on the far north side of Waterton Park, and the Blakiston Trail was south of that, it seemed like a sensible location to figure out where they'd gone off track.

"It's south," she said. "That's a good enough place to start."

"Why does it matter if it's south?"

"Well, we're on the north side of the park right now, heading in. Anything south *should* take us closer to civilization." She shrugged. "We might even be able to see where Twin Lakes is from there."

"Cool! And if we see the lakes, then I say we cross the ridge and walk south. Find Twin Lakes campground. Catch up with the rest of the class." Ash did a solo fist pump. "Bingo! We're back in time for supper."

"Sounds good to me. Let me fix the straps on my pack and—"

Ash was off before she could finish.

Vale pulled her backpack on, double-checked that she had everything zipped, and jogged across the clearing to where Ash had headed into the trees. The snow was slippery, and her feet slid in the melting slush. She looked up and groaned. If Ash was hungry, his hiking pace certainly wasn't showing it.

After a burst of running, she reached his side. "Trying to lose me?"

"Whoa! Sorry. I didn't realize." His pace slowed immediately.

"Thanks, Ash."

They walked in companionable silence for a few minutes before Ash spoke. "I wasn't trying to lose you before," he said. "I'm just excited to get back to the others."

"Me too."

"So let's hurry. Okay?"

Vale laughed. "I *am* hurrying, Ash. You're, like, a foot taller than me."

He gave her a confused look. "What's that got to do with anything?"

"Your legs are longer, which means your stride is longer too. Each step you take is a step and a half of mine. That distance adds up."

Ash frowned.

"Just trust me," Vale said. "It's physics."

He gave a one-shouldered shrug. "Guess that makes sense." And he slowed his pace again.

The snow became deeper as they moved farther up the slope. When going side by side became impossible, they took turns walking one in front of the other. The person walking in front broke trail through the foot of snow while the person following got a break by walking in their footsteps. It was slow, but effective.

Vale grew increasingly sweaty as the incline rose into a sharp tree-covered slope. There was no path, so there were no switchbacks to ease the hike, and Ash seemed intent on going straight up.

For an hour, they headed through the trees, pausing at regular intervals when the pace became too hard or the hunger too much.

When the forest thinned, Ash headed straight up the incline. Vale caught herself against a tree.

"Wait," she panted. "I need a second."

He glanced back. "What?"

She struggled up the next rise before she answered. Looking back behind them, her heart sank. The entire area was unfamiliar. There was no sign of a clear path whatsoever. They'd *definitely* come in on a game trail.

"I—I need a minute to catch my breath."

"*Another* break?" Ash looked longingly at the open slope above them. Yesterday, he'd been hiking on only four hours of sleep. Today, he was rested but worried, the urge to find Twin Lakes driving him forward. "But we're almost there."

"Yes. Just a minute—"

"But we've gotta get to the ridge."

"I know, but I can't—" Vale rubbed a line of sweat on her cheek away. "Look, Ash. I get that you're, like, a human mountain goat or something, but I need to *pace* myself."

He laughed. "My gaming buddies would crack up if they heard you say that."

"Maybe so, but it's true. Your legs are long. That makes it way easier for you to climb."

"I'll slow down again," he said.

"Actually, could you just weave a little bit? Make switchbacks."

"Make *what*?"

"Switchbacks. Those turns in the trail that"—she used her hand to make a zigzag sign—"flip back and forth to make the incline easier."

"You mean like skiers do?"

"Exactly, only going *up* instead of down."

Ash peered at the slope. "I guess I could, but it'd be faster if we went straight up."

"It won't be faster if I can't make it to the top." She pressed her hand to her side. "Let's just"—she made the same zigzag shape with her hand—"switch back and forth, okay?"

"All right. Works for me." Ash started away from the trees. "I'll break trail first."

With their new switchback pattern, the hiking—though steep—grew easier. When Ash's legs were exhausted from slogging through the deep snow, he let Vale take the lead. She took them almost to the end of the tree line, then Ash switched off again.

As they hit the open snow on the mountain's shoulder, Vale took the front. Now that they were gaining in altitude and in the sun, she was almost too warm. She tugged open her jacket, sighing as the chill air licked over her neck.

"So tired . . . of . . . hiking," Ash panted.

She looked back over her shoulder. "You okay?"

"Fine. Just bored."

"You want to play a game?"

"A game?" He gave her a crooked grin. "Like what?"

"I dunno. How about two truths and a lie?"

He laughed. "You're going to lose that game, Vale. I know *all* your dark secrets."

"Hardly." She coughed. "So you in or not?"

"Of course." He took two quick steps, closing the space between them so that they walked one behind the other. "You go first."

"All right. I can tie my laces behind my back—"

"Truth! I already know you can do that."

"Shh!" Vale said. "I'm not done yet. You've got to wait until I say all three."

Ash laughed. "You're going to have to come up with better clues than that."

"Fine. As I was saying . . . I can tie my laces behind my back." She glanced at Ash; he was grinning. "Second one is that I'd go into a burning building for Mr. Bananas, and my last one is that I have an A in every subject."

Ash's brows pulled together.

"Your guess?" Vale said sweetly.

"But . . . one of them has to be a lie. Right?"

Vale glanced back again and winked. "Uh-huh. One is."

"But . . ."

"You don't know?"

Ash frowned. "It doesn't make sense. They're *all* true."

"Nope."

"Which one?"

Vale laughed. "Oh, how the tables have turned!"

"No way! You'd let Mr. Bananas die? That's harsh!"

"I never said that!"

"But I *know* you're an A student . . . and I've *seen* you do the shoelaces thing. I don't—"

Vale broke into a peal of laughter.

"Seriously," Ash said. "What one is the lie?"

Vale peeked back at him. "I have a B minus in phys ed."

“Wait . . . Really?” Ash snorted.

“Uh-huh. My dark secret’s out.” She smiled. “All right. Your turn now.”

“Okay,” Ash said. “How about these . . .”

For a long time, they went back and forth, testing their knowledge of each other and laughing as they switchbacked up the mountain-side. Sweat ran down the center of Vale’s back despite the thick layer of snow on which they walked. Far below, in the valley they’d left behind, small melted patches opened up bare areas on the ground. Above the tree line, the peak neared. They just needed to get over the hump of snow-covered rock.

Vale was searching for a way up when she heard Ash snicker. A second later, something thudded into the center of her back. She looked over her shoulder.

“What’re you . . . ?”

She shrieked and jumped sideways as Ash lobbed a snowball at her. It bounced off her shoulder and scattered, showering her hair with flakes.

“Oh, you better RUN!” Vale laughed. “Did you forget which one of us played softball in middle school?”

“Stop! No! I didn’t—”

“Get running, Ash!” She reached down and grabbed a handful of the slushy-soft snow—*perfect for snowballs!*—then pressed it together. “’Cause I’m taking you DOWN!”

“Don’t!” Ash laughed. “It was a joke, Vale! I only—”

Vale pulled back, lifted her knee, and forced all her strength into the throw. It spiraled from her grip, spun perfectly, and smacked Ash dead center in the imagined bull's-eye of his chest. Snow spewed outward, dusting his face, eyebrows, and hair. Ash kicked a spray of snow her way. Suddenly they were laughing and shouting, frolicking in the snow with childish joy. For a moment, at least, the fears of the day were forgotten.

"Other trails?" Janelle repeated. "What do you mean?"

All three parents in the room turned as Constable Wyatt stood and headed to a large aerial map that hung on one wall. He gestured to the band of mountains that extended past Red Rock Canyon into the interior of BC. "To be honest, the entire area is covered in paths," he said. "Some are old First Nations' trails, half-grown over. They go throughout the woods. Others are game trails. There are even some that were once used by the trappers who traveled between Waterton and the BC interior in the 1930s and '40s." The officer stepped closer to the map, drawing lines with his fingertip through the shadows that marked the shift in elevation. "This, here, is Twin Lakes." His finger moved west. "And this, here, is Sage Pass. There's a trail that goes *there* too. It's not clearly marked—not like the hiking paths we have in the park—but if Vale and Ash got onto it, it'd be hard for them to tell the difference." He sighed. "Certainly if they were wandering around in the dark."

Mrs. Shumway burst into tears, and her husband looped his arm over her shoulders. "So what do we do? How do we find which one of those trails they actually took?" he asked, voicing Janelle's own question.

"There's already a search team on the ground," the officer said. "But it's a large area to cover, since we don't know where they went off course. We're assembling another volunteer force to assist in the search."

Janelle cleared her throat. "Then I'm going with them."

The snowball fight near the top of the ridge stopped all progress. Ash lunged and dashed, evading Vale's increasingly accurate volleys. Gusty winds blew snow back toward him, blinding Ash as he danced out of her way. At the top of the ridge, a C-shaped cornice of snow hung—a frozen wave—blocking their way. Below it, the wet, slushy snow near the top made every foothold difficult, and now that they were out of the trees, there were no handholds to catch himself when he fell.

Ash scooped up a handful of snow and lobbed it back over his shoulder at Vale. "Stay sharp, Shumway!"

She laughed as the snowball thudded into the snow at her feet. "Missed me! Better work on your aim."

"You moved! My aim's as good as—"

A snowball smacked Ash's face, dusting his eyebrows white. Laughing, he clambered away from Vale, loping horizontally along the slope rather than going straight up.

"Wait for me!" Vale called.

He glanced back over his shoulder. She had fallen behind him in the past few seconds. They were separated by twenty feet or more, a line of footsteps linking the two of them like a chain. Ash's feet slowed. "All right, but—" A snowball smacked him in the leg. "Oh, you sneaky bastard!"

"Get ready!" she laughed. "Secondary attack starts . . . NOW!"

Another snowball followed the first, and Ash pushed himself into a half jog, whooping and laughing. "I'm outta here."

"Slow down!" Vale yelled. "You can't ditch me!"

"There are no rules in"—a white projectile appeared in his peripheral vision, and he dodged it at the last second—"a snowball fight!" He picked up another handful of snow, tossing it back. "Cheater!"

"Slow down!"

"No way!"

"Ash, come ON! That's not FAIR!"

Ash took a few steps up the snowy drift, slid, and fell. Another snowball hit his shoulder. Laughing, he lobbed one back in return. The snow was up to his knees now, growing deeper with each step. The drift over the rock was a treacherous combination. He got four steps, then slipped again, jarring his knees as he went down. He tried again and again. Each time he fell, he caught himself, until his hands were numbed from the cold.

"Seriously!" Vale called. "I really can't keep up!"

Ash glanced back to discover Vale was nearly at his side. "Liar!" He laughed. Another ball hit him in the back, spraying up his neck. "You're fricking lethal, Vale!" He palmed a handful of snow and threw it in a high arc that swung up for a long moment, then came down on her head.

Hoots followed his words. "Oh, I'm gonna get you for that!" Vale grabbed a handful of compacted snow and pulled one leg back, aimed, and released.

With a shriek, Ash jumped to avoid the snowball. His feet hit a crust of snow—causing the surface to shift—at the same time as his voice boomed outward. "NO!" The sound echoed up the slope like a drum, only it didn't fade away. It grew louder.

Both Ash and Vale turned in shock as above them, a slab of snow the size of a car cracked away from the overhang and began to slide toward them.

"Avalanche!" Vale screamed. "Run!"

They were on an open slope. There were no trees. The snowslide was almost entirely above them. A single thought shot through Ash's mind.

We're going to die when that hits us.

CHAPTER SIX

"We're gonna die, you know."
"Maybe. But if we die, we're gonna die walking."
ROBERTO CANESSA AND NANDO PARRADO, *ALIVE*

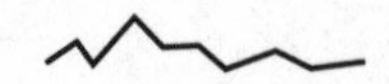

THE TEENS STARED in horror at the massive slab of snow tumbling toward them. A primitive part of Ash's brain pushed him to run before he'd consciously thought to do it. Vale was already in motion, ten steps ahead of him. She stumbled and caught herself in the knee-deep snow, then ran again, heading straight back along the path they'd just cleared, Ash close on her heels. The ground rumbled as the slide neared. He didn't look back—didn't dare!—just pushed himself as fast as humanly possible.

When Ash was playing a video game, there were moments when he lost himself in the action. Time slowed. His mind expanded. In those moments, he was swept away by the sheer exhilaration of the competition, caught up by the adrenaline that surged through him as he worked through an online campaign, one challenge, one fight after the other.

With the avalanche rumbling toward him, he caught onto the same degree of clarity. His thighs ached as he forced his way through the deep snow, one footstep after another after another. He didn't slip. Didn't hesitate. *There's no time.* Each movement was perfect. Each footstep orchestrated to get him out of the way. Vale, however, was losing speed.

Her legs are too short, Ash thought. *She's not gonna make it.*

Reaching her side, Ash grabbed hold of Vale's arm and dragged her forward. *Faster . . . faster . . .*, his mind chanted. Vale stumbled, and he jerked her back up. He let go of her elbow to grab her hand. The first pebbles of snow pelted the backs of their legs. Ash sprinted forward, dragging Vale with him. The snow became a churning mire around their legs, pulling, tugging, trying to knock them down. The ground began to move!

Behind them, a sound as loud as a freight train roared past.

And then . . . *silence.*

Ash and Vale didn't stop running until they'd reached the trees. They'd covered the entire distance in less than a quarter of the time it had taken them to hike it the first time. Vale was gasping, her mouth the O of a fish out of water. Ash let go of her hand and caught himself against the trunk of a tree. He coughed and gagged.

Holy crap, that was close!

Ash stared back the way they'd come. The entire slope was scraped bare. The glint of brownish rocks glittered in the sunshine. He took a few steps away from the trees and looked down the slope. The trees below them had been knocked clear, the slide burrowing itself like a fist into the forest's edge. Broken spikes of tree trunks, split like kindling, stuck out from the snow.

A giggle of sheer panic broke free of Ash's throat. He buckled over, holding his hands against his thighs as he laughed. "We fricking *owned* that!" His hoots grew louder, tears filled his eyes. "We MADE it! We survived!"

No one answered.

"Vale . . . ?" He lifted his head to discover he was standing alone in the snow. A movement caught his eye. Vale was walking slowly back the way they'd just come.

"Vale . . . ? Vale! Where are you going?"

She glanced back and then, strangely enough, she laughed. "The path's wide open now." She pointed to the rock face, scoured clear by the slide. "The snow's gone. Let's figure out where we are."

Ash jogged forward, the aftermath of the close call leaving him jittery. "Hold up!" he called. "I'm coming too. Wait for me!"

Vale grinned and waited.

They stood at the top of the ridge, a hump of brown rock drying under their feet, while in the distance, the snowslide was a white footprint in the green-gray tree line. Ash stared at the phone's screen. *Please connect . . . please . . .*

"Anything yet?" Vale asked.

Ash's heart sank. "Still no connection." He swore under his breath. "Hold on a sec. I'm gonna try a different place."

Five minutes later, he returned from the quick jaunt along the rocky ridge.

"Any luck?"

He shook his head, too upset to say the words aloud. *We're in Canada, for God's sake! Why isn't there any reception here?*

"Guess Ms. Holland was right about no reception," Vale said.

"I'm almost out of power anyhow." Ash held down the off button—he needed the power to last until the next time he tried—then shoved the phone into his pocket. "Waste of time for us to climb all the way up here."

"Maybe . . . maybe not."

He looked up to discover Vale standing at the edge of the ridge, staring south. She had a compass in her hand.

"You see something?" Ash peered down into the valley, searching. It was a rippled blanket of trees. A thin layer of snow covered the ground, growing heavier on the higher slopes. If this was a game he was playing, he'd just take off and explore, but the rules were different. Here every decision took incredible amounts of time to complete. Like game lag, but in *hours* rather than in seconds. Worse yet, in the mountains there were no second chances. These were their lives they were gambling with.

"There," Vale said, pointing. "That blue mark. What's that?"

Ash followed the line of her arm. A faint blue glimmer, like a jewel, was nestled in the forest at the bottom. Near it, a slightly duller blue shimmered behind a screen of pine trees. The fear disappeared in a rush of excitement.

"It's Twin Lakes!" Ash shouted. "That's it! We're almost there!" He headed down the far side of the ridge.

"Wait! Don't leave me behind!"

He glanced back in confusion. "I wasn't leaving you."

“Good.” She jogged to his side. “Just . . . don’t.”

“I want to head down.” Ash pointed. “Those lakes must be where Ms. Holland and the others are, right? If we start now, we can be there before dinnertime.”

Vale lifted her hand to shade her eyes as she peered into the distance. “I . . . I’m not sure.”

“What do you *mean*, you’re not sure? You’re the one who pointed it out, Vale. It’s two lakes.”

“Yeah, but the second one seems awfully small.” She squinted. “I’m not even sure that second bit of blue *is* a lake, if I’m honest about it.”

Ash grinned. “It’s gotta be a lake!”

“It looks like *something*, but I’m not sure what. At most, maybe a boggy area.”

He started down the slope. “I say we go check it out. Then we’ll *know* it’s a lake.”

“And if it’s the wrong place and it’s *not* Twin Lakes? What then, huh?”

“Trust me. It’s *not* the wrong place.” Ash took sliding steps, dropping in elevation as he went. “It’s easy walking if we go this way,” he said. “There’s a path right through the trees.”

“A trail?”

“Not a real trail—no—but I can see a way to get down.” He pointed. “See that line? It’s a straight drop down to the valley.”

“I . . . I’m not sure.”

“C’mon, Vale. Just go with this. I can *see* two lakes down there.” Ash walked on. He was almost at the tree line when he heard Vale puffing behind him. He paused until she reached his side.

"What if someone is looking for us?" she said.

"Then we'll help 'em out by finding them first."

She pointed through the trees. "But I only see *one* lake clearly. The other one might be anything at all."

"Doesn't mean the other one's not a lake too. Just means it's smaller." He shrugged. "Besides. If it's the wrong lake, then we're no worse off than we are now. Right?"

"I . . . I guess so." Vale turned to stare out at the faint blue smudges: two of them side by side. "You're right. It's probably two. So let's hike down. It might not be Twin Lakes, but at least it's south."

"South?"

"Yeah. The town of Waterton is south of us. South is the direction we should be heading." She nodded. "It's a good idea, Ash. Let's go."

A grin broke across Ash's face, so wide and bright he seemed to shine from within. "And it's a lake, right?" He held out his empty water bottle. "Not sure about you, but I'm thirsty."

"Oh man, me too."

"Good, then it's settled," he said, already hiking again. "We head down to the lake. Meet up with the class."

"Sounds like a plan to me."

As they reached the first trees of the forest, Ash looked over, his eyes twinkling. "Hey, Vale. You know how trees get onto the internet?"

She smiled. "Uh . . . nope."

"They log on."

It took them most of the afternoon to pick their way down through the trees. This side of the mountain was covered in deadfall, the remnants of a forest fire dotting the landscape with blackened spears of long-dead trees. It slowed them more than Ash wanted, and he knew if they were still walking once nightfall arrived, they'd be in the same trouble as the night before. Low-lying clouds had begun to fill the valley, the landscape growing dimmer with every passing hour.

Thirst was Ash's constant companion. He ate snow to stave it off, but it never entirely quenched his thirst. The lakes were still miles away. He and Vale laughed and talked, trying to lighten the situation.

"Would you rather live an extra fifty years or stay sixteen forever but die twenty years early?" he asked.

Vale snorted. "Neither."

"That's *not* how the game works. You've got to choose."

"Fine. Then I choose the fifty."

Ash stumbled. "Even if you get all wrinkly and ancient? Have you ever seen people who live to one hundred and twenty? They're like giant raisins."

Vale grinned. "That's really *mean*, Ash."

"But it's true!"

She shook her head. "I'd still take the fifty extra years rather than stay young. I kind of think it's going to be fun growing up."

"Huh. Really?"

"Yeah. You get to see the future. Play with grandkids. Enjoy new technology."

"Whoa! Didn't think of that," Ash said. "All the new video games!"

"Exactly." Vale giggled. "My turn now: Would you rather be able to read people's minds or influence people's thoughts?"

"Thoughts, definitely! I'd make 'em do what I wanted." He dropped his voice to a robotic drone. "Vale Shumway will do all my homework for me."

"That sounds an awful lot like . . . a supervillain in the making."

"Oh, come on. Wouldn't you?"

She shrugged. "I don't know."

"But what's the point in getting into people's heads, then? I mean, why just *hear* what they're thinking? Why not change it instead?"

"I guess I kind of wish I knew where I stood with some people."

Ash was quiet for a moment, remembering the relentless teasing Vale experienced at school and the online harassment that had ended several happy years of their gaming together. "I guess that makes sense."

She gave him a tight smile. "All right. Next question."

"Would you rather be trapped in an avalanche or . . . ?" He gave her a devilish smile. "Crushed by REGRETS?"

"Trapped in an avalanche," she said, then began to laugh. "No! NO! Switching my answer. Crushed by regrets. Less chance of death."

"Nice one." He grinned. "That was a trick question, you know."

"I know, Ash. I know."

The wind picked up midday, and their laughter faded. Soon they were walking in silence again. With each minute that passed an uneasy feeling—like a stone—grew deep in Ash's gut. When they passed the midway point on the treed slope—but still hadn't seen an actual trail—he *knew* Vale had been right all along. The first lake twinkled like a sapphire. The second was little more than a marsh, full of cattails. The patch was fed by the lake they'd seen from above. That single lake was completely alone. *Lost*, just like the two of them.

Another hour of hiking took them to its shores. The wind sent icy spatters of sleet onto his head, but Ash was so thirsty, he hardly noticed. He fell to his knees and dug his water bottle out of his pack. It had been empty for hours, and his tongue felt thick and woolen with thirst. He pulled off the lid and dunked it under the water.

"Do you think it's safe to drink the water?" Vale said warily.

"I'm going to take my chances." He lifted the bottle to his lips. It was filled to the brim with lake water, bits of flotsam swirling in the bottom, but he chugged it down without a second thought. The icy water sluiced down his throat, quenching his thirst. His teeth ached from the cold. Ash didn't care. He filled it a second time, drinking in greedy gulps.

He set the bottle down to find Vale watching. "What's up?"

She stubbed her toe on the ground. "Does it taste okay?"

He shrugged. "Tastes fine to me." Vale shifted foot to foot while Ash took one last drink and tipped his head back. "Ahhhh! So good." He double-checked that the lid was on and put the refilled bottle into his backpack.

Vale unzipped her pack and pulled out her own canteen, crouching down at the water's edge. "I'll risk diarrhea over dying of thirst."

Ash broke into raucous laughter. "That's fricking disgusting!"

"Not as disgusting as getting beaver fever and not having toilet paper to deal with the runs. My dad picked up giardia on one of our camping trips. He had stomach issues for weeks. It really sucks."

Ash's laughter faded as his stomach churned. Suddenly the water he'd swallowed didn't feel so good in his stomach. "That's . . . not so good."

"No. But hopefully it won't come to that." Vale finished filling her bottle and took a long drink. She let out a happy sound of relief. "That's so good. You don't have a chocolate bar hidden in that pack somewhere, do you?"

He groaned. "I wish! I'm so hungry, I'd kill for a Mars Bar."

"I'd sell my best friend for a milkshake."

"Me?" Ash said in mock horror.

Vale giggled. "Of course. We're talking an honest-to-God milkshake, right? You seem like a fair trade."

"Ouch!" He thumped his chest. "Right in the feels."

Vale snorted with laughter.

Ash grinned. "Don't feel bad. Truth is, I'd sell out *all* my friends for a burger. You included, Vale."

She laughed. "Not just *any* burger, though: It's got to be a meal! How about a Teen Burger, fries, and a root beer float? A bacon cheeseburger sounds like heaven right about now."

"Man," Ash said. "That would be *amazing*!"

"It really would. When we get out of here, A&W's going to be my first stop." Vale's stomach made an audible gurgle, and she laughed. "But for now, we've got water. That's a start. Right?"

"A good one."

Ash wasn't sure *how* it had happened, but things felt *good* again. They weren't safe—and this *wasn't* Twin Lakes—but at least they had each other to rely on.

"Well, I don't know about you," Ash said. "But I'm cold."

"Yeah. Me too." Vale lifted her face toward the sky. Around them, the ground was still covered in a thin layer of snow; more was falling. "We're going to have another dump of snow overnight. We should make a fire. Dry off if we can."

"How does that foil trick you talked about work?"

"I'll show you." Vale held out her hand. "Can I have one of those gum wrappers?"

"Sure."

Ash found them in the bottom of the bag and unwrapped a stick of gum. His mouth flooded with saliva at the mere thought of it. He *wanted* to swallow it—to eat every single stick that he had left—but he forced himself not to. Instead, he took out a stick and held it toward Vale.

"Here," he said. "It's not a meal, but it tastes good."

"Thanks, Ash." She popped the gum into her mouth and sighed in pleasure. "Sooo good."

"I know, right?"

She groaned. "I'm still hungry, though."

"Me too."

"Fire first. Then we'll think about food. We've got to hurry; the snow is starting to stick." Vale headed to the nearby trees, searching the lower branches one after the other. She muttered to herself as she worked: "Should've brought a book. Then at least we'd have some kindling. Ugh! Just need something that'll burn . . ."

"What're you looking for?"

She looked back at him. "I need some old-man's beard."

"Some *what*?"

"It's a kind of lichen that grows on the branches of trees." She reached up and tugged a handful of black tangles from the branches, then held them out to Ash to see. "There's this one and another kind of moss, bright green. Both are good kindling."

"On it."

Ash moved around the lake, grabbing bits and pieces. When he had a handful, he headed back to where Vale was sitting, a pile of moss, twigs, and a few larger branches neatly stacked beside her. She looked up as he arrived.

"There you are," she breathed, then glanced at the forest behind them. "Stay close, all right? I think there's something in the woods."

"Deer again?"

"Don't think so," she said. "It sounded big."

"Another cougar?"

"I hope not, but it's . . . it's something."

Ash dropped his moss and lichen into the pile next to her. "Then we'd better hurry up with this fire."

She nodded and pulled out the flashlight, then popped out the battery. "We're going to make a prison lighter."

Ash chuckled. "You've been to prison, huh?"

"No, but I read books and I watch TV. You should try it sometime," she teased. "Get out of the basement once in a while."

"You know me. If it's not a game, I'm not interested." He winked. "*You* used to be exactly the same."

"Yeah . . ."

"You could still get involved. D&D is great. It's hands-on and—"

"You know," Vale said, interrupting. "Books might not be your thing, but there's this show called *Orange Is the New Black*—" Vale put the kindling into a little pile with the lichen on the bottom and a small tripod of twigs on top. "Anyhow, they use prison lighters in the show. I remember seeing a YouTube video on how it actually works. All you need is a battery and a bit of foil." Vale took the gum wrapper and folded it in half, then carefully tore a half circle from the center so that only a thin bit of foil held the two ends together. "You let the foil touch either end of the battery and . . ." Vale pressed the two ends down. "Oh no!"

"What's wrong?"

"I tore through the gum wrapper. It doesn't have a connection now." Vale held out her hand. "Can I have another wrapper?"

Ash handed her the second of the three wrappers. Vale went through the same process of folding and tearing. She worked methodically, her eyes focused on the line of foil. The valley was growing darker by the second. Vale didn't seem to notice.

"Let's try that again," she said quietly, then pressed the two ends of the foil on the terminals of the battery. Seconds passed . . . half a minute . . . *Nothing happened.*

Ash cleared his throat. "Are you sure that—"

"Bingo!"

A small flame danced in the center of the foil. Ash stared at it in awe. It was so small, but it held the potential of heat and safety. As he watched, Vale lit a piece of lichen, then another. The flames greedily spread through the green furry layer to the wooden twigs. When this held, she added bigger pieces, and then full branches. Soon there was a cheery fire dancing in front of them.

"Wahoo!" Ash hooted. "That was fricking AWESOME!"

"Thanks," Vale said with a grin. "I'm glad it actually worked."

"You hadn't tried it before?"

"Nope."

"Cool, cool! That's pretty impressive." Ash held out his hands, sighing as heat spread into them. "You got some mad survival skills there, my friend."

Vale snorted. "You've got skills too, Ash. You found water, didn't you?"

"I declare us . . ." Ash stood and raised his arms. "THE SURVIVAL SQUAD!" Birds burst into flight from nearby trees at his booming voice. "Commander Valeria Shumway and her trusty second, the illustrious Ashton Hamid . . . questing into unknown lands!"

"Is this another attempt to get me to join your Dungeons & Dragons group?" Vale said. "'Cause I don't—"

"Zerging their way through the dangers of the nether realms on a campaign to find CIVILIZATION!"

Vale's giggles turned into cackles, and then hoots. Ash grinned and began to laugh. Suddenly they were both cracking up, the sound echoing joyously through the clearing with the crackling fire. It was snowing in the forest. They were lost. They were hungry. But for the first time since they'd been caught in the rain the night before, they were warm. Vale grinned at him.

“So we’ve got fire,” Ash said. “Shelter’s next, right?”

“I’ll start the lean-to if you get the branches.”

“Sure thing. And I’ll pay for the burgers if you hike out of here to pick ’em up.”

Vale laughed. “It’s a deal, Ash.”

CHAPTER SEVEN

"I have made fire!"

CHUCK NOLAND, *CAST AWAY*

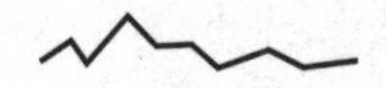

VALE HAD AN armful of branches when she heard Ash gasp. She spun around so fast she almost dropped them. "What's wrong?"

Ash stood slack-jawed a stone's throw from the half-constructed lean-to, his tall silhouette traced by orange bands of firelight. "Geez. Would ya look at that?" He dropped his branches to the ground and pointed upward.

She lifted her chin, searching for a cougar in the treetops. *Nothing there.* Vale's gaze rose higher, caught by something in the dark sky. Her eyes widened in shock. In the time they'd been gathering wood, the clouds had parted.

"Oh wow . . . ," she whispered.

The night sky glittered with starlight. Unlike the dimmed view Vale got from her backyard in the city, the mountain perspective was breathtaking. A million stars shone like diamonds strewn across a black velvet cloak. The Milky Way, usually a smudge in the darkness when Vale saw it from her window, was awash with pinpricks of dancing light.

"They're so bright," Ash said. "I've never seen anything like that."

"Me neither." Vale had gone camping before, but never in the backcountry. The KOAs where her family stayed were glorified parking lots with bathrooms and cooking facilities, streetlights on all the corners. Here, a thousand stars she'd never noticed now vied for her attention. The sight of it was dizzying.

Ash took a step away from the fire and staggered. "It feels like . . . like I'm going to fall *up*, or something."

"Up?"

"Seriously, though. It's weird, Vale. The sight of it . . . makes me feel stoned. You know?"

Vale giggled. "Uh . . . nope. I *wouldn't* know."

Ash laughed. "Okay, well, it doesn't look real somehow. Like it's a special effect from a game or something."

"Maybe it's that we're used to the light pollution."

"Guess so." Ash turned in a slow circle. "This is beautiful. Crisp. Bright. Weirdly . . . perfect somehow."

"Agreed."

They stood in the darkness, the scent of pine and wood smoke surrounding them as they stared up into the vaulted dome of the sky. They might have stayed like that for far longer, but a sound in the bushes tore Vale's attention downward.

"Did you hear that?" she hissed.

"Hear what?"

"*That*. The sound over there." She stared into the sooty black beyond the firelight. "Something's moving in the trees again."

"Like . . . a ghost?"

"No, not like a *ghost*, Ash! This is real life, not some game we're playing."

He let out a nervous chuckle. "Right. Sorry. I . . ." He cleared his throat. "That just kind of popped out. So, what was it?"

"I don't know, but I think it might be the animal I heard in the trees when we were gathering wood." Vale backed toward the bonfire. "It's back . . . and it's closer."

"Where? I didn't hear anything."

"By those two big trees." The burning wood popped loudly, making Vale jump as sparks rose into the air. "Hold on. I'm going to grab the flashlight."

"You can't!"

"Why not?"

He gestured to the fire. "You said we needed to save the battery so we could use it as a lighter."

"Right, but I need to know if—"

"Just tell me where it is," he said. "I'll check it out."

"Ash, I don't think that's a good idea."

"It's probably nothing." He winked. "And we've established it's not a ghost. So where'd you hear it?"

"By that bush over there by that bunch of pine trees," she said, pointing.

"Big or small?"

"I couldn't tell. It moved the bushes . . . but it *sounded* big when I heard it before."

"Can you see it now?"

"Er . . . Not clearly. But—" Vale squinted. "There! Yes. Something moved over there by those two trees. You see the dark shape? There's something *behind* that bush. It's moving around in the shadows."

"Uh-huh . . . Yup. Got it." Ash reached down and took hold of the unburned end of a large stick. He pulled it from the fire, shook the embers from it in a spray of sparks, and lifted it above his head like a makeshift torch. "Hold on a second."

"Wait!" Vale cried. "You can't just walk over there!"

"I can't just stay here and do nothing."

Vale stared in horror as Ash headed into the darkness. Long seconds passed. The shape in the shadows was no longer moving. Vale took a hesitant step forward. *Is that something by the two trees?* She took another step. *It looks like something, but—*

With a shriek, Ash turned tail and bolted back toward her, torch held high. Vale screamed. There was no place to go. No place to run!

Ash cackled as he reached the firelight. "Do NOT go over there!"

"What?!"

He dropped the wood back into the fire, leaned over, and put his hands against his thighs, his laughter growing more raucous by the second.

"Seriously, Ash. It's not funny!" she shouted. "What is it over there?"

He looked up and grinned. "A skunk. And if he wants to camp out in those bushes, I say we give it to him."

Vale looked over to the shadows, then back to Ash. A smile slowly crossed her face. "A skunk?"

"Uh-huh." He grinned. "Not a ghost or a goblin or a bear or a cougar. Just a good ol' skunk."

Vale giggled. "Figures."

"Oh! And I thought of a joke while I was creeping around in the dark."

"Of *course* you did, Ash."

"You want to hear?"

"Sure."

Ash nodded. "Why do you always find demons in the same game level as ghouls?"

"No idea."

"Because demons are a ghoul's best friend."

And with that, Ash and Vale began to laugh.

Even after the new lean-to was finished, Vale couldn't get rid of the feeling that they were being watched. Twice she turned, certain that *something* waited in the darkness, but the bushes were silent.

Nerves strung taut, Vale took a walk around the fire's bright perimeter, searching the shadows. *Nothing there.* A few minutes later, the skunk waddled out of the bushes. Vale and Ash scrambled back out of its way. It strode past the camp as if they weren't even there, took a drink from the lake, then headed off in search of a quieter abode. Still, Vale's uneasiness lingered.

It's probably nothing, she told herself. *Just creeping myself out.*

She sat beside the fire and stretched out her legs, letting the warmth seep into her aching limbs. They'd walked as far today as they'd walked yesterday, but without food. The pain of hunger was an unending ache in her stomach. She lifted the water bottle and drank deeply. For a moment, the pain subsided, but her lightheadedness stayed.

Again, the sense of being watched returned and Vale looked up. She caught Ash watching her. "Something wrong?" she asked.

"No, uh . . ." He cleared his throat. "I know you hike and all that, but have you ever gone camping in the woods like this before?"

"Camping, yes. But certainly not like this." She gave a weary laugh. "This is *nothing* like the KOA."

Ash tossed another stick onto the fire. "The KOA?"

"Kampgrounds of America—misspelled with a *K*," Vale said. "It's pretty fancy, actually."

"Fancy, huh?" Ash laughed. "I could do with some of that right about now. This whole overnight trek was my first camping trip. I've never stayed anyplace rougher than a Super 8."

"Really?"

"Yeah . . . my mom's just not into the whole camping thing. She likes everything neat and orderly."

"How about your dad?"

Ash's smile disappeared between one breath and the next. "I, uh . . . Not sure. Never asked him."

Vale frowned. "But surely you must have talked about it at some point."

"Nope."

"But . . ." Her words faded uncertainly. There was more to this story. She could see it in Ash's hunched shoulders and the way he stared at the fire. She wanted to ask more, but didn't dare. Vale obviously knew his parents were divorced—there'd never been a "Mr. Hamid" in the picture in all the years they'd been friends—but she'd never once heard Ash *talk* about his dad. During a decade of hanging out, his absent father had never once come up. Now he had.

They sat in silence. Vale hardly dared to breathe. *Just great, Vale. You've really put your foot in your mouth this time*, she could imagine her father saying.

Ash looked up. "When my parents split up," he said, "Leo and I stayed with Mom. So . . . my dad wasn't around so much."

"Sorry about that."

He snorted at some private joke. "Oh, don't be sorry. My dad's a dick—always has been."

Vale frowned. Ash so rarely spoke of his father; she didn't want to say the wrong thing.

"Anyhow. My mom's allergic to bee stings, so she doesn't like the outdoors that much. She just . . ." Ash shook his head. "She doesn't. So I never went camping when I was a kid."

"Well . . . that's cool, I guess."

He side-eyed her. "Cool?"

"I mean, for someone who's never camped before, you're doing pretty awesome."

"Thanks . . . I guess."

"No, really, Ash, I—I mean it. I—" Vale laughed. "Sorry, it came out weird. I . . . I'm making it worse. Aren't I?"

"Nah." He smirked. "You're usually so pulled together, I kind of enjoy you blurting things out. It's . . ." He waved his hand as if trying to find the right word. "Refreshing."

"Refreshing, huh?" Vale giggled. "My dad hates it. Says I'm 'unladylike' when I say things without thinking."

"Your dad sounds like a dick too."

"No, he's really not," Vale rushed to say. "He's a good guy, just . . . kind of old fashioned." She sighed. There was *more* to this story too. Like the way her father seemed unable to acknowledge her sexuality. Or how she never really felt like she could talk to him honestly about her feelings. "My dad and I have our issues," she said stiffly. "It's . . . it's weird. We can't talk. Or we *can* talk, but there are times when Dad doesn't really *listen*." She cringed. "Sorry. TMI."

"It's fine. Good to know that your family's screwed up too."

"I guess so," she said, and turned her attention back to the fire. "Maybe everyone is messed up, at least a little bit. I mean, if you look close enough . . ." Her words faded. That was what bothered Vale about talking about her family. No matter where you came from; no matter how good your family looked on the outside, *everyone had baggage*.

"So Valeria Shumway's secret weakness finally reveals itself . . ."

Vale shot him a dirty look. "Ash . . ."

"Knows everything about camping, but not so good with real-life humans," he teased.

"Don't be a jerk." She laughed.

"Oh, I'm not judging. There's a reason I stick to gaming. Lets you focus on strategy and skill in a controlled environment rather than forcing you to make small talk with people you don't know."

"But you talk to *everyone*, Ash. You're friends with, like, the entire school population."

Ash snorted. "Thanks."

"You remember that first day in kindergarten?" she asked.

"Uh . . . barely."

"You walked right up to me and introduced yourself. Your full first, middle, and last name." Vale giggled. "Oh God. Do you remember what you were wearing?"

Ash groaned. "Please don't—"

"You were wearing a *suit*! A tiny little three-piece suit, and your lunch kit looked like a brief—"

"Stop."

"—case, and you were all prim and proper, and I just . . ." Vale broke into a gale of laughter. Her memory of tiny Ash was a perfectly crisp photograph, and it was so *unlike* the gamer she knew now, she hardly knew how to reconcile the two of them.

"I'll have you know, my *mother* dressed me that day," Ash said dryly.

"But it—it was a—suit—" Vale laughed harder.

"I came over to you," he said, "because the teacher was freaking me out with all her rules." Ash shook his head. "I figured you were safe 'cause you looked like you knew what you were doing."

"Back in kindergarten?" Vale's giggles continued. "Ah . . . the power of deception. I was terrified."

"Nah. You were solid, even then. I could tell."

Vale grinned and wiped tears of laughter from the sides of her eyes. "Thanks, Ash."

"I'm a very good judge of character, you know."

"Oh, I know."

Ash pulled out a piece of gum from his pack, unwrapped it, then paused. He broke it in half. "Want some?"

Vale's mouth flooded with saliva. "I . . . yeah. Is that okay? Do you have enough?"

"Last one. You might as well enjoy it too."

She took the piece from his fingers and popped it in her mouth. "God, I don't even *like* this flavor, but it's *so* good."

Ash chuckled. "Here," he said. Vale looked up to see him holding out the wrapper between two fingers. "We need that for the prison lighter, right?"

"Yeah. Thanks."

Vale tucked it deep into her pocket. All joking aside, fire was the difference between life and death. Hunger could be ignored for the time being. *Cold would kill*, and controlling the fire was trickier than Vale expected. The wood in the valley by the lake was wet from the snowfall, and the campfire threatened to go out unless she tended it constantly. She shivered and added another piece. It sizzled and smoked before bursting into flames. Ash, a short ways away, was caught up in his own thoughts as he too fed the fire.

As the hours of darkness lengthened, the temperature dropped and new snow began to fall. Vale shivered. Some primitive part of her mind had begun to recognize that they needed to move. Though she knew there *must* be a rescue being staged at this point, she and Ash had walked for hours without the other members of their group. They could be many kilometers off track. With the area so densely wooded and animal tracks crisscrossing the snow, it would be difficult to see them from above. They were lost. And as much as she'd hoped for it, this lake was clearly *not* one of the Twin Lakes. It was in a solitary valley with no trails as far as Vale could tell. To wait here meant being trapped by the winter snows. They hadn't arrived yet, but they *would*. And that would make getting out of the mountains next to impossible.

Vale tossed the last branch of wood they'd gathered into the fire and looked up. "I think tomorrow we should head south."

"South again? Why?"

"Because this *isn't* one of the Twin Lakes."

"It could be," he said wistfully. "We haven't searched the entire valley. There might be another, bigger lake somewhere."

"No. If there was another lake, then the rescuers would already be here. Twin Lakes is where they'd start looking."

"But we don't know that."

"No one is here, Ash. We're alone." She let out a tired sigh. "We probably should have stayed where we were."

"I *thought* we were close to Twin Lakes," he said. "All right? That's where the class was headed when we got lost. It *seemed* like a good guess at the time."

"I never said it was your fault. We *both* decided to come into the valley."

Vale waited for him to answer, but he hunched his shoulders and stared into the flames instead. The fire around which they both sat had dwindled down to embers, the bits and pieces of wood belching out smoke that made Vale cough. She reached for a piece of firewood, but the pile was down to twigs.

With a grunt, she climbed to her feet. "I'm getting some more wood."

"I can help."

Vale glanced back over her shoulder. "No, Ash," she said tiredly. "It's my turn. You stay warm."

Away from the firelight, the landscape fell into velvety blackness, shadows morphing with the indigo spikes of trees. Vale grabbed a pine bough and tugged, but it was a green branch and it wouldn't tear free.

"Come . . . ON!" She jerked, and her hand slipped on the needles. Vale stumbled back and came down hard, her ankle twisting underneath her. "Ouch!"

"Vale . . . ?" Ash's voice came from the direction of the dying fire. "You okay over there?"

"I'm fine," she said. "I just tripped and . . ."

Vale's words died in her throat as something large—as big as a human, or bigger—rustled the bushes on her other side. Her breath caught. *Don't move. Don't make a noise! DO NOT DO ANYTHING!* For a few long seconds, the animal stayed in place, the sound of its woofing breath announcing its presence. Then it turned away. The sound of breaking branches marked its departure into the forest.

Vale's mind was a white scream of terror.

"Vale . . . ?" Ash called again. "You still there? I . . . I think I heard something."

She scrambled to her feet, took two steps toward the fire, and her ankle gave out. Pain shot through her from foot to knee, and she fell back to the ground. Vale hardly noticed. *Got to get back to the fire!* She struggled upright and lurched forward, limping. *Back to camp!* When her ankle threatened to give out again, she caught hold of a nearby branch. *Need to get back to safety!* She hobbled forward the last few steps and tumbled to the ground in front of the low-burning fire.

"What happened to you?"

She looked up at Ash with terrified eyes. "S-something in the trees! I-it's big. *Really* big!"

"A cougar?"

"Don't know. I think it might be a bear." She crawled the last few feet to the fire, her fingers numbed by snow.

"Whoa! A bear?" Ash gasped. "Are you fricking kidding me?"

"I wish I was! We need to build up the fire. Build it *big*! And we've got to keep it going all night."

Ash stared into the blackness that surrounded them. "You're sure you saw—"

"I don't know for sure it was a bear, but it was *big*, all right? I saw it break through the brush. It huffed at me."

"That's it, then . . . That's our boss fight." His eyes widened, and he spread his hands wide. "The big finale, a game's last rung before you win. The final challenge you have to conquer before you can take the prize." He gestured to the valley and the trees around them. "We've been sitting here, thinking our fight was about being lost, but that's only half-true."

"It . . . it *is* true, though."

"But there's *more*!" He stepped closer. "The bear is our boss fight. That's what we have to survive."

Vale swallowed hard. "I really hope not."

"But—"

"If we try to fight a bear, we're going to lose, Ash. Both types of bears are too strong."

"Types?"

"Black bears are the smaller of the two, but they're still way stronger and faster than a person. You might be able to use a stick or something to scare them away, but it would be dangerous. As for grizzlies . . ." Her voice tightened as the panic returned. "You can't win against them, Ash. The best thing you can do is to just play dead and hope they stop attacking."

"Boss fi—"

"No! Just no. This isn't a *game*, Ash!" She grabbed the remaining twigs near the fire and threw them into the flames. "We need a bigger fire. We need it now!"

Ash seemed like he was going to say something else, but he closed his mouth and nodded. "All right," he said, climbing to his feet. "I'll get the wood. You sit here."

"Don't!"

"One of us has to get the wood, Vale. There's no other choice."

"But—"

"Just sit here. I'll be right back."

Vale wrapped her arms around her knees, fighting the urge to cry. She wanted to go home. She wanted to climb into her own bed and pull the covers up to her neck and play with Mr. Bananas. She wanted to text Bella and tell her about the worst hike of her entire life. Instead, she and Ash were stuck out in the woods. Vale was hungry and tired and her ankle was messed up. She was lost.

Now there was something in the woods.

Ash returned with a handful of branches and set them down beside her. "Here," he said. "You're good with the fire. You build it up again."

"But—"

"I'll get more wood."

Vale watched him head back into the darkness, a sick feeling in her throat. But a few minutes later, he was back with a heaving pile of branches tucked under his arm. Ash might not know a lot about camping, but she had to admit he was a good worker.

"Thanks," Vale said as he tossed the branches down.

"No problem." And then he was off in the woods again.

After four more trips, they had a pile as big as their shelter and a brightly burning fire next to it. For the first time since Vale had heard the animal in the woods, the tightness of her chest began to ease. When Ash came back the last time, dragging the tangled mess of a stump—roots still attached—from a long-dead tree, she gave him a wan smile.

"That's a lot of wood," she said.

"Well, you said we've got to keep the fire going all night. Right?"

"Yeah, I did."

"We need wood, then."

He tossed a few more branches onto the pile and took his seat on the damp ground next to her. For a time, they stared at the fire, the only sound the snap and pop of pine sap in the embers.

"Your leg," he said. "Is it okay?"

"It's my ankle, actually, and yeah. I think so." Vale rolled up her pant leg and winced. Her ankle was purple. "Er . . . maybe not."

"Can you walk on it?"

"Slowly."

"You should ice it," Ash said. "Bring the swelling down." He grabbed a handful of snow. "Here. Hold it against your ankle." He placed the snowball against her skin, and Vale yelped. "Sorry," he said. "That bad, huh?"

"Uh . . . yeah." She put her hand on the snow, holding it in place. The pain slowly eased. "Thanks for thinking of that."

"No biggie."

Vale chewed her lip. "I kind of screwed things up for us, didn't I?"

"What d'you mean?"

"I can hardly walk. That's going to be an issue tomorrow."

Ash let out a tired sigh. "Sprains are never as bad once you've iced them. When I hit my first growth spurt, I was clumsy as hell. I've done in my ankle more than once. We can bind it up tomorrow morning when it's time to get out of here." He grabbed the scarf—the one he'd been wearing as a hat—and unwound it from his head and neck, then handed it to her. "Here. This should work."

"You think so?"

"I *know* so. I've had sprains that look way worse than that one does."

"Thanks, Ash."

"It's fine."

"Just take the thanks, okay?"

He chuckled. "Fine, then you're welcome."

Vale took a slow breath and blew it out. "Look, I'm . . . I'm sorry for what I said before. I didn't mean to say coming here was your fault." She looked up, finding Ash watching. "I thought I saw two lakes. I did. And it was a good idea to come here." She picked up a handful of kindling and tossed it into the fire. "Besides. We've got fire and water now, right?"

"Right." Ash nodded. "Your ankle feeling any better?"

"Yeah, it is."

Ash moved closer to the fire. "Thanks, Vale."

"For . . . ?"

"For knowing what to do. For reading books and listening to Perkins and Holland in class. For knowing about bears and stuff. For just . . ." He laughed. "For getting the two of us through this."

She smiled. "You're welcome."

Debra Shumway hadn't slept since yesterday. She couldn't. Not with Vale, her youngest child, lost in the woods. Thinking of Vale brought a new surge of tears. Debra sniffled and pressed a wad of damp tissue against her nose. She'd been crying since the midnight phone call, but this evening's discovery had made it ten times worse.

"We've got the first reports back from the searchers," Constable Wyatt said, shuffling the paper on his desk. "Things are no longer so clean cut."

"Meaning what?" Debra asked.

"There was a heavy snowfall in the area last night," the officer continued. "Our original concern was hypothermia, but today we . . . have new concerns."

"New concerns?" Brad said.

"Yes. This afternoon, a searcher entered the valley north of Avion Ridge. They found evidence that Vale and Ash spent the night there."

Zara Hamid sat up straighter. Ash's mother had barely said a word since last night, though she'd written notes in a small tattered journal the entire time. Debra admired her calm, though she didn't understand it.

"North?" Brad repeated. "But I thought the searchers were looking in the area *south* of Twin Lakes."

"They were," the officer said, "but a helicopter on its way out of the park passed over Avion Ridge and . . ."

Debra looked from her husband to the officer. "And what?"

"And they saw evidence of a possible campsite."

Debra's breath caught, her heart pounding so hard she felt dizzy. "But that's *good*, right? I mean, if they made a camp, then they probably had a fire. And if they had a fire, they could have survived—"

"Ma'am, when I told you to prepare for the worst, I meant that."

"Then what?!" Debra cried. "What did you find? What—?" Her voice broke.

In the chair next to her, Ash's mother, Zara, reached over to Constable Wyatt's desk and pulled out several tissues from the box. She offered one to Debra and dabbed her eyes with the other. It struck Debra—in a strangely disconnected way—that although Zara seemed calm, she was barely holding it together. She too was close to breaking.

"A team headed into the valley north of Avion Ridge late this afternoon," Constable Wyatt explained. "The searchers found the camp. There was a lean-to. Lots of footprints in the woods, and, er . . ." The officer clenched and unclenched his hands, as if uncertain what to do with them. "They also saw there'd been an avalanche."

"But it's only October," Brad said. "There can't be enough snow to cause something like that."

"Actually, no. There's been snow in the upper regions of the Rockies for weeks now. It started late September, and with yesterday's turn in the weather—rain followed by the snow—the conditions were primed for a slide." Constable Wyatt tugged at his collar. "That's what I called you here to explain. When the team went into the valley, they found tracks. Two sets, actually."

"Ashton," Zara whispered.

"Yes, and Vale's too," the officer said. "They followed their tracks south into the trees and up the ridge to the south."

"Tracks . . ." Debra's fingers tightened around the tissues in her hands, her heart pounding so hard she could hear it in her ears. "So Vale and Ash are trying to walk out. They're trying to get back to Twin Lakes."

"That or Waterton. Yes. That's what the searchers figured anyhow," the officer said. "It seems they'd made a camp the night before, but it looks like a cougar spooked them."

Debra gasped. "A cougar?!"

"There was a kill found, not far from them. A *deer*—" Constable Wyatt rushed to explain. "Not *a person*. But it was near where they were sleeping, and my guess is that Vale and Ash decided to get out when they saw it. They headed due south, right into an area primed for a snowslide."

Debra glanced over at Zara. Ash's mother had an air of rigid control; her jaw was tight, but her eyes glittered with tears.

"But . . . I don't understand," Brad said. "If they were alive this morning, then they're probably still okay. Right? It's almost freezing now, and if they're both moving, they should be okay. The searchers could—"

"Sir, their tracks go right into the path of the avalanche."

Zara made a choking sound.

"Oh Jesus," Brad muttered.

Debra covered her mouth, fighting the urge to scream. "No . . . no, no, no!"

"We have men and women on the ground now; they're going through the entire slide, square foot by square foot, using poles to search for bod—" Constable Wyatt cleared his throat. "We're doing everything we can to find them."

"B-but they're still looking for our daughter?" Debra said. "I mean . . . there's still hope that they could be alive, right? They could have gotten out of the snow, or dug a tunnel and crawled out, or . . ."

"There is a slim chance," the officer said, "but I need you to understand, there's a very real possibility that your daughter Vale . . ." He glanced at Zara. "And your son, Ashton, were caught in that avalanche. Their tracks go into it"—he took a slow breath—"but they don't come out on the other side."

"But you don't know that for sure! You don't—" A sob broke free of her throat, tearing away the rest of her words. *Vale can't be dead. She CAN'T!* Debra had been so certain the search teams would find her daughter last night. Today's discovery of the abandoned camp, the tracks in the snow, and the avalanche changed everything.

"I'm sorry, Mr. and Mrs. Shumway. Ms. Hamid. The teams are continuing to look, but with night falling, there's little they can do. We've got an avalanche recovery crew who've come down from Banff. They're joining the searchers from Lethbridge and Waterton. They'll stop for the night, then go back out at dawn to—"

"But Vale's still out there! She's out there *now*! She's lost—she's—" Debra slumped forward in her chair, choked by sobs.

A hand brushed her leg. "Breathe, Debra, honey," her husband said quietly. "It's going to be okay." Brad rubbed her knee in a repetitive, absent manner. It was meant to be consoling, but at the moment, it made her want to scream.

Constable Wyatt stared at the surface of his desk. Across from him, in the other chair, Zara held her face in her hands, composure shattered. *She looks*, Debra thought, *the way I feel.*

"So what now?" Brad asked. "What happens next?"

"They're sending out a helicopter in the morning," Constable Wyatt said. "I'll keep you posted if there's any new information. For now, let's just pray that the two of them made it through the avalanche alive."

Debra closed her eyes and prayed like her life depended on it.

Ash was nodding by the fire when Vale nudged him with her toe. He blinked himself awake.

"You go to sleep," she said. "I'll stay up and keep watch."

"All night?" Ash said through a yawn.

"Someone's got to keep the fire going." She glanced out at the darkness, then back at him. "I haven't heard anything lately, but that bear—or whatever it was—could still be close."

He stood and stretched his back. "Nah. The shelter's plenty close to the fire. Let's just put on a bunch of wood and both get some rest."

"But—"

"It's going to be a long walk tomorrow. South, right?"

Vale nodded.

"So we put on a piece of wood that'll last and hit the hay." Ash headed to the pile of wood. There were plenty of branches waiting, but he sought out the tangled ball of roots that was attached to the rotting stump he'd torn from the ground. *This* would burn for a few hours at least. He dropped the stump into the fire. It smoked for a few seconds, then burst into flames. "Yeah," Ash said, "that should hold until—"

Vale screamed and scrambled back from the fire on hands and feet.

"What the—" Before Ash could finish his question, the carpenter ants reached him. They crawled up his legs, finding paths under the layers of clothing to bite. Ash stumbled, almost falling into Vale who was peeling off her garbage-bag outer layer to reach the jacket below.

"Ants!" she screamed. "The stump is full of wood ants!"

Ash was too busy to answer. The carpenter ants were four times the size of the small ants that he recognized from his yard at home . . . *and they were angry!* The insects came in a black wave, biting whatever flesh they could find. Ash writhed as they crawled inside his clothes. The wood ants that reached his bare hands bit, but didn't let go, and their figure-eight-shaped bodies hung, attached by mandibles, to his skin. He yelped and jumped back from the fire—slapping them off before tumbling in the snow. He scratched and shook, trying to free himself of the biting insects. At his feet, Vale rolled like a dog.

After what felt like ages, Ash got the last of the ants off. In his rush, he'd tossed his jacket off to the side, near the bushes. His shirt lay discarded on the lean-to. He gathered them both, carefully checking them before returning to the fire. Vale was panting like she'd been running. Her hair had come free of its ponytail and swirled around her face in a riot of curls. She had stripped off her outer layers and stood on her one good leg, shivering, in her jeans and T-shirt. She held each piece of clothing up to the fire as she checked the seams before putting them back on.

Ash shivered and zipped up his coat. The snow was falling fast. Even the fire wasn't holding the icy grip of winter at bay. He looked through the pile of branches and found a large stick. Along with the stump, it should last a few hours.

"Do you think it's safe?" Vale asked.

"Only one way to find out." Ash held the end of the stick into the fire, waiting, terrified, for ants to come pouring out of the cracks and up his arm. The flames licked their way upward. Embers grew on the tip of the branch. *No ants.*

"There," he said, tossing it onto the fire. "I think that piece and the stump should last a while."

Vale yawned. "Ready to get some sleep?"

"Yeah. Let's head in."

It took what felt like ages before Ash finally slept. Twice he took out his phone. Each time there was no reception, so he turned it off again. Sixteen percent, even on low-power mode, was barely enough to last for the length of a phone call, and that was only if he could get enough reception to call for help. *Need to get up high again.* Trouble was, Vale's twisted ankle was going to make climbing impossible.

He frowned down at the girl who slept at his side. In the dim glow of the light stick—the last one Vale had—he could see the stress this experience was putting on her. Vale's face was drawn, her cheeks hollowed out, and lips pinched. She looked *hurt*, and that bothered him. Vale was Ash's best friend, and right now she was doing more for their survival than he was. *Not like I can hunt for food or something . . .*

At the thought of food, Ash's stomach let out a low rumble of protest. Images of his mother's homemade mansaf—leg of lamb—on top of markook bread and roasted vegetables hung in the air before him, enticing him with their imagined tastes. The last piece of gum was long gone, nothing left to distract him from the hunger pains that tortured him. Stomach aching, Ash squirmed uncomfortably as he waited for sleep to take him. *Just stop thinking about food!* It was a Herculean task, but eventually he forced himself to focus on the sounds around the lean-to. He categorized them. *Bird. Rodent. Crinkle of the emergency blanket. Wind in the trees . . .*

Slowly his body relaxed, Vale's warmth a welcome comfort. His lids fluttered closed as moments from today flickered in a random montage: *Him and Vale climbing the mountain . . . The snowball fight . . . Ash stomping the snow and the cornice giving way . . . Grabbing Vale's hand as they ran from the avalanche . . . Vale seeing the lake in the valley . . . The hike down . . . The animal in the darkness . . . Helping Vale with her twisted ankle . . . The carpenter ants in the stump . . . Vale in the shelter and him taking his place beside her . . .*

Sometime later, Ash woke in the dark, heart pounding.

What was that?

He opened his eyes, taking in the faint green glow of the light stick and Vale, a warm bundle in front of him, and the opening of the lean-to with the fire down to embers a stone's throw away. Ash was warm, surprisingly so. In fact, he felt the way he'd felt that long-ago night when he'd fallen asleep in the doghouse. It was almost like he was nestled between two—

Ash's breath caught. *Oh crap! There's something lying right behind me.*

Terrified, his senses stretched out into the shadows. Ash could feel the branches of the lean-to, but against the narrow barrier of them, something *else* lay. It was large and warm. He could feel its slow breath rise and fall. Panic rose like a wave inside him. *It's lying next to me. It's just outside. The animal that Vale heard in the forest. It's here!*

Whatever it was, it felt big.

With trembling fingers, Ash reached back over his shoulder. He brushed aside the pine needles and branches that formed the shelter's wall. He held his breath and pushed farther . . . farther . . .

He touched stiff fur.

Ash jerked his hand back so fast he smacked Vale in the back of the head with his elbow. She made a snuffling noise and turned her head.

"What're you—"

Ash pressed his hand against her mouth; Vale's eyes widened in shock. *Outside*, he mouthed.

Vale shook her head in confusion. *What?*

Ash let go of her mouth and leaned in until his lips were directly against her ear. "The animal you heard is outside," he hissed.

He felt her stiffen. "A bear?"

"I think so. It's on the other side of the shelter . . . leaning on me."

CHAPTER EIGHT

"I'm glad you're here, Katie. And I owe you one."
"You owe me for a lot of things, but this is not one of them."
JERRY SHEPARD AND KATIE, *EIGHT BELOW*

VALE STARED AT ASH, waiting for the punchline. *He can't be serious . . . can he? Did he just say there's something on the other side of the branches?* When Ash didn't move or speak again, Vale lifted her chin and peeked over his shoulder. The pine boughs *were* pressed against his back, but that could be anything. It had snowed again. That didn't mean—

The sound of a huffing breath—loud and much too near—shocked all thoughts from Vale's mind. The branches shifted inward as the animal on the other side resettled itself against the lean-to. A whooshing sound broke the silence. Ash leaned closer. He stared at her with wide, frightened eyes.

MOVE! he mouthed.

Vale nodded, her heart heaving in her chest. She leaned back, rolled sideways, then froze, unable to go any farther. Her legs turned to jelly. What if the animal on the other side of Ash was the same one she'd seen in the woods? *Can the two of us handle a bear?* her mind screamed. They were huge, at least twice the size of an adult man—far exceeding a person in weight and strength—and they were highly territorial. In the animal world, bears were apex predators! *We have no weapons! Nothing to fight with. No way to escape. We're going to die here!*

Reeling with panic, Vale gasped for breath.

Ash bumped into Vale's shoulder. "Move!" he whispered. "I need out."

"I-I'm going."

"Go *faster*!" he hissed.

Vale grabbed her coat and inched backward, but moving around in the dark in silence was impossible. Terror filled her limbs with lead, making every movement stilted and jerky. Ash shoved again. She pushed forward. Her hand slid on the emergency blanket and the foil crackled. Hearing it, the animal outside the shelter jerked awake, stumbling to its feet. The branches behind Ash bent inward, then snapped back, as the walls crashed down.

There was a brief moment when Vale couldn't move. *We're going to DIE!* And then instinct took over. Heart pounding so loudly she could hear it in her ears, she fought her way from the shelter. Something smacked her sprained ankle. She yelped. Ash slammed into her butt.

"Go!" he shouted, no longer trying to be silent. "Get OUT!"

Crying, gasping, Vale scrambled out of the disintegrating lean-to as fast as she could. Ash followed. Half a second later, the last few tree branches fell inward and covered their packs and the area where they'd been sleeping in a shower of snow and branches. She stood up and lifted her gaze to the darkness of the camp.

Vale froze.

Around them, at least thirty yellow eyes glittered from the shadows. Her shoulders tensed as her mind struggled to determine what she was seeing. In the near-complete darkness, the only thing she could tell was that they *weren't* alone.

"Ash," she whispered. "You seeing this?"

"What in the world . . . ?"

Ash stood up next to Vale just as the herd of elk that had wandered into the camp turned as one. The animals stared at the two teens. One lifted its snout and snuffled the wind, puffing white clouds of breath as it tried to pick up their scent. *That was the sound I heard in the woods*, Vale thought. None of them moved, barring a spindly-legged calf that had wandered too close to the lean-to. It stumbled in the tangle of branches and snow, then shook itself off, the snow sifting off its stiff fur.

"Are these a different kind of deer?" Ash asked.

"Not deer. Elk. But I've never seen one up close before." Her hands tightened into claws at her side. "You're not supposed to get this near to them."

"First time I've seen one."

The small herd watched them, as if assessing the danger the teens posed. The half-grown calf wandered away from the destroyed shelter and back toward the other elk from its herd.

Ash leaned closer to Vale. "Are . . . are they dangerous?"

"Sometimes."

"When?"

"When it's mating season, or when they think one of their babies is in danger." Vale struggled to remember what other details she knew. Elk weren't *usually* aggressive, but provoked, they could stomp a person to death. It all depended on the time of year. *When are they rutting?* she wondered, but the answer wasn't there. "Either way," she said, "they're wild animals. We should be careful around them. Give them space."

Ash nodded. "Got it."

It was dark, the stars winked out by restless clouds. A soft layer of snow covered everything. More was falling. The circle of firelight was small, the fire having burned low in the past hours. Even now, tongues of flame danced over the last chunk of the stump, which grew smaller by the minute. The elk churned uneasily around the clearing.

"Why are they doing that?" Ash hissed.

"I don't know."

A cow elk and a calf moved nervously past them, heading into the darkness. The herd milled. Somewhere in the shadows, a bull elk bugled. On the other side of the camp, another answered.

Ash stepped closer. "What's happening? Why are they making that sound?"

Vale's hands began to sweat, and she rubbed them on the side of her jeans. "I . . . I think they might be rutting."

"Rutting?"

"Mating. The males fight to see who is strongest. Elk can be aggressive. I just wish I could remember what time of year that happened."

A branch broke—nearer now—and both Ash and Vale turned. "I can't see anything," Ash said.

"Hold on. I'll build up the fire." Vale had just reached down to toss a piece of firewood onto the flames when a noise broke through the darkness: Bushes crackled with the passage of a large animal.

Hearing it, several of the nearby elk sprang into action, bounding away from the fire and the lake, heading straight into the black night, leaving the teens behind. A male elk appeared from the shadows and lowered his head. He pawed the dirt, swinging his antlers back and forth.

Ash leaned closer. "What's that one doing?" he whispered.

"I don't know, but I think—"

An elk's bugle—loud and angry—broke the silence. The animal crashed through the trees, passing a stone's throw from Ash and Vale.

"They're going to fight!" she yelped.

The two elk slammed their antlers together with a resounding crack. Entwined, they huffed and grunted, their fight bringing them closer and closer to the edge of the fire.

"We need to move!" Ash said, bolting from her side.

"Ash, wait! You can't just—"

Another male elk, coming from the other direction, stumbled out of the shadows, blocking Ash's path. Seeing him, it lowered its head. *Charged.*

"Ash!" Vale shouted, limping out of the way of the pair of elk still fighting a few feet from her. "Get BACK here! You'll get stomped!"

The elk followed Ash back toward the fire. Ash rolled, narrowly avoiding the animal's antlers. "Where?" he gasped. "Where can we go?"

Terrified, Vale scanned the clearing. The lake was ice cold. They'd be dead in minutes if they waded into the water. The trees were full of rutting elk. Climbing a tree would have been an option, but they'd stripped off most of the branches they could reach.

The first pair of elk broke apart, and the larger one bugled again. A challenger came forward and the winner backed up as the bull elk took position. The pair pawed at the ground, then smashed together, the hooves of one scattering a line of coals out of the campfire. The two of them shied away from the fire, then returned to the ongoing fight.

In a rush of understanding, Vale saw what needed to be done. "That's it!" she cried.

"What's it?"

"The fire! We need to build it up."

Ash nodded. "Got it!" He sprinted into the darkness.

"Where are you going?" Vale shouted.

Ash rushed around the other side of the fire and grabbed the remaining branches that were left in the pile of kindling. He tossed them into the flames. The needles lit first, flames flashing brightly, then fading into choking bellows of smoke as the fire died down. Two muscled bull elk—caught in a fight to the death—stumbled into Ash, knocking him aside.

Ash scrambled out of their way and crawled back around the other side of the fire. "It's all smoke," he shouted. "I don't know what's wrong!"

The larger of the two elk swung his head, antlers hitting Vale on the arm and nearly taking her to the ground. It swung back again, hoofs reaching the embers of the dying fire. She ducked out of the way. "Ash, hurry! We need the fire going!"

Ash threw on another stick. More smoke belched out, the light dying. "I can't get the stupid fire to light!" he yelled. "I don't know what I'm doing wrong!"

"It needs more air!" Vale took two limping steps toward the shelter's remains and grabbed a handful of branches they'd woven into a lean-to mere hours before. She tucked them under her arm, grabbed more, then dragged the wood to Ash's side. The elk had stumbled a few feet away; the sounds of their huffed breath sent a frisson of panic through Vale's spine. *Need to hurry!*

"It's not burning," Ash said. "There's wood and hot coals but—"

"The fire needs oxygen," Vale said, crouching next to him. "Blow on the embers." She took a deep breath and directed a gust of breath at the brightest part of the coals. With a hiss, they flared from dull red to yellow orange. The branches nearby popped into flame.

"Whoa!"

Another elk bugle broke the quiet of the clearing. The elk charged, and Ash scrambled out of its way. With the fire going, the bull elk shied a little farther outside the circle of light. "It's working! They're still fighting, but we've got a little room now."

"Let's build it higher." Vale tossed in another handful of kindling, then leaned down. "Keep blowing as you add more wood." She climbed to her feet and hissed in pain as her ankle protested. "Don't add any new branches until the first ones are burning."

"Got it." Ash darted to the destroyed hut, grabbed more, and returned to the fire.

Ankle throbbing, Vale did the same. She pulled pieces of wood from the base of the dismantled shelter, then dragged them to the campfire, switching places with Ash. Somewhere in the forest, more branches broke. The third bull elk—separate from the fight for dominance—caught sight of Vale. It lowed its antlers.

"Watch out!" Ash shouted.

With a cry of panic, Vale stumbled back out of the way, narrowly avoiding razor-sharp hooves as she tumbled to the ground a few feet from the fire. The elk charged again.

"Go!" Ash bellowed. "Get AWAY from us!" He grabbed Vale's arm and pulled her aside as the bull elk changed direction last second, swerving away from the fire. Ash stood in front of Vale—blocking her from view—his voice high pitched with panic. "Get OUT of here!"

Seeing the flames, the animal huffed and stepped back. It swung its antlered head low, then moved away from the fire, stepping back into the perimeter of darkness.

"Th-thanks," Vale gasped.

"No problem." He held out his hand and Vale grabbed hold of it, letting him hoist her to her feet. On the far side of the clearing, the two elk fought on, while the hunched shape of the third bull elk appeared for a moment on the edge of the firelight, then dissolved back into the shadows again. It bugled.

It's circling the camp. It's watching us.

Vale and Ash worked faster. The fire was growing, but not quickly enough. *Need more wood!* Vale turned, the pain of her ankle almost taking her to her knees. She gritted her teeth and kept going. There was no way around it; if they wanted to stay alive, they needed to be able to see.

Vale tossed the broken boughs onto the campfire. These ones lit at once. She grabbed a burning stick and held it aloft as she hobbled back to the fallen lean-to for another handful. Ash did the same in the forest. Arms full, Vale limped toward the fire. She turned to go, but Ash grabbed her arm, holding her steady.

"Stay!" he gasped, fear sharpening his words. "The elk is in the trees again!" He pointed. "You go back and it'll charge you for sure."

Vale turned to look at where the shelter had stood only minutes before. The elk pawed the ground, then took two stiff-legged steps toward them. It swung its head. "It's waiting for us to leave the fire," Vale whispered.

Her gaze darted around the clearing. Two adult male elk circled each other, ready to fight. Behind them, the small lake glittered. She winced. She and Ash were trapped, unable to move. She edged as close to the rising flames as she could and stared into the darkness. Vale's pant legs grew so warm, the skin on her legs began to smart. She didn't move; neither did Ash. The elk was there in the shadows. Invisible. *Dangerous.*

"Let's stay here," Ash said. "We have enough wood for a bit. It's . . . it's safer."

Safer . . . but not safe, Vale thought. She knew that Ash was thinking it too.

Vale woke with a start. She was curled up on her side on the muddy ground, the dying fire warm at her back, the chill morning air draining the heat from her exposed flesh. She opened one eye. The sun was a bright circle in the sky just above the mountain range—it couldn't be much later than seven or eight—though the warmth of the day still hadn't arrived. Vale sat up and stretched as she looked around the trampled campsite. The evidence of the night's trauma was everywhere: the remains of the destroyed shelter, elk prints in the snow, scattered ashes, and snow trodden black with mud.

Vale scanned the valley. The ragged peaks that surrounded the lake were newly covered in a veil of snow. Wispy clouds hung halfway up the valley wall, the sun slowly burning them away as day arrived. The forest lay silent. The lake calm. Vale frowned when her gaze came back down.

Ash was nowhere to be seen.

Fear caught hold of Vale's throat and tightened into a vise as she climbed slowly to her feet. She gasped as she took her first step. The swelling of her sprained ankle had eased in the past hours, but it was still sore. She took a few steps away from the smoldering campfire, hot tears pooling along her lash line.

"Ash . . . ?" she called.

Nothing.

"Ash!"

No answer.

Panic hit her in a rush. "Ash, where are you?"

The wind whistled through the trees, indifferent to her concern.

"ASH!" she bellowed.

Her words echoed up out of the valley, then faded into silence. It was bright and sunny, but Vale felt like a cloud had passed in front of the sun. She searched the snow, terrified. *There was blood on the snow after the cougar attack. If something happened to Ash, there'd be blood . . . Right?* She hobbled slowly around the camp. *If he was stomped by an elk, I would have woken. He would have screamed.* The ground was covered in a layer of melting snow, the footprints turning to mud with each passing minute. If some animal had attacked Ash, it hadn't left evidence.

Maybe, she thought, *he went to relieve himself. He'd want a little space for that, right . . . ?* The knot in her chest eased. *Yeah. Maybe that's where he is.* The thought made her aware of the fullness of her own bladder. Vale took a few steps away from the campsite and crouched in the bushes to pee. She faced the woods, watching in case Ash returned. With the sun rising in the sky, the snow on the ground had grown pocked and blotchy, meltwater blurring away the tracks through the woods. Animal-and-human passage soon gave way to patches of damp grass and mud. It wouldn't be long, Vale figured, before she'd be warm enough to take off her jacket.

She limped back to the destroyed shelter and picked through the remains of the branches. Every once in a while she glanced up, always expecting Ash to appear. *He never did.* Under the slushy layer of melting snow, she uncovered her backpack—now crushed and waterlogged—but still zipped closed. She shook out the three garbage bags on which she and Ash had spent half the night and hung them over a tree branch. Two were badly tattered, but Vale wanted to keep everything she could.

She stood up again, and something caught her eye. "That's Ash's pack." She reached into the pile of snow and shook it out. Barring the water bottle—which Ash had had with him by the fire the night before—everything else was inside. Vale stared at it, heart pounding. *Surely he wouldn't leave camp without his backpack! Right . . . ? RIGHT?!* She just didn't know.

For the next few minutes, she tidied the campsite they had created.

That done, Vale gathered a new pile of branches. Each step she took made walking easier. *Ash was right about the ankle.* Near a thicket of dead fallen trees, she found where Ash had pulled the stump they'd burned the night before. She frowned at the sight of the unearthed pile of roots, black carpenter ants drawing lines through the dirt as they rebuilt their nest. Vale gave them a wide berth. She paused now and then to catch her breath. She was lightheaded from hunger, but after a moment's rest she pushed herself to continue. Eventually, she had a small pile of kindling, and a neat bundle of branches beside it. A thin trail of smoke rose into the sky. Fifteen minutes of hard work and everything was in order.

She nodded to herself. *Once Ash gets back, we can start walking again.* When she lifted her gaze to the horizon, the expression faded. The valley was empty as far as she could see. The elk had moved on. Only the howl of wind as it moved over the peaks interrupted her solitude. Vale's vision blurred as tears filled her eyes. The terror that she'd kept almost at bay was back, clawing its way through her chest. Fears that dogged her on a daily basis roared to life as tears trickled down her cheeks, dripping off her chin. It wasn't a mistake, and there was no use denying it.

Ash had left her behind.

Ash took the steep incline as a challenge. *One more step*, he thought grimly. *Just focus on one more step.* He didn't let his thoughts go back to the camp he'd left behind, didn't let himself think about Vale waking up alone. (His guilt wouldn't let him.) Ash had left her sleeping by the fire. There'd been no way for him to leave a note for her, so he'd headed off without looking back. If things worked out: *Great!* If they didn't . . . Well, Ash wouldn't let himself think about *that* either.

Legs shaking, he kept his eyes on the ridge where he was headed. The forest thinned the higher he got, but the snow got deeper. The past two days in the woods felt like level grinding: the tedious process of learning skills and going on side quests in order to build experience points so a player can gain levels. Ash was done with that! He wanted action, change. *Out of this fricking nightmare!* He could see the end of the trees in the distance, and he forced himself through knee-deep snow toward that line. *I'm gonna fix this, Vale.*

Unlike the animals who made these high alpine slopes their home, Ash's body wasn't built for climbing through snowdrifts. His Keds were mud caked and sodden. His foot slipped in a wet patch of half-melted sleet, and he fell forward, smacking his head against a tree branch. The movement jarred the breath from his lungs, and he saw stars. *Hate being so WEAK!* Shaking, Ash paused for breath. He touched the top of his head, then pulled his fingers away to inspect them. There was a smear of blood, but nothing worrisome. With no first aid kit, there was nothing Ash could do about it anyhow.

Frustrated and desperately hungry, he started walking again. *Got to keep going, keep moving.* Each step brought him higher. If he could get anywhere near the top, he *should* be able to get reception for his phone. He grinned, imagining his success. *Get one bar and we're scot-free!*

Fifty more steps brought him to the last of the scrubby pines that clung to the slope, and with one final push he broke up above the tree line. "Yes!" Ash leaned forward, taking a moment to catch his breath and regroup. There were times when he and his fellow players stayed up days in a row, playing battle after battle in multiday tourneys. In those endless hours, Ash would guzzle energy drinks and eat junk food, losing track of time as he pushed himself to the max. *Nothing compares to this.* Survival here was a different thing entirely. There were no health potions to counter the palsied twitching of his muscles, starved of glycogen. There was no teammate to give him a break while he grabbed a bite to eat. There was only him and the hours of climbing. *And Vale.* He fought for each step as much for his friend as for himself. This was hard work . . . *impossible work!* But he was doing it for both of them.

"Nothing to it but to do it," he muttered. He tried to take a step, but his shaking legs wouldn't move. He clenched his teeth and took a deep breath. "Get your ass in gear, Hamid!" With an angry grunt, he threw himself back into motion.

In the alpine zone where he hiked, the snow was wet and slushy, bits of it clinging to his jeans. Around him, the air grew thin. Each foot higher made the climb harder, and his breath came in sharp gasps. Sweat trickled down the center of Ash's back, and he tugged open his coat, overheated from exertion despite the chill. Faint shadows blurred the edges of his vision.

One more step, a voice inside him chanted. *One. More. Step.*

His goal was the area directly below a snowcapped peak. It was a ragged line of rock, the snow scoured away by the hands of the wind. From the forest, it looked like an easy climb, but up close it was treacherous. Ash reached the sheer wall and leaned against it. Wheezing, he stared back the way he'd come. His heart sank. *There was no other lake anywhere.* He had no idea where he was, but it definitely wasn't near Twin Lakes.

"No!"

His gaze dropped lower. Straight below him was the blue shimmer of the lake where he and Vale had made their camp. She was probably awake by now, and she'd definitely be angry at him once she realized he left. *You know, Ash, I COULD have walked on my ankle. You just needed to ask.* He smiled sadly to himself. Vale might have the best intentions in the world, but with her ankle twisted, there'd been no other choice.

With grim determination, he turned back to the rock wall and began to climb. It was Ash's chance to save *her.*

Vale's terror was sudden and intense. *Ash is GONE! He left me behind! My God, I'm all ALONE!* Tears flooded her eyes as the truth she'd avoided all morning arrived with the weight of a truck coming to a stop on her chest. *This CAN'T be happening*, her mind chattered. *He CAN'T leave me here! Not NOW!* Vale's gaze jerked around the camp, then the forest, then the distant mountaintops.

But I'm the reason we're lost. This is it . . . he gave up on me!

"NO!" She cupped her hands around her mouth. "Ash!" she screamed. "Ash, come BACK!" Vale took two steps and stumbled, her ankle blossoming with a white-hot firebrand of pain. Heartbroken, she hardly noticed. "Ash! ASH! Where ARE you?"

Vale's whole life, she'd struggled to fit in. The schoolyard taunts of elementary school—mostly written off by exhausted teachers as "boys being boys"—had expanded into full-on trolling in her middle school years. She'd been a gamer then. But the constant online trolling had tipped the balance. To escape it, she'd given up the pastime she'd loved.

Only Ash had stood by Vale's side.

Vale had tried to find a new place to fit. Bella and the LGBTQIA online community had helped tremendously (even if it hurt that a few members of that community didn't recognize aro-ace as a valid orientation). But she was still left with her daytime hours. And as high school began, new bullies made Vale their target. Mike had personally gone out of his way to subject Vale to his reign of terror. Even her parents' well-meaning actions echoed Vale's precarious place in the social strata. "Date someone," they said. "Give it a try." From morning to night, Vale struggled. She made friends . . . only to have them disappear once Mike and his cronies got them in their sights. And all the way along, Vale had waited—terrified—for the moment when Ash too would walk away from her.

He just had.

Horrified, she recalled the last two days. She'd gotten the two of them lost. Her stubbornness and refusal to back down had made them late. Was it a surprise Ash left? *This is my fault!* Sobbing, Vale headed out into the woods that surrounded the small camp. *Ash walked away! He's GONE!* She searched the ground for tracks, hoping against hope to find a line of footprints to follow. Elk prints had churned the snow into mire. Muddy prints mixed with leaves, blocking any clear path. "Please," Vale whispered. "Please let me find his path . . ." Hiccups tore through her as she stumbled, fell, stumbled again. She glanced back up when the trees closed in.

The lake was still there. She could see it.

She came back and headed away in another radial spike, searching for Ash's path. Her eyes were raw from crying. A moose crossed her path, but her search didn't slow. Panic broke over her, leaving her heaving for breath. Coming back toward the camp, her shouts redoubled.

"Ash!" she sobbed. "ASH! Where ARE you?"

For two full hours she took forays into the forest, making a perfect pinwheel of her own prints in the rapidly melting snow. But with each passing minute, the chances of finding Ash dwindled. He was gone, pure and simple. Realizing it, Vale finally slid to her knees in the shadow of a larch and gave way to heartbreak.

Her whole life she'd been terrified of being abandoned. It had finally happened. She was alone. She was lost. And the only one who could save Vale was herself. Her tears slowed, and she found herself empty of emotion. The wind pushed through the branches, cutting into Vale's coat and leaving her shivering. With leaden feet, she finally stood, and slowly limped back to camp. She walked toward the campfire, then froze.

In the hours she'd been searching, it had gone out.

"NO!" She grabbed a dried branch and tossed it onto the embers. This time, however, the needles didn't catch. "Oh no, no, no . . ." Vale jerked the branch off and leaned close. "Come on . . . Just need to get it going again." Her heart thudded as she blew across the coals. She watched and waited. *Nothing.*

Vale scrambled upright and jogged to a nearby tree, ignoring the throb of her ankle. The lower branches were stripped of lichen. Frustrated, she staggered toward the next thicket, reached overhead and grabbed what few pieces she could reach. She limped back to the cold campfire.

Vale dropped to her knees. She added a bit of lichen, hoping against hope that there was enough heat left to ignite it. She blew again. The ashes swirled up, blinding her, but the coals did little else. "Not NOW!"

Hands shaking, she put her fingers above the embers. The coals were *warm*, not hot, no longer burning.

"Why NOW?"

Vale blew hard. *Nothing.* She leaned closer, pressing a number of tiny branches, moss, and lichen up against the coal. She blew again and again, but the flames wouldn't catch. Fresh tears filled her eyes as Vale grabbed her bag and shook it onto the ground. She grabbed the battery. "The last wrapper," she whispered.

With shaking hands, she searched her pocket until she located the final piece of foil.

She knelt in the ashes and tore the wrapper into a thin line, then held it against the poles of the battery with trembling fingers. She waited for the gum wrapper to ignite. "Please . . . just . . . work . . ."

Seconds passed. A minute.

Nothing happened.

With trembling limbs, Ash pushed with the last of his strength and reached the top of the cliff face. For a long moment, he couldn't move. His energy was gone, body spent. Ash's feet dangled precariously over the edge, and he lay folded in half, his upper body on the narrow horizontal ledge that formed the top of the ridge. On the other side was another valley, but the wind was flicking a haze of snow up, and he couldn't see beyond a few feet in front of him. He was cold and wet, his body long past exhaustion.

Ash's lashes fluttered closed. *Just going to rest a bit . . . Get back my strength.*

He might have stayed that way for a minute, maybe five. Time had lost meaning for Ash. Behind his closed lids, a game appeared. It was *Builder Craft*—something Ash had played obsessively as a child. The game allowed its players to create their own universes, shaping the world like blocks of clay under their virtual hands. Half-asleep, Ash imagined mountains rising cubically around him, and valleys falling down into the hazy far lands of unloaded data. Somewhere above Ash's head, a pulsing hammer appeared. It hacked the ridge on which he lay. The rock broke into cubes, tumbling toward the valley. The hammer smashed down again. Ash twitched as more rubble fell to the valley below. It wasn't until his body began to slide backward—headed for a fall—that he scrabbled for a new handhold.

"Sheesh!" he gasped. "What the heck?"

Ash took several icy breaths. He squinted down the other side of the ridge. With the rush of wind-blown snow, he might as well have been looking into a snow globe. He shook his head. The fog that filled his mind was still there, but it was tempered with adrenaline. *Got to move. Pass out and I'll die.* With numb fingers, he tightened his grip on the rock, his gaze drawn inexorably downward to the last thirty or so feet he'd just climbed. At the bottom was a scree slope. The jagged rock varied in size from dinner plates to microscopic shards and many of these sharp-edged stones pointed up like teeth. Ash's fingers tightened their grip on the cliff. Getting up had only been half the battle. Getting down would have its own challenges.

Think about that later.

Hands shaking, Ash reached into his pocket and pulled out his cell phone. He pressed on the power button, watching as it flared to life, the "low-power mode" appearing seconds later. Ash glanced at the battery meter.

12%

"Crap!"

Ten percent was practically shutdown time. At home, he'd plug it in and walk away at fifteen. But here on the mountain, Ash needed that 10 percent to last long enough to make the most important phone call of his life.

"Please just work . . ."

Ash waited as the phone searched for connection. There were several long seconds when nothing happened. Ash's hand grew sweaty around the phone. Though the ridge led to a sharp peak, he was currently as high as he could possibly climb without ropes and carabiners. This should work, and yet—

A single reception bar appeared, and his breath caught. "Yes!"

He popped open the phone app and typed in 911. There was a long moment before it began to ring. The phone crackled, and the ringing stopped. Ash grinned as he waited for the reply.

Nothing happened.

He looked down at the screen. *No connection available.* His gaze flicked to the battery: *10%.*

"No fricking WAY!"

Frustrated, Ash dialed 911 a second time. The bottom of one slick-bottomed Ked, precariously wedged in a toehold, began to slide, but intent on his phone, he barely noticed. Ash waited as it began to ring a second time, a third . . . Suddenly he heard a click.

A connection warning flashed on-screen.

"Not now!" Ash hissed. He stretched his arm out, trying desperately to recapture the wavering connection. If he could only get one call in, he'd—

Ash's sneakered foot slipped.

Momentum pulled him away from the rock face. His center of balance shifted, and the phone tumbled through his fingers.

With a scream, Ash fell.

CHAPTER NINE

"Everything happens for a reason. The reason is a chaotic intersection of chance and the laws of physics."

WELCOME TO NIGHT VALE PODCAST

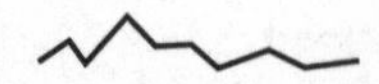

WITH A SCREAM of fury, Vale crumpled to the ground. Tears streamed down her face. She put her forehead to her knees, and sobbed. All the disappointments of the past couple of days came boiling up to the surface. The fire was out. She was lost. She had no idea where she needed to go other than south, and—as of this morning—she was utterly alone. Ash had either walked out or gotten lost (a terrifying possibility). Either way he was gone. The pain of those two thoughts stripped her of the last of her dignity. Tears washed her face and hands, sobs choked her.

A single thought slowly pulled Vale from her panic. *If I freak out, I'm NEVER going to get out of here.* She lifted her chin and wiped her face with grubby fingers. Hiccups rippled through her chest as she fought for control. *Ash may be gone, but there are searchers looking for us. A smoke signal will help.*

She looked down at the foil and battery in her hands. For a gum wrapper to function as a lighter, you needed a narrow band at the center where the foil would overheat. Inspecting the thin metal strip, Vale realized that the section she'd ripped was too thick to connect. The wrapper was damaged, but still viable. She could fix it if she was careful.

Vale took a shaky breath. "Just need to slow down," she said. "I'm rushing, and when you rush, you make mistakes." She wiped the tears from her cheeks, took a slow breath and blew it out again. "I've got the tools for a fire. That's more than most people have. Got to stop wasting time feeling sorry for myself, and fix this."

She nodded to herself, then caught hold of the too-thick line of foil and carefully thinned it with the edge of her nail. Finished, she set it aside.

"More kindling means a better chance the flame will catch," she said, her calm returning. She stood and walked into the forest where she'd searched for Ash. This time, her gaze was up in the trees. She gathered pieces of twigs and old-man's beard. Returning, she crouched again.

"I can do this. I can," she said fiercely. "I'll make a smoke signal. Yes. That'll help." She nodded to herself. Her ankle was still too sore to hike all the way out of the mountains, but it *would* get better. In the meantime, she had plenty of wood in the valley. She had water to drink. She could last a day or two while her ankle healed. And if Ash was *lost* rather than simply gone, then the smoke could lead him back.

Yes, Vale thought, *a smoke signal is a good start.*

As her breathing returned to normal, she leaned close to the small pile of kindling and held the two ends of the foil on the battery above the lichen. She said a silent prayer as she watched it. Twenty seconds passed . . . thirty . . .

A bright flame blossomed in the center of the foil.

Heart pounding, Vale lowered it to the old-man's beard. It spread slowly, and then jumped to life. Vale added more twigs. It grew brighter, moving from the twigs to the larger branches, and then finally to the coals that she'd allowed to go cold in her panic.

Vale leaned back on her heels. "There," she said. "That's the first step. I can do this. I can!"

With the campfire burning again, Vale crawled back to her feet. She looked around her. The lower branches of the nearby trees were all gone, stripped for firewood and shelter the day before, but there were plenty of trees to choose from a little farther out. She smiled.

"Just need to be smart and I'll survive."

Ash scrabbled blindly for handholds as he whipped down the bare rock face. One fingernail caught an edge and tore free. His knee smacked a jagged edge and flayed open. Skin tore from his cheek. It had taken him at least an hour to climb the last thirty feet of open cliff, three heartbeats to reach the bottom.

He slammed into the scree slope with both feet and rolled on instinct. The rocks were piled loosely like gravel, and they gave under the pressure, dropping him another ten feet down the slope, but when he tumbled forward, he slammed his right shoulder down hard. A sickening pop echoed in his ears, pain arriving seconds later. He rolled down the slope. The shifting pebbles moved under him, the sheer force of his fall shifting the surface downward. Ash slid to a stop halfway to the trees.

Game over.

Ash lay on his back, staring upward at the bright blue bowl of the sky. Pain filled every part of his body. His arm flopped at a weird angle, something pressing up under the skin of his collar. His fingers were shredded from a thousand rock razors, his head aching. A single thought appeared: *I'm alive. I didn't die.* It was impossible, and yet it was.

Ash felt like he'd been in a car crash. Inch by inch, he tested his body. Both feet ached from the impact, but neither felt broken. Same for his legs. Ash let out a sigh of relief. *That's lucky.* He wiggled his hands. Both responded, though the palms of them were shredded from the rock, and two fingers on his left hand were missing fingernails; a third nail hung half on, half off. *Deal with that later.* He moved on to his arms. His left arm was fine, but tears filled his eyes as he tried to move his right. It dangled loosely, as if it had been torn from his chest, then taped back on. It didn't *fit* properly anymore. He took a sharp breath. A stabbing pain arced through his side. His rib cage was a mass of agony.

Broken ribs, he thought. *That's going to make breathing an issue.* There was a calm detachment to his thoughts that worried Ash. It seemed like he was on the outside the way he was in a game, looking down on his broken body—an adviser rather than a participant. *Get up. Walk back to Vale*, the other voice told him. *There is no other way.*

Using his left arm, Ash pushed himself upright. His right arm slumped down against his side in a way that left him fighting the urge to vomit. He breathed hard for several seconds as he waited for the feeling to pass. When it did, he forced himself to his knees. *So far, so good. Keep going.* He wobbled as he scanned the rocky slope. He had been lucky in his fall. A few feet one way and he would have hit the boulders. A few feet the other, and the cliff would have been too steep to slow his fall. Ash staggered. His right arm swung out, something grating under the skin between his neck and chest. He dry heaved. When he could breathe again, he reached for his zipper, but even undoing his jacket to check the damage was impossible. Gasping, he let go of the zipper.

This is so bad!

As the urge to vomit passed, he forced himself to search the area where he'd first hit the ground. There were bits and pieces of glass, a part of the battery, and nothing else. Without a metal detector, there was no way Ash was going to find enough of his phone to put it back together. *The phone is dead*, he thought. *I'm going to die out here too.* The realization was an afterthought. A side note on the bottom of a page. He sat down again, gasping as his broken collarbone stabbed painfully under the skin. For a long time, he stared at the scree slope. He didn't move. Didn't care.

Going into shock, the voice inside him announced. *Sit here long enough, that'll kill you too.*

That was the dark thought that spurred him into action. Ash forced himself back to his feet. Wobbling, he took a single, jarring step, then stopped as his ribs screamed in protest. *Keep going.* He took another step. The pain lanced from shoulder to fingertip, and he wobbled, faint and out of breath. *Move. You've got to MOVE.* Ash took another step, and another, and eventually he made it to the trees. A familiar smell reached his nostrils, and he sniffed the air, then lifted his gaze.

Far down in the valley, a faint gray smear appeared above the lush green of the pine forest. Vale had a campfire burning. A faint smile flickered over Ash's mouth, then faded away as the pain hit. He wished for one desperate moment this really *was* a game and that he could warp directly to her side.

Need to get back to Vale.

He gritted his teeth and took another step.

"What do you mean, 'there was a signal'?" Debra cried. Her husband Brad reached out for her hand and squeezed. She clung to him.

"I mean," Constable Wyatt explained, "that we've been monitoring all the satellite signals coming from the area of the park, and for a brief moment—around eleven this morning—they caught a cell phone signal."

"But I thought you said that was impossible!" Brad interrupted. "I thought you said there was no cell phone reception inside the park."

"There usually isn't," Wyatt said. "But sometimes, at the right height, in the right conditions, a phone can briefly connect. And if we've got a connection then there's a possibility that—"

"But where did the call come from?!" Debra cried. "If it's a *phone*, you'd be able to figure out where it came from, wouldn't you? Using GPS?"

The officer steepled his hands on his desk. "The phone call was dropped a few seconds after it connected, so we couldn't use GPS to get a location on it."

Debra's breath caught. "Oh my God. So you can't even tell who was calling?"

"Yes and no," Constable Wyatt said.

"What's that supposed to mean?"

"It means we don't know *who* was on the line," the officer said, "but we were able to trace the number. We are certain that the call came from Ash Hamid's phone."

Debra felt the floor tilt underneath her. "Then someone survived the avalanche. Vale or Ashton . . . at least one of them is still alive."

Constable Wyatt nodded. "One or both, almost certainly."

There was a benefit to hiking away from the trees near the lake. For one, it gave Vale a sense of where she was. Her mind made a map as she slowly gathered supplies. This valley was smaller than the one they'd come in from, but it had its own share of resources. Midafternoon, she'd found the first of them.

"Chokecherries!" Vale laughed as she limped forward.

In the southwestern end of the valley, the forest thinned, and a patch of berry bushes took their place. The berries were dark and bitter with a hard pit, like the fruit that gave them their name. Vale had never enjoyed them when she'd eaten them before, but after two days of fasting, her mouth flooded with saliva at the first taste. She grabbed a handful, chewing as best she could despite the hard cores, then spat the inedible pits out on the ground. She grabbed a second handful, eating more slowly so that she could get more of the berries into her stomach, which had awoken with the rumble of an angry giant.

For the next half hour, she ate her fill as she wandered farther and farther into the stand of berry bushes. Surrounded by the plants, she forgot the need for firewood or shelter or a way back home. *Food!* Vale had almost forgotten how good it felt to be full. The sharp flavor filled her mouth, and her stomach—full for the first time in days—stopped its restless cramping. If there'd ever been a meal to remember, it was this.

A sound nearby—something low and rustling—tweaked her attention. Vale lifted her head and listened. In the distance she could hear the trill of birdsong. The relentless wind. And under all of that, the small sounds of the forest.

Probably just the wind.

With her focus on eating, Vale took another handful of berries, munching them as she watched the woods. Minutes passed, but the uneasy feeling didn't fade. A branch broke somewhere in the depths of the forest. She turned, searching for movement. Nothing moved. But the feeling was there, her senses sharpened into alertness.

"Ash . . . ?" she called warily.

No answer.

The sense of being watched grew stronger. She took another furtive glance over her shoulder, then brought her attention back to the bushes. The chokecherries hung in bunches, some so ripe they were falling from the stems. Vale filled her pockets, then lifted the bottom of her jacket up to create a crude bowl and began to pick in earnest. *Next time I come*, she thought, *I've got to bring one of the plastic bags. That way I can—*

Another branch broke in the forest, this time a stone's throw from her. Heart pounding, she stepped back from the bushes. She leaned to the side, searching for the source.

There's something out there. But what . . . ?

Another branch broke—a little bit closer—and Vale hobbled a few steps farther out, trying to pinpoint where the sound had emerged. She had just opened her mouth to shout to Ash when the bushes on the other side of the glade rustled. A furry head emerged from the screen of bushes near Vale's feet.

Adrenaline rushed through her body, and she stumbled back. *Is that a badger?!* Panicked, she dropped the edge of her jacket and the berries she had so carefully gathered tumbled to the ground at her feet.

The animal took another step out of the shadowy foliage. As it emerged, its blondish-red coloring appeared and Vale frowned in confusion. While the creature had the stocky body she expected from a badger, it had no distinctive black-and-white stripes marking its face. Vale had been camping and hiking her entire life. She *knew* badgers were dangerous. *What is that?*

It took two more steps forward, finally emerging into the light. Vale's fear abruptly disappeared. "It's just a marmot," she said with a shaky laugh.

The size of a small beaver, marmots were reclusive burrow-dwelling creatures who posed no threat to humans. Vale grinned as she watched it move through the glade, oblivious to her presence.

Seconds slowly passed. Vale was about to reach down to pick the berries up again when the marmot abruptly turned its head, as if hearing something Vale hadn't. It scurried away from Vale.

She stared after it. *I wonder what—?*

A new motion to the far side of the berry patch drew Vale's attention. Large and furry—a wall on legs—it pushed past the leaves out into the open. Vale's stomach dropped.

Oh my God! That's a bear!

CHAPTER TEN

"There's something out there waiting for us, and it ain't no man."

BILLY, *PREDATOR*

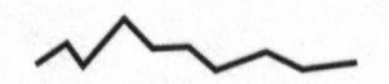

JANELLE HOLLAND JOINED the other searchers in the early afternoon. It had taken her nearly a full day to get the paperwork for the school division in order and the police reports finished, to say nothing of dealing with three *very angry* parents. She'd arranged to take the two emergency days allotted by her teaching contract before she crashed for six solid hours in the barracks of the police station. Waking, she'd caught a ride with Constable Wyatt back to Red Rock Canyon. The parking lot teemed with vehicles and new searchers getting ready to head out.

"Be safe out there," Wyatt said as Janelle climbed from the squad car. "Stay with your team. Watch out for wildlife."

"I will."

"Bears in particular," the officer added.

"Understood."

"If you find anything, have one of the wardens call it in to town. We've got helicopters searching the area. They can pick you up."

"Got it."

The officer opened his mouth, then closed it again. He frowned. "And just be . . . careful, Janelle. There *are* bears out there."

She nodded and walked away.

The bear was three times Vale's size, with blondish-brown fur, a flat, sloping face, and a large hump over its shoulders. It reached into the bushes for a mouthful of berries, and she got a clear look at its dished profile and massive shoulders. Her breath caught, terror arriving like a kick to the gut. *My God! It's a grizzly!* More dangerous than their black bear cousins, they were to be avoided at any cost, but *especially* when feeding. Vale had just wandered into the same berry patch this grizzly had claimed. If it saw her, she was dead!

The bear grabbed another mouthful of berries and leaves and tugged them off the branch, eating them with openmouthed enjoyment, lips smacking. It hadn't seen her . . . *yet*. It would if it kept going this way.

Vale fought the urge to run. Do that, and she'd surely be chased. Stay calm, and she had a chance. Snippets of her father's camping advice flashed to mind. Grizzlies were the most dangerous of the forest animals. They kept to high alpine slopes. They hunted only when they needed to, but they were fiercely protective of kills. You should never hold eye contact with one. They'd take it as a challenge. Grizzlies were fearless; they'd take on *any* animal . . . and they'd almost certainly win. The best advice was to back away. Be quiet. And if they attacked you, play dead.

"If it comes to it, Vale, you just lie there and let the bear chew on you."

"But how am I supposed to do that, Dad?"

"You be quiet. Go limp. 'Cause the longer you scream and kick, the longer the attack will last . . ."

If Vale had been wearing her backpack, she would have set it down in front of her as a distraction, but everything Vale had was back at camp. She hadn't even been carrying a bag with her!

The grizzly lumbered forward, snuffling the bushes. *Fifty feet . . . forty . . . thirty . . .* Vale's breath hitched. If the bear saw her standing here, this was it. *The end.* No one would ever know what had happened to her. The grizzly took a few steps closer. She was caught between the urge to run and stay.

Can't move! But I can't stay here either!

Suddenly, the sound of leaves moving interrupted. *The marmot!* Hearing it, the bear swung around, turning its back to Vale. It roared. The sound echoed through the glade with an intensity that turned Vale's knees watery. The bushes rustled again, and the bear stepped toward the source of the sound, huffing angrily. *The marmot is in the berry patch!* The grizzly took two stiff-legged steps, heading directly into the foliage. It growled low in its throat, moving toward the sound. First its front shoulders disappeared, then the back legs and finally the tail as the bushes closed behind it.

Vale sprinted away from the chokecherry bushes without a second thought. Behind her, the bear roared a second time. Her shoulders tensed, and she skidded to a stop. A second passed . . . two . . .

and then the grizzly roared again. This time, the sound was farther away.

The bear's going after the marmot.

With this in mind, Vale jumped back into motion. *Need to get out of here!* Adrenaline surged through her body, sharpening her senses. Her ankle ached with every step, but she didn't slow. She could feel the dying warmth of the sun on her shoulders, feel the nip of the late afternoon air, smell the pine forest and the sour-sweet tang of the berries she'd trodden underfoot. She struggled the last few steps to the camp she'd left behind. The fire was burning cheerfully, the lean-to waiting. Spending today putting the camp back together suddenly felt like another mistake.

"My God! I can't *stay* here!" Vale hissed, grabbing her backpack and tucking things into it. "Need to get out of this valley."

A marmot and a skunk, even elk, Vale could avoid. But a grizzly? She was in its territory, and there was no way that would end well. As the sun dropped in the sky, Vale came up with a plan: Pack tonight. Start walking tomorrow morning. It'd be slow going, but she'd stand a better chance of surviving if she did.

Vale tossed the foil emergency blanket into her bag, then headed for the shelter.

It doesn't matter how slowly I go, as long as I don't stop.

In the twelve hours since Ash had walked away from their camp, the snows had mostly melted, but bits of slush clung in the shadowy north sides of the hills, making the hike back to camp an obstacle course. Each step he took was torture, each breath a new level of pain. There was a sick, grating sensation deep inside his rib cage, and it grew sharper with each jarring footstep. *Broken ribs*, his mind noted. *Bone grinding against bone.* No matter how carefully he walked, the ragged flares of pain grew, expanding until it filled every thought.

Walk, the voice yelled. *Walk or DIE.* There was no in-between.

Ash was halfway through the trees when the sun began to set. During the lingering twilight hour when the sky shifted from purple to black, the temperature lowered. His breath hung in the air in white wisps, his fingers numb. Still Ash pressed on. The pain didn't matter, nor did the cold. Nothing mattered except the driving need to put one foot in front of the other.

Got to keep moving. Got to get back to Vale.

The trees grew closer together as he dropped in elevation. Unable to see clearly, Ash stumbled and collapsed. Stars flashed in his vision as pain stabbed up through his wounded arm, and he lost consciousness. He woke a short time later, shivering and cold. The abraded skin of his face lay against a skiff of snow. His nose was stuffy with blood. He tried to move, then fell back. Ash's right arm was useless. It dangled obscenely at his side. Something inside his shoulder was off, and he had no way to fix it. He tried to move, but the effort left him fighting the urge to scream.

Got to keep walking. Got to get back to Vale. MOVE!

Resisting the urge to lie down again—to give up—he forced his left arm underneath his chest and pushed with all his might. His muscles shook as he hoisted himself upward, crawling from his knees to his legs once more. The world spun around him. He tottered.

Just . . . Keep . . . Going . . .

He forced himself to walk again.

The sky darkened to solid black, and the stars came out, followed by the moon. Twice Ash tripped and fell to the ground, tearing up his knees. The pain gave flashes of insight. Something was broken inside him, and unless he got help, he wasn't going to get through it. *Walk, Ash! WALK!* Panic forced him to continue.

With the arrival of nightfall, the sounds of the forest faded. For a long while, there was only the crunch of his footsteps and the wind through the trees, and then a *new* sound reached Ash's ears. From far away, in a valley to the northwest, came a plaintive howl. Ash's knees went weak, a primitive fear—hardwired deep into his DNA—arriving in a rush of terror.

"Wolves," he gasped, and struggled to make his shaking legs move faster.

In more than one of the RPG games Ash played, wolves were predators. He knew absolutely nothing about them in real life (and Vale wasn't here for him to ask), but the fear he felt was intense.

A few seconds after the first howl, a second wolf's voice answered from the valley to the south. Ash stumbled, almost fell, righted himself again. *Need to hurry!* Ash knew he'd never survive an attack. A third howl joined the chorus, then a fourth. Ash's breath grew sharp.

Got to HURRY!

As the cacophony of howls filled the night, the scent of smoke reached his nostrils. He turned. Through the screen of trees, a dot of light appeared. The sight of it renewed his strength. He staggered forward, pushed on by the sound of howling. The fire was warmth.

The fire was safety. And—inasmuch as it could be in the middle of the Rocky Mountains—the fire meant *home.*

With this in mind, Ash shoved past the pain.

Soon he could make out the lake. A sturdy new lean-to had been built in a knot of trees close to its shores, and a bright fire cast a dancing light before it. A minute later, the silhouette of Vale appeared as she moved from place to place, gathering items, carrying them out next to the fire, and tucking them into her backpack. Ash smiled, though the expression hurt.

Should have told her I was leaving this morning. It was stupid to take off like that.

"Vale," he said, but his voice came out as a hoarse whisper, barely audible over the wind and wolves.

Ash stumbled a few more feet. His strength was gone. *The camp was so close!* He wove unsteadily toward the edge of the clearing, his vision slowly spiraling down into a pinprick. His legs gave out as he stepped from the woods and he caught himself with his good arm.

"Vale!"

She spun around, her mouth falling open. Her face was white with terror as she stumbled back toward the fire.

"V-Vale . . . ?" he croaked.

Her eyes widened. "My God! Ash," she gasped, "is that you?" Her expression flicked from fear to concern in a heartbeat. "What happened?"

"I—I was trying to—to . . ." He wobbled, words escaping him.

"I thought you left me." She dropped the wood down in the pile, heading toward him. "I thought—" Her eyes widened as she neared. "Oh my God! You're covered in blood. What happened?"

"I—I tried—I—" He staggered.

"Whoa! You look awful. Sit down before you . . ."

Ash didn't hear the rest. Sight and sound faded as he tumbled to the ground, his face cradled by the moist soil. And in his mind he just kept falling.

Vale's brain wouldn't add up what she was seeing. *Ash is back!* She wanted to know *why* he left, but as soon as she dropped her backpack and limped to his side, her confusion was tempered by fear. He looked like he'd been put through a blender.

She crouched at his side. "Ash?"

No answer.

Vale shook him, and he mumbled something incoherent. "Ash? What happened to you today?" With him unconscious, there was no way to be sure, but it looked like he'd taken a beating and lost. Vale's stomach dropped. *Or the bear I saw attacked him.* She rolled him onto his back, exposing the right side of his face. "Oh no, no, no . . . Not this!"

Temple to cheek had been scraped and slashed. By *what*, Vale couldn't hazard a guess. It was definitely too evenly scored to be a bear attack, but it looked like he'd run his entire right side down a cheese grater. Bits of skin were caked in the clots of blood, and his right eye was almost completely swollen closed. Her stomach rolled as she saw the flecks of dirt packed into the mess.

Vale shook him. "Ash? I need you to wake up. What happened?"

Nothing.

Vale tipped his face so she could see the other side. Barring a few bloody marks in his hairline, it looked all right. She tipped his face back so she could see the right side again. Her stomach churned. "Ugh . . . Gross," she moaned. "I'm going to have to clean that up. Aren't I?"

Ankle throbbing, Vale sat back on her heels and stared at him for several seconds. She, Ash, and the rest of the students doing a camping trip as part of their physical education class had been forced to sit through three sessions of first aid training. It had been mostly theoretical, but Ash's injuries were all too real. Vale drew on those classes now. She undid Ash's coat and eased it down his arms. He cried out but didn't wake as she reached his shoulder. Curious, Vale pulled the collar of his T-shirt out of the way.

"Oh heck no."

His collarbone was definitely broken. A dark red bruise marred the area from neck to chest, and an inverted V of skin showed the bone jabbing through the layers of flesh. It hadn't stabbed through the skin, but Vale wondered if it might. She looked away and took several slow breaths, forcing down the urge to vomit. She turned back, and her gaze dropped to his arm. "Gross, gross, gross . . ." His entire right arm looked a couple of inches too long. A wave of nausea lifted Vale's stomach and dropped it again. *The arm's out of joint.*

"Deal with that later," she muttered. "Got to check vitals first."

With Ash out for the count, it was easy enough to assess him. He cried out when she dragged him toward the fire, but didn't wake. Prodding his ribs elicited another cry of pain. *Ribs must be broken too*, Vale thought. Neither of his legs were broken—he'd walked back to camp—nor his arms. Vale stared at him for several long seconds, fear slowly winding its way around her chest. There was a bear in the valley. Elk too. The lake was obviously drawing animals in, and that meant that the longer they stayed, the more likely a confrontation would be.

Vale chewed her lower lip, fighting the urge to scream. *At least he didn't abandon me.* Frustrated, she let out an angry huff, then scooted over to his left side. "Have to ask you what happened later," she said. "But for now, let's figure this out." *Maybe this is for the better*, she thought. *If Ash was awake, he'd be in pain.* "Just going to get you fixed up, then try to wake you up again. We can't stay here. You know that, right? We just can't." The coat Ash wore was still tangled around his arms, so she tugged the sleeves past his hands and slid the jacket out from under him. She set it aside, then put her hand to his neck. His skin was hot to the touch. Vale frowned. "You're running a fever. That's not good."

There were too many things wrong with him, and she didn't know where to begin. If he'd been awake, she would have given him the acetaminophen she had in the kit to dull the pain, but he hadn't woken despite her rough handling. Vale's attention turned back to Ash's prone form.

"First things first," she said grimly. "Got to deal with the ribs."

She had no idea what to do with the arm, but she *did* know that the only way to manage broken ribs was to bind them up. If Ash had been able to sit up, it would have been easy. The issue was that Ash was out cold. She tugged his shirt up and out of the way. The blood drained from her cheeks.

"Oh, Ash . . . ," she murmured. "This is so bad."

Ash's torso was a mass of bruises. On the right side, the bruises varied from deep purple to bright red, with a few punctuated spots of color on the other side. She touched the darkest spot on his ribs and pressed lightly. Ash flinched under her hand. She jerked her fingers away and took a shaky breath. *Definitely broken.* This whole situation was so impossibly awful. *He's going to die if I don't help.* Vale was trapped by that knowledge. With a shake of her head, she turned her gaze to her own ankle and unwound the scarf from around it.

"Need to work with what we've got here, Ash," she said with a frustrated sigh. "I'm going to *try* to be careful, but tell me if it hurts too much, all right?"

Ash slept on.

She took one end of the scarf and shoved it under him, then leaned across him so she could reach around the other side. Her chin dropped down to his chest, and she grimaced. She could just barely get her arms around Ash's chest, but no farther. He was more than a foot taller than she was, and the height made all the difference. She couldn't catch hold of the other side of the scarf. Vale couldn't lean on his broken ribs to do it either.

"All right," she said, letting go of the fabric and sliding her hands free. "First plan failed. Guess we'll try something else."

Vale hobbled over to Ash's right side, surprised that her ankle didn't feel any worse unwrapped than wrapped. She crouched down next to him.

"What to do, huh . . . ?"

She didn't *want* to touch his damaged shoulder, but there was no other choice; it was in the way. Ever so gently she lifted his arm and laid the forearm above his head, the way she so often put her arm as she slept. She'd just lowered it to the ground when she felt something pop under her fingers. Vale gasped and jerked back, letting go of Ash's arm.

"Oh God. What have I done?" But Ash didn't scream or show any discomfort at all, and—as Vale leaned in to inspect the arm—it no longer seemed quite as stretched out as it had before. The dislocation had pulled back into position, leaving Vale with room to deal with Ash's ribs. "Well, that's good, then. Hold on," she said as she slid her hands under one side. "Just got to—"

She tipped him up slightly, and Ash shrieked in pain: "STOP!" His eyes opened for a second before rolling back up into his head.

"I'm sorry!" Vale yelped, almost dropping him. "I just need to wrap this."

Ash's head lolled to the side, unconscious once more.

She caught hold of the end of the fabric and tugged it tight, then moved to the other side and did the same thing a second time. This time Ash gasped but didn't scream. The third time, he didn't make a sound at all. The damaged ribs were bound, his arm in place. Vale turned her attention to his face.

"Oh gross . . . this is going to be nasty," she said as she got a good look at his features. One eye was completely swollen, but by firelight, Vale could see the mess of scrapes and contusions. The mud that packed them was what worried her. "Ash, I know you can't hear me, but . . . this one's going to hurt. Okay? I'm sorry about that."

Vale set his coat on top of him and grabbed her water canteen. She jogged to the nearby lake and filled the bottle. When she returned, she set the canteen into the fire, waiting while the water boiled. During the time it took, she checked Ash's vitals again. He seemed to be breathing more easily, and didn't cry out when she checked him. He didn't wake up, though. She took a few minutes and laid his damaged arm across his chest. There was nothing she could do for the collarbone, but at least this way it wasn't trying to poke through the skin. His breathing grew slower until Vale bumped him.

He moaned and his eyelids fluttered.

"Sorry. I don't have a sling, Ash," she said. Vale frowned down at him, then reached for the two backpacks. From Ash's she pulled out his bandanna, but it was far too small to work as a sling. He had a long-sleeved shirt there too, but Vale had no scissors to cut it with. She set it aside. Vale turned to her pack. She grabbed the first aid kit and laid out the contents. "Tape! That'll work!" She took a long loop of the tape, moved it around his neck, and wrapped it securely around his wrist. It was a simple tether, but it prevented his arm from flopping. "That'll keep it in place for now."

Happy with her progress, Vale checked the water again and found it bubbling. Bandanna in hand, she soaked the fabric in the boiling water and carefully washed away the worst of the soil and blood from Ash's face. The skin underneath it was bloody and raw. Vale's stomach tightened, the uneasy feeling of being completely out of her depth returning. She dried the skin with Ash's spare shirt—the cleanest material she had—then opened up the antibiotic ointment and spread it across the side of his face. She picked up the gauze pads and compared the size. They were far too small to cover the abrasions. And even if she used all of them, there would be a large patch of exposed skin left over. The bandanna was soaking wet. Frowning, Vale stared at the contents of the pack. *Got to think outside the box.*

Her gaze drifted from one thing to another, and then—

"The pads!" Inspired, Vale unwrapped the first of the three menstrual pads that she had brought with her. She held one up to Ash's face. "Perfect size!" She lowered the pad down to the broken skin—happily seeing that it covered everything from temple to cheek—then taped it securely in place. Vale giggled to herself. Ash looked like the Phantom of the Opera. "When you're roughing it, you've got to use what you've got to use."

Vale sat back on her heels and flinched as her ankle throbbed. Busy with Ash's injuries, she'd almost forgotten it. Her gaze returned to his face. That was as much as she could do for his wounds for now. She'd need to talk to him to figure out where else he was hurt. Vale leaned over him.

"Ash? You awake yet?"

He didn't answer, but somewhere beyond the firelight, a branch broke. Vale jerked around. The woods were dark, but the sense that something was *there* in the shadows stayed with her. Worried, Vale tossed wood onto the flames until the campfire danced with light.

Another branch broke, and Ash moaned in his sleep. Vale glanced nervously around the safe perimeter of firelight. This place had water, food, and wood, but it was *not* a secure campsite. The watering hole drew animals from the entire valley.

"I've got to get you into the shelter," she said. "I'll stay up and keep watch."

As carefully as she could, Vale caught hold of Ash's belt loop and the front of his shirt and dragged him into the lean-to. He groaned but didn't wake. She crawled back out again, grabbed his coat and laid it on top of him. Ash's face was sweat sheened, and he'd begun to shiver. The anxious feeling that had started with the sound in the woods grew until it filled her chest.

This is bad. Really bad.

She tucked Ash's coat around him, then unzipped her own and added it on top. On that, she placed the emergency blanket. His teeth were chattering so violently that Vale went outside and pulled several pine boughs from the wood pile and laid them over his legs. The needles weren't much for insulation, but it would have to do.

Clad only in her T-shirt, jeans, and boots, Vale crouched by the fire, shivering as the night grew cold. The forest was indifferently silent, the animal that had frightened her now gone. Vale glanced toward the shelter where Ash slept. *He should have woken up by now.* A wave of frustration rose inside her, and tears blurred her vision. She rubbed them angrily away. There was nothing she could do. Not anymore.

As the moon rose, Vale checked a jagged stump of wood for ants (there were none) and then tossed it into the fire. It would last, she knew, for many hours. Vale shivered. *Need to get some sleep. Tomorrow's going to be a long day.*

If a bear came, it came. For now, she needed rest.

Vale crawled inside and lay down under the two coats at Ash's side, staring across the jackets at his ravaged face. This wasn't like it had been when they were in school together—talking and joking—this was time to analyze, to consider what needed to be done. Ash was hurt. He might die. And there was nothing Vale could do about it except keep going.

I'll figure out how to save us both tomorrow.

Ash awoke someplace dark and quiet. Confused, he tried to move, then fell back as a wave of agonizing pain caught him completely off guard. His shoulder felt like fire, his chest caught in a vise. He lay still, fighting for each breath. When he was motionless, the myriad agonies inflicted on his body receded into the background. Staying still was the key.

Not dead, then, he thought. *Well, that's good.*

Ash breathed in shallow pants. He was chilled and damp, his body racked by shivers. When his pain faded enough that he could manage, his lashes fluttered open and he struggled to focus. The room where he lay was completely dark, the air icy. Somewhere—in the distance—he could hear wood snapping. *Where am I?* No one answered.

Ash's thoughts were slippery. He couldn't remember what turn of events had brought him to whatever place this was, but it felt *bad*, and he didn't know why. Confused, he forced the memories into order, pulling them back like a tangled thread. He could remember the mountain and something about a *Builder Craft* hammer. He could remember his sneakers slipping on the foothold and him falling . . . but little else. Even thinking about that left him exhausted, and he let his eyelids droop closed once more. *Think about it later. So tired . . .*

When he woke again, there was a flicker of light in the darkness.

The air had grown warm. He squinted in confusion. A short distance away from a rough half-circle doorway, a cheerful fire burned, casting its warm golden glow on Ash's body. He lifted his head, then hissed in pain. He lay inside a homemade shelter, a bed of pine needles softening the hard ground under him, two jackets over his chest and more pine boughs over his feet. He twisted his neck, searching the shadows.

"V-Vale?" he said.

A shadow blocked the open side of the shelter. "Ash? Did you say something?"

"Y-yeah."

"Oh thank God you're awake." He couldn't see her face, but he could hear the relief in her voice. "I was getting worried. You're hurt . . . *bad*."

"You should see the other guy." He tried to laugh, but a stab of pain shot through him and it came out as a yelp.

"Try not to talk too much," Vale said. "I'm pretty sure you've got broken ribs."

"Er . . . yeah."

The shadow in the doorway grew in size. Vale crawled up next to Ash, frowning down on him. She wasn't wearing a coat anymore, and her cheeks were bright pink like she'd been running. "I wrapped your ribs as best I could while you were passed out," she said. "But let me know if I did it up too tight."

"It's fine." Ash coughed and tears filled his eyes. Now that he was awake, the full effects of the damage had returned to his awareness. Even his throat hurt. "Thirsty."

"Hold on," Vale said. "I'll get you something to drink."

She left the shelter, and Ash's head tipped to the side, watching her go. Details from yesterday returned. He'd made it back to camp, but it had changed in the hours he'd been away. For one, this shelter was bigger than the one that had been knocked down the night before—perhaps twice the size. There was room for someone to sit up and move around. Plenty of room to stretch out. For another, the fire was far closer to the entrance. Heat bounced down on Ash, warming him. He was unpleasantly hot, and he shoved the jacket down with his good arm.

She fixed the camp while I was gone, he thought. Guilt crept through him. *Should have told her where I was going before I left.* He closed his eyes, fighting down the urge to cry. Tears weren't going to change anything.

He was interrupted by the sound of Vale returning. She climbed into the shelter, and a warm scent rose alongside her. Ash's stomach growled. Vale leaned closer. She had her water canteen in hand, but the liquid it held was a deep red, something bobbing on its surface.

"Wh-what is that?"

"Chokecherry soup," she said, then laughed. "I'm going to warn you, though: It's bitter. And I don't have anything else to offer. But it's better than water for filling your stomach."

"Chokecherry?"

"It's not as bad as it sounds," Vale said as she scooted nearer. "Just lie where you are. I'll hold it to your lips. It's not very sweet, but it'll fill you up."

Ash nodded, and Vale brought the metal canister to his lips. The scent of berries—sharp and tangy—hit him, and he could barely stop from slurping as the first bit of liquid reached his tongue.

"Slow down," Vale said. "Just go slow. All right?"

The soup was little more than crushed berries and water, heated over the fire, but to Ash it was the best thing he'd ever tasted. The liquid was bittersweet—like unsweetened cranberry juice. He drank greedily. Vale pulled the jacket back over him and tucked it in the way his mother had done when he was little. He was too busy drinking to complain.

Vale cradled the canteen until he paused for breath. "How's that?" she asked.

"Good."

"Ready for more?"

Ash nodded, and little by little, he drank the rest of the chokecherry soup. His stomach was full for the first time in days. He was warm. And though the pain was there, it no longer drew all his attention at once. Vale lifted the water bottle away from his lips and wiped a stray dribble with the sleeve of her shirt.

"I'm going to stoke up the fire again," she said. "It's still a long time till morning. You sleep."

Ash sighed rather than answer.

When he woke again, Vale was inside the shelter, crawling around him. She lifted the side of the two coats and slid in beside him.

Ash turned. "Vale?"

"Sorry," she whispered. "I didn't mean to wake you."

"You didn't."

"Oh, well . . . that's good, then." Vale lay down next to him, her face blending into the shadows. For a long time she lay in silence.

"Thank you," Ash whispered. He reached out for her with his left hand, groping blindly in the dark. "For helping me tonight. I mean it."

Under the coat, Vale's hand found his and squeezed his fingers once before letting go. "No problem, Ash. That's what friends are for. Right?"

"Right." Ash took a shaky breath. His throat ached, and unshed tears burned his eyes. There was so much *more* he needed to say to her. "Vale, I—"

"Shhh . . . It's late, Ash," she said. "We need to sleep. We can talk more in the morning."

"All right." Ash felt her move up against him, and he closed his eyes. "'Night, Vale," he whispered.

"G'night, Ash."

And in the shelter, the two friends slept.

Vale jerked awake as something bumped into her back. The transition from slumber to panicked alertness was immediate, and her arms pinwheeled in terror. One fist smacked down on something large and warm.

"Ouch! Vale! Watch it!" Ash yelped.

She sat up, struggling to orient herself. "Wh-what happened?"

Vale squinted through the shelter. In the watery predawn light, little had changed. Outside it, the fire burned steadily. The forest around them was silent.

"I . . . I tried to get up." Ash coughed, then winced at his ribs. "It didn't work."

"Why didn't you wake me up?"

"I wanted to do it myself."

Vale ran a hand through messy hair, pushing it off her face. Now that she was awake, the need to leave the valley was present once more. "Why?"

"'Cause I thought I could do it."

"Ash, your collarbone is busted. And from what I could see last night, I think your shoulder was dislocated too. You've got to take it easy, or you're going to make it worse."

"I know that—I just—I didn't want to ask you to—" Ash groaned.

Vale's eyes widened. *That* sounded like pain, and that scared her. "Seriously—what's going on?"

"I need to GO, okay?! And I didn't really feel like asking for help."

Vale went from indignation to sheer horror in less than a second. *He needs to pee, obviously!* "Oh God," she gasped. "I didn't know. I'm sorry, I—"

"Stop talking and *help me*! I think I'm going to wet my pants."

Vale crawled around him, appearing on his other side. She pushed the coats away, and Ash shivered. "I'll help you sit up. Ready?"

Ash nodded.

"On the count of three," Vale said, sliding her arms under his armpits. "One . . . Two . . . THREE!"

Ash yelped as she pulled him into a sitting position. "I need—to get—outside," he said. "Please. I—I can't hold it anymore." He crawled one-handed from the shelter. It was still relatively dim in the valley, though a faint smudge of pink marked the clouds along the eastern horizon. Dawn was on its way.

Vale scrambled out after him. "Just wait a sec!" She caught hold of him under his arms. "Get your legs under you, Ash," she ordered. "I'm going to help you stand up."

"On three?" he asked as he got his feet in position.

"Uh-huh. Three." Vale's grip tightened. "One . . . two . . . *three*!"

Ash choked back a scream as she pulled him to his feet.

"Did I hurt you?" she asked. Ash's face was grayish under his tan, beads of sweat on his forehead. "I'm sorry, Ash. I tried to be careful, but—"

"Gotta go." Ash took a step and wobbled, but Vale caught him before he fell.

"C'mon," she said. "I'll walk you. Let's move a little bit into the trees." Her voice dropped. "But not too far."

"Fine. Just hurry."

Ash staggered away from the shelter, Vale tucked under his side. She helped him go as far as she dared, then pulled him to a stop. Ash yelped like a dog who'd been kicked.

"No farther," she said. "Here is fine."

"But I need to pee."

"There's a bear in the valley," she said.

"A bear?!"

"Yes, and I had a run-in with him yesterday. I don't want to risk another one."

"Fricking crazy!"

"Yeah. Tell me about it." Vale stepped away from him. "You good from here?" She stepped back, but didn't leave. *The last thing I need is him falling down again!*

"I, um . . ." Ash tried to undo his jeans with his left hand, but his scabbed and nail-less fingers wouldn't work right. "Ugh!"

"What's wrong?"

"Nothing." He jerked angrily at the button of his jeans. It didn't budge. "Come ON!"

"Seriously. What's the problem, Ash?"

"I—I . . ." He let out a high-pitched laugh. "I ripped off a couple nails. I can't undo my jeans."

There was a long pause. "Are you kidding me?"

Ash glared at her over his shoulder. "Do I *look* like I'm kidding?"

"No . . . ?"

"I know this is awkward, but I really need to pee!"

"Right." Vale's cheeks burned bright red. Awkward *doesn't even come close to this!* She cleared her throat. "I can undo the button and zipper for you. But you have to do the rest."

He nodded grimly. "Fine. Do it."

Vale stepped closer, her voice wavering with panic. "You'd better never tell *anyone* about this," she growled. "Promise?"

"Got it."

"Seriously, Ash. You breathe a word and it's Friends Off." She shook her head. *My God, what'll Mike do if he hears?*

"Yes. I get it, Vale. Now hurry!"

Terror prickled Vale's chest. "Promise me, Ash! You never said you—"

"I promise, okay?" he yelped. "Now hurry up! I feel like my bladder is going to explode."

"Fine." Vale fumbled the button and jerked down the zipper with trembling fingers. Her cheeks burned as she stepped behind him. "You're going to have to do everything else yourself," she said in a choked voice. "I'm . . . I'm not going there."

"Thanks. I'm good," Ash said.

Vale heard Ash groan. For a second she thought he'd hurt himself, but a moment later, the tinkling of urine began. He sighed loudly. Hearing it, Vale giggled. *At least that's in working order.*

"What's that?" Ash glanced over his shoulder. "Why're you laughing?"

"Sorry," she said. "I'm—I'm sorry I laughed, you just sounded so . . . happy." She bit the inside of her cheeks to keep from grinning.

"Relieved is more like it," Ash said. "Seriously, Vale. At this point, I honestly don't care." He grunted and Vale heard fabric rustle. "All finished, I just—" There was a long pause. "I . . . I need a hand with the button again, if you're cool with that."

"Uh . . . yeah. I can do it." Vale averted her eyes as she reached for the button. *Just pretend it's not Ash. Look at the trees. Look ANY-WHERE else!* Her fingers finally got the button in position, and she did it back up. "There you go."

"Thanks."

"You need help to walk back to the shelter?"

Ash took a step and winced. "If you could spot me, that'd be great. I'm not feeling so hot right now."

"Spot you?"

"Don't let me fall."

Vale took her place at his side and wrapped one arm gently around his waist. "Now *that* I can do." She smiled. Far to the east, the first bands of sunshine painted the valley in shades of gold and she squinted at the rising sun. They'd made it to day three.

"Thanks, Vale. I owe you one."

"After crawling into camp last night in the shape you did? You owe me *more* than one, my friend. I'm going to have to start charging you for all the rescues."

"Maybe you should start a tally."

"A tally?" She snorted.

"Yeah. Survival Squad lives to see another day. Ash zero. Vale three."

Vale looked up at him. Her throat ached to see her friend like this, but at least he was back. *He didn't leave me after all.* "We're both alive. Given the challenges, I'd say we're both three for three."

"Guess so."

She winked at him. "We're tougher than we look, Ash. Don't let the rumors sway you."

Ash chuckled. "You ever hear the rumor about the computer virus?"

"Don't think so . . ."

"Forget it," Ash said. "I don't want to spread it all over."

Vale began to laugh.

CHAPTER ELEVEN

"Shit just got real . . . again."

HEC, *HUNT FOR THE WILDERPEOPLE*

VALE EASED ASH down so he could sit against a tree trunk near the fire.

"You okay?" she said.

He cringed as he reached the ground. "Yeah," he panted. "Doing all right, I guess."

Vale frowned. It was clear Ash was doing *anything* but all right. He looked like he was about to vomit. "Just rest here a minute," she said. "I'll get us some water." With a final look back, she left him to refill her metal canteen with lake water. *Don't let the bear come back*, she silently pleaded. *Like this, Ash will be completely at its mercy.*

The early morning lakeshore was calm. A thin layer of ice hugged the rocks on the edge, but it was already melting. Vale dunked the canteen under the surface, keeping an eye on the trees around the lake. She wasn't the only creature in the woods who was using this lonesome alpine lake for a water source.

When she returned, Ash was trying to add sticks to the fire, one-handed. Each movement—no matter how small—was followed by a sharp intake of breath. *He's hurt bad.*

"Let me do that," Vale said, taking the branches.

"Th-thanks. Just feeling a little cold right now."

He coughed, drawing Vale's attention. Ash looked like he did so many Monday mornings: long hair hanging in his face, eyes ringed by purple smudges from lack of sleep, clothes drooping on his lean frame. But there were other, more worrisome differences. His cheeks were pink and flushed, skin clammy. She put a hand to his forehead, then jerked away.

Ash's fever was back.

"Let's get you warmed up," she said, and went back out to gather more wood.

With the fire rebuilt, Vale sat down next to Ash and pulled out the baggie she'd filled with the last of the berries from her pockets. They were squished and pulpy. (At home she would have turned up her nose at the mere suggestion she eat them. Here in the woods, the sight of them almost brought her to tears.)

We don't have enough.

With the bear feeding in the berry patch nearby, there was no chance to go back for more. Ash coughed, then yelped, and she glanced over at him, struggling to catch his breath.

"You okay?" she asked.

Ash shook his head, pain tightening his features. "Hurts . . . to breathe."

"Sorry, Ash. Just . . . just rest, okay?"

He didn't answer.

Vale frowned as the truth settled around her. *Ash can't walk out. Not yet. We CAN'T leave today.* That meant at least another day in the valley with the elk and the bear. It meant another night of standing guard, keeping the fire going to scare the animals away. Ash couldn't even stand up on his own. Would he be able to walk tomorrow? Fear tightened its grip on her, and her breath grew sharp.

Vale closed her eyes and took several slow breaths. *I'm going to think about it later. For now, I've got to help Ash.*

Vale used her thumbnail to cut through each chokecherry and pop out the pit, then poured the half cup of pitted berries into the canteen water. She set it next to the fire while she headed off for more wood. The fire was heat. The fire was hope. It was every bit as important as the water, not just for safety, but as a signal.

By the time she came back, the water inside the canteen was steaming, the chokecherry pulp bubbling away. The sharp sweet smell made her stomach growl. Vale glanced over to Ash. He was still propped against the trunk, but in the past few minutes, he'd nodded off. His lids were closed, face drawn in pain. Her breath caught. Vale hated to see her friend like this.

The weather, which had been warm enough yesterday to melt the snow in the little valley, had taken a turn for the worse in the past twelve hours. Leaden clouds filled the sky above the northern ridge, hinting at more rain. Worry was a dark flower inside her, pushing to bloom. If they wanted to be saved, they needed to save themselves. And that fact made everything so complicated! From the moment Ash had wandered into camp late last night, incoherent and broken, she'd been caught between two warring urges: get out of the valley where the bear was, or stay and let Ash heal so he could walk out without doing more damage to his body. Neither option was good.

Ash's going to need a lot of help if he's going to go anywhere . . .

Ash began to snore softly as sleep took hold. His head dropped to the side, mouth opening. Bruises colored the skin on his arms and face, and his tan complexion had taken on an ashen pallor. He'd run a fever during the night, throwing off heat like a furnace. It worried Vale like a sore tooth, something she could only ignore for so long before she accidentally touched her tongue to it, and the sharp pain was back.

If Ash doesn't get medical help, he's not going to survive.

The thought twisted inside Vale's gut. Her sore ankle was nothing compared to his battered body. There was no way Ash could hike far—not in his condition—but the longer they stayed here, the more likely a confrontation with the grizzly became. Vale checked the chokecherry soup. The scent of it had her mouth watering, but she pulled it aside to cool before she took a sip. Her gaze flicked to Ash. *He'll need some energy if he's going to get better.*

Ash's snores grew deeper, and then he suddenly coughed, the unexpected movement jerking him awake. He groaned and opened his eyes to find Vale watching. "Everything okay?" he asked sleepily.

"Yeah, fine," she said, then forced herself to smile. "You were just snoring there for a minute."

"Ugh . . . sorry about that."

"Totally fine," Vale said. "My cat snores too, you know."

"Mr. Bananas snores?"

"Uh-huh."

Ash laughed, then cringed. "Ow . . . that hurts."

"You feeling any better?"

"I'd be lying if I said yes."

"Fair enough."

Ash straightened up, but he bumped his damaged arm as he moved. He hissed in pain. "So do I look as bad as I feel?"

"Worse. You've got a, uh . . ." Vale giggled. "A sanitary pad stuck to your face."

Ash's expression was almost worth the joke. "I've got a *what*?"

"A pad," she laughed. "You know? Like . . . a menstrual pad. That's what I had to use on your cheek."

"What the hell?" Ash's good hand came up.

"Stop!" Vale swatted his hand back. "You can't pull it off."

"But that's gross!"

"Why is that gross?"

His eyes widened. "Because . . . because it's a fricking PAD!"

"A fresh one!"

"But they're for a girl's—a girl's—"

"Period. You can say the word, you know."

"Disgusting!"

"Oh for God's sake," Vale snapped. "When you have a period—"

"Stop! You're not helping." Ash lifted his hand and touched the pad. "So gross."

"The pad was sealed in plastic. And it was big enough to cover the side of your face. You've got road rash all the way down your cheek and jaw." She shook her head. "Stop being such a baby about it."

He stuck his tongue out at her.

"Really, Ash?"

"I'm *not* being a baby," he said.

"Are too."

"Am not."

"Actually, you are."

"Ugh." Ash touched the dressing gingerly, his fingers moving from one end to the other. "You know, it doesn't feel like a pad."

Vale snorted with laughter. "And would you even *know* what one felt like?"

"Uh . . . no. Not really, I guess."

"Didn't think so."

"I'm not a girl, and I only have a brother." Ash frowned. "Didn't you have, like, a first aid kit with you? Couldn't you have used that?"

"I did, and yes—I used that too, but the cuts on your face were too big to cover up with the itty-bitty gauze pads. I used what I had, all right, Ash? And the pad was it. You're lucky it wasn't your *Immortal Defenders* sweatshirt."

There were several long seconds of silence. Ash smiled, though the expression looked weary. "Well . . . thanks for thinking of it, Vale."

"You're welcome. But don't go poking at it, all right? Your face needs some time to heal. Some of those cuts are deep." She leaned closer. "Do you promise not to touch them?"

"I promise." He paused, then said: "I still say you'd be great on a campaign. Honestly. You really would."

Vale laughed. "Not giving up on that lost cause, are you?"

"Nope. You'd be awesome at D&D. You're good at figuring out what needs to be done, making plans, giving directions . . ." He waggled the eyebrow not covered by the pad. "And you're *especially* good at bossing people around."

"Bossing?" Vale laughed. "I don't!"

"You do. But it's all good." Ash chuckled tiredly, then winced. "Ouch, ow! Ugh . . . That hurts!"

Vale's smile disappeared. "The ribs are bad, aren't they?"

"They hurt like a bitch."

She frowned. "We're not going to hike anywhere today."

"But—"

"You need a day to rest up. So do I. We'll take a bit of time, be ready for tomorrow. Sound fair?"

Ash's eyelids slid half-closed. "Uh . . . yeah. Sounds good to me." A shudder ran through him. "Wish I wasn't so cold."

Vale tossed more branches onto the fire. "So are you going to tell me what happened to you in the woods?"

He opened his eyes. "What do you mean, what happened?"

"You showed up last night and passed out. When I saw your face, I thought maybe the bear had gone after you."

Ash laughed again, then cringed. "Ouch. Nope. No bear."

"Then what?"

He nodded to the far southern range. "I climbed to the top of the mountain, and I . . . I fell. Took a lot of splash damage when I hit the ground."

"Sheesh, Ash." Vale glanced out across the valley. In the distance, early morning clouds obscured the peaks, but she knew their danger. "You could've died out there."

"Gotta be honest. I'm surprised I didn't."

"You are *so* lucky."

"Not really," he said. "I never did get the phone call through."

Vale's heart sank. "So that's what you were trying to do."

"Uh-huh. Almost got through, and then . . ." He shook his head. "Lost the signal and fell." He glanced over at Vale. "What did you think I was doing out there?"

"I, um . . . well . . ." She turned away. How did you tell your best friend you thought they'd left you behind? That you'd been waiting for him to abandon you for the last few years? That yesterday you'd believed it had finally happened? "I guess I didn't really know." She shrugged as she looked out over the valley. It was morning, but the weather wasn't warm like it had been the day before. There'd be rain or snow in the next hour. "I thought maybe you'd decided I was dead weight and headed off on your own."

She heard Ash grunt and turned to find him clutching his ribs as he scooted over to her side. "Wait!" Vale gasped. "Don't move, Ash. Your ribs—"

"Are already busted," he said, then settled down beside her. His face shone with perspiration. "I wouldn't do that," he said fiercely. "That's not me."

"Do what?"

"I wouldn't leave you behind."

Vale felt her throat tighten. "Well . . . thanks."

Ash reached out with his left hand and caught hold of her sleeve.

"I'm serious here. I wouldn't. Okay? That's a dick move. We're friends. Right?"

"Uh-huh." Vale nodded.

"Well, friends don't do stuff like that."

Ash's face was tight with pain, and Vale had a sense that he wasn't *just* talking about taking off. She wondered what *else* he meant. "Guess not," she said quietly.

"You've got to trust me. I'll watch out for you, Vale. I will."

"Fair enough. But then you've got to trust *me* too."

Ash rolled his eyes. "Is this about the pad again?"

Vale smiled. "Not really. It's just—it's everything. Okay? You've got to trust me, Ash. I've got to trust you. We can work this out together."

He squeezed her arm and let go. "Sounds fair."

"So you ready for something warm to drink?"

"Hell, yes. I'm starving here."

Vale grinned. "Good. 'Cause this is the last of the soup." She pulled the canteen from the edge of the fire and checked the temperature with the tip of her finger. *Warm, but not scalding.* She held it toward his left hand. "You take it," she said. "Drink it all. You need the energy."

Ash didn't reach for it.

"What . . . ?" she asked warily.

"I'll take half. You take the other."

"No. You're hurt. You should—"

"I'm not taking it all, Vale. Argue with me and I'll refuse to drink any." Ash narrowed his gaze. "So is it a deal?"

"I . . . I guess."

He took the canteen from her hand. "Good. 'Cause that's how Survival Squad rolls."

And while Ash drank, Vale thought of all the ways she was going to keep the two of them from dying, because there was no question. Their survival was currently resting firmly on her shoulders.

Midday, Vale announced she was going to try her hand at hunting.

Ash stared at her, confused. His whole body felt like it had been put through a shredder, and Vale was turning into an old-timey woodsman. "I . . . don't get it," he croaked. "Hunt what?"

"Fool hens."

"I don't . . ."

"We saw one when we were near Avion Ridge. They're birds," she said. "They don't panic when you get near them. I figure if I go slowly enough, I'll be able to walk right up, maybe use a shoelace to snare one, or club it with a stick."

Ash frowned as he struggled to remember the bird they'd seen back at the lunch site. In the back of his mind, a brown-and-beige-dappled bird appeared. It had seemed pretty unfazed by the students in the area, but it could still fly. "Wouldn't it be easier to hunt for eggs?"

"Wrong time of year," Vale said. "But we still need to eat. And I don't know about you, but I'm starving."

Ash closed his eyes, letting his thoughts spread to the rest of his body. Truth was, hunger was the last thing on his mind right now. The pain was all-encompassing.

"Ash . . . ?"

He opened his eyes to find Vale looming over him. "Uh, yeah?"

"You kind of passed out there for a minute."

"J-just resting," he said. A shiver ran through him. A moment ago he'd been burning up; now he felt like he'd been doused in ice water. "Y-you were saying?"

"I'm going to try to find something for us to eat, Ash." Her words were slow, as if explaining to a child. "The berries aren't enough. We need to keep up our strength. You need to eat. So do I." She frowned. "I'm going to leave you here by the fire for a bit. All right?"

"Okay." His lids slowly closed once more. "I'll just . . . wait for you."

Vale laughed, though it sounded anxious. "You do that. And call if you need something, okay?"

"You got it."

"Back in a bit." Vale tossed another log into the fire, then pulled a large stick from the pile next to the shelter, before heading out into the woods. Ash watched her until she disappeared into the shadows, hoping against hope that her suspicions about the spruce grouse were right. His eyes slid closed, and he sent out a silent prayer.

Please keep Vale safe . . .

She headed out in concentric circles around the camp, pushing through the brush as she searched. Ash watched her for two circuits, but sometime in the third, he dozed. One moment he was watching Vale, the next he was floating in the dreamland between pain and sleep.

Time passed.

Asleep, Ash rose to the top of the mountain once more. The phone was in his hand, only this time it connected, and for some reason, his *father* was the one who answered. "Dad!" Ash shouted. "You've got to find me! I'm lost in—" And then his sneaker slipped, and he fell. His foot jerked out at the same time he awoke.

Vale sat across from him. She hunched over the fire, doing something to what looked like a furry pillow, splashed with blood.

Ash took a breath to speak: "What're you—" The smell of burning feathers filled his lungs. He coughed, then groaned as a stabbing arc of pain lanced across his ribs.

Vale jerked up in surprise. "You're awake again."

"Yeah," he croaked. "What's that smell?" He fought the urge to cough. "Fricking gross."

"I'm trying to get rid of the feathers. Plucked some, but couldn't get them all out. I figured I'd burn them off. I . . . I'm not so good at it." She shook her head. "Sorry."

"So you got a bird?"

"Yeah. But it's pretty small." She sighed and put the pitiful creature directly into the fire. "I guess we can forget about eating the skin. Just focus on the meat." She looked up and gave a quick smile. "You rest, Ash. I've got this."

"Thanks."

"You need to go to the bathroom?"

"Uh . . . yeah. Please." Ash coughed, then moaned. "Can you help me up again?"

Vale headed to his side. "On three, okay? Ready? One . . . two . . ."

She tugged, and Ash bit back a scream. She helped him move a few feet from the fire. Ash fought the urge to rage. *Hate being this weak!* But there was no other choice. He *did* need the help.

"This is far enough," Vale said as she unbuttoned his jeans, then stepped behind him. "You go. I'm going to wait. Tell me if you start to feel lightheaded, all right?"

Ash closed his eyes, relaxing. "Yeah. You got it."

A few minutes later, they were back at the fire. The unmistakable smell of cooking poultry reached his nostrils, and Ash sighed. "God, that smells so good." He had no idea how Vale had caught the bird, but he didn't care.

"Should be done in a bit," she said. "You doing okay?"

Ash tried to answer, but his eyes were drooping again. Even the short walk had depleted his energy. "F-fine." Shivers rippled through him.

"You warm enough? You want me to build up the fire a little?"

"Yeah, if you don't mind."

"No problem." She pulled several pieces of kindling from the pile and added them to the fire at his side. "Just let me know how I can help."

"God. You've done *everything* so far. I'm dead weight, Vale."

"You're not."

"Am too," he grumbled.

"Ash, stop. We're friends. *This* is what friends do for each other."

Ash tried to answer her, but there was a painful lump in his throat. *Friends.* Vale had saved his life last night, but on any day of the week, Ash couldn't even stand up for her against Mike and the other jerks in the class. Tears prickled along his lower lids. *I'm a bad friend.*

Suddenly, the words he'd thought, but could never figure out how to say, were tumbling out.

"I . . . I'm sorry for not saying anything against them," he said. "For thinking it, but never—" His voice broke.

Vale lifted her head. "What're you talking about, Ash?"

"B-before, at school. When the guys were harassing you in c-class. Making fun of y-you. I—I—" A hot tear rolled down his cheek. "I should've t-told them to screw off. I never did."

"Ash. You're hurt. This doesn't matter right n—"

"I need to *say* it, all right?" His voice cracked. "I'm a bad friend; I—"

"You're not."

Ash was crying now, his voice hitched and broken. "B-but I should have stopped them. I—I thought about it, but . . . but . . ."

Vale took a stick and pushed the smoking grouse to the side of the fire, not holding Ash's eyes. She took a shaking breath. It was the same kind of sound his mother made when she was about to cry and trying not to show it. "It's okay, Ash," she said thickly. "I understand."

He let out a choking laugh, then grimaced as his ribs grated. "Yeah? Well, you're a better person than me," he said, "'cause I *don't.* It's m-messed up. F-friends don't do that."

Vale caught his eyes across the fire. She was crying, and that made him feel worse. "I get it."

"Get what?! I'm a jerk."

"No." She shook her head. "It's hard to make yourself a target. I . . . I understand that."

"You shouldn't."

She sighed. "It's fine, Ash."

"It's not." He reached out for her hand even though the effort made him feel sick. Vale looked at his open palm for a second, then slipped her hand into his. "I'm sorry, Vale, so fricking sorry!" he said fiercely. "I—I should have done something to h-help you. I . . ." He let go of her hand and wiped tears from his eyes. "I wish I had."

Vale scooted up next to him and wrapped her arms gently around his shoulders. "It's okay," she said in a choking voice. "I'm fine. So are you. We're *friends*, Ash. Let it go."

He leaned against her and closed his eyes, waves of remorse riding through him. "And what if I can't?"

To that, Vale had no answer, so they sat in silence instead.

The teams of searchers switched off throughout the day and night, and Janelle found herself mingling with a motley group pooled from the local community. There were firemen and ranchers, local townspeople, and several park employees in the group. They started at Red Rock Canyon, moving deeper with each passing hour. They ate and camped along the trail, supplies brought in by helicopter.

Janelle had never been so tired in her life.

Reaching the clearing south of Avion Ridge, Janelle located a uniformed woman who appeared to be in charge. She glanced at the ID badge: *Warden Aya Banks*.

"Where are we searching today?" Janelle asked her.

Warden Banks turned. "Heading out toward Sage Pass. There's a group out there already. We'll trade off with them so they can get a few hours of sleep." She hoisted her pack onto her back. "You one of the new volunteers?"

"I am."

She nodded. "Then grab your things, and let's get ready. We need to find these kids as soon as we can. Warden McNealy and the others have already headed out. We need to hurry."

The anxious feeling in Janelle's chest tightened. "Did something happen . . . ?"

Aya frowned. "Not yet, but there's more snow coming. We need to find them before then."

"Why before?"

Warden Banks paused. "Do you know much about the snowpack in the mountains?" The way she phrased it had the same bone-weary patience Janelle often found herself using with her students.

"No," she admitted. "I don't. Is there some reason I should?"

"See there?" Aya nodded and pointed to the far western slope of the mountains. "That, there, is Sage Pass. We figure that's where those two kids got off track."

Janelle winced. *Where MY two students got lost.*

"But they left the pass sometime later. Doesn't look like they got caught in the snowslide," Warden Banks said, "so we figure they must be headed south now."

"But that's good, right? I mean, Waterton is south."

Aya's face grew dark. "No. It's not good at all."

Janelle stared at her, fear coming fast and tight around her.

"There's a chain of mountains and a valley between where those kids likely are and the passage to the town." Aya sighed. "One of the mountains is called Starvation Peak . . . and below it is Starvation Valley. *That's* where they'll get caught if they keep walking. And that's why we've got to find them."

Janelle swallowed hard. She wanted to ask *why* but didn't dare. There was a scream building in the back of her throat, and if she let it out, it would never stop.

"Back in the eighteen hundreds," the warden continued, "there was a group of indigenous people who used the mountain routes for travel. A band of them—Kootenai, most likely—were going through the pass when the snows came early." She paused. "Much like this year."

"The snow," Janelle whispered.

Warden Banks nodded. "The tribe was trying to get back out to the plains, but the snow came, and they were caught—the entire group of them—in a narrow pass. Once it started snowing, they couldn't get out. The sides were too steep and the mountains too tall. They were trapped and . . . they starved."

Janelle felt the ground shift beneath her. *That's where Vale and Ash are headed.*

"So when I say we have to find those kids," the warden said, her voice gentling, "I'm not kidding. I'm telling you because there's another snowfall forecast tomorrow, and once it starts, it's not going to stop."

Janelle nodded. "Then it's up to us to find them today."

Warden Banks nodded. "Exactly. Because if we don't, their bodies won't be found until spring."

The spruce grouse was gamey and tough, but it was food, and for that, Vale was grateful. *Now we just need to stay warm.* Despite being surrounded by a forest, this task was harder than it seemed. The clouds drew in like a curtain, bringing with them a fine mist of rain that never truly fell, but never actually stopped raining either. It was like standing outside an icy shower. The damp leached through Vale's clothes, settled against her skin, and forced the cold deep in her bones. She took nervous forays out into the forest, always alert for animals.

She'd been lucky with the first spruce grouse, but her attack had spooked the others and there were no more to be seen. There *were* berries out there, however. It just took time to find them. After half an hour of searching, she located a few stubby bushes with sparse clumps of chokecherries that amounted to a couple of cups. A few minutes after that, she found an even smaller patch of huckleberries, though the remaining berries that clung to the branches were small and tart. Each time she came back to the camp with more firewood and a few more berries, but it was slim pickings compared to what she'd found in the glade with the bear. Still, it was *something.*

She had just returned with another handful to add to the bag when Ash began to cough. He groaned and reached out for his ribs with his good hand.

"Oh God! That hurts."

"Want to lie down?" Vale asked.

"Not yet. I have trouble breathing when I lie down too long."

A sliver of fear ran the length of Vale's spine. "Right."

Ash was clearly in pain, and Vale worried about the fever. Something was wrong, and it was more than just his ribs. Vale rustled through her first aid kit and pulled out the acetaminophen tablets. She squinted at the label on the plastic package, then popped out two.

"Here," she said. "Take these." She dropped them into his hand and brought him a bottle of water to wash them down.

"Thanks. You have more of them?"

Vale glanced down at the four unbroken blister-sealed packs. "A few . . . but not enough."

She headed out twice more that afternoon: once to gather a handful of berries, another time to locate firewood. When Ash was caught up in a fit of coughing near nightfall, she gave him the next two acetaminophen tablets and insisted that he sit inside the shelter out of the rain.

Vale built a roaring bonfire. Eventually, she used up the pile of branches and had to move on to the larger, fallen trees that surrounded them. (She checked each one for wood ants before she dragged it to camp.) At one point, Vale found an entire dead tree that was small enough to drag with her. Inspired, she pushed the entire log into the fire at one end, and as it burned, she moved it inward into the flames. It reminded Vale of the way you could sharpen a pencil down to nothing. It was a solution that gave her time to stop gathering wood. She crouched down and scooted into the relative warmth of the shelter.

"Ash? You feeling any better?"

He was lying on the bed of pine boughs, but he opened his eyes as she came nearer. His face was flushed again, the fever making his dark eyes bright. "Yeah," he croaked. "Doing just great. Can't you tell?"

"Mind if I join you in here? I've got a good fire going, but it's getting cold."

"Sure." He coughed, but it was cut off almost immediately by a groan of pain. "But I'm not much company right now."

"You need anything? Some water?"

"No thanks."

"Some more pine boughs to lie on? I could grab a few to soften—"

"I'm fine."

"Need to go to the bathroom? I can help you walk, if—"

"Vale, just stop!" he said in a sharp voice. "I'm messed up and I feel awful, but otherwise . . . fine. Just hang out for a bit. Talk to me."

"About what?"

"I dunno. Like . . . anything. Just distract me, all right?"

"I . . ." Vale frowned. That he *wanted* distraction worried her. "Ash, are you *really* okay?"

He laid his head back and closed his eyes. "Totally fine, just . . ." He coughed, then cringed. "Just talk, Vale. Distract me."

She took a slow breath. "Okay. So, what're we going to talk about?"

"How about what you plan to do after high school?"

Vale groaned. "Ugh . . . I don't even want to *think* about that yet."

Ash opened one eye. "You kidding?"

"No, I'm not kidding. I just don't want to decide. I . . . I know I need to figure out my college plans, but right now I just want to get through high school."

Ash frowned. "But I thought for sure you'd have everything planned by now. You always told me you wanted to be a biologist. Study animals and stuff."

Vale shrugged.

"No, seriously, Vale. You *always* talked about that when we were kids."

"Yeah, well . . . it still interests me, but I don't know if I'm ready to take that leap or not."

"Why not?"

She glared at him. "'Cause I just don't *know*, okay?"

"Uh . . . yeah. I get that. But not knowing sounds weirdly . . . *like me.*"

Vale laughed. "What do you mean?"

"I dunno. It just doesn't make sense. You're Vale Shumway. You're supposed to *know* that stuff."

Vale snorted with laughter.

"No, really," Ash said. "You're in all the honors classes. You're on student council. You volunteer for all the cocurricular—"

"I'm the least popular person in the entire school."

"Hey! That's not true."

She laughed. "Yeah, well. You have to say that 'cause we're best friends."

Ash frowned.

Vale shrugged. "I guess right now I'm just trying to . . . get through each day. The thought of *purposefully* extending that kind of torture just freaks me out a bit."

"What do you mean?"

"Yes, I love reading about things, but college is *more* than just studying." She sighed. "I'm worried that college is just going to be a brand-new bunch of Mikes and Brodies."

"You don't know that."

"And you don't know it *won't* be." She laughed, but it had a bitter edge. "It's hard, Ash. I won't lie. Thinking about four more years of that *after high school* just . . ." She sighed. "It exhausts me."

Ash propped his head up on his good hand. "So change it."

"Like that's so easy."

"It is, Vale! You just have to find the right people to hang out with. Have fun. Get out once in a while."

"The right people?" Vale stared at him. "I hang out with *you*, Ash. When I'm online, I have Bella. How are those *not* the right people?"

"I don't mean it like *that*."

"Then what?"

"I mean—you and me—we were always friends, but I never really felt like I truly 'fit in' until I got into the right gaming communities."

"But you *always* play video games, Ash." She rolled her eyes. "God, even I played video games back in the day, but that doesn't mean—"

"It has to be the right people. The right groups," he said. "You stopped playing in middle school."

"Because I was getting trolled."

"And I hated that. I did. But I don't play with those guys." He frowned. "Not anymore. And it wasn't until I found the right kind of people online that I really felt like I had a place. Like I . . ." He frowned as he searched for the words. "Like I had *my own people*. And that brought its own confidence. It's not just online either. It's just finding people with common interests."

A wistful smile crossed Vale's lips. "Is that why you keep trying to get me to play Dungeons & Dragons with you?"

He ducked his chin. "Maybe."

"That's really nice, Ash."

"It is! I mean, if you like D&D, then maybe you'll give gaming a try again."

"I don't think so."

"Listen, Vale. I live here in Alberta, but the people I play with are from around the world. They share the same interests. They have the same passions, the same games they like to play . . ."

As Ash spoke, Vale felt herself pulled into his excitement. He spoke of his gaming friends with the same joy she felt when surrounded by her friends—like Bella—who she'd met online years earlier. But there were too many hours in the day when she *wasn't* surrounded by open-minded people. Vale watched Ash as he spoke, his voice rising and falling with enthusiasm. *Maybe that's the difference*, she thought. *He's found where he fits. Where he can be himself. I'm still looking.*

". . . and in the end, it really isn't about the game at all," Ash said. "It's about having fun with friends. My mom's always on me about what a waste of time it is, but I dunno. I've met some of the coolest people in the world online." His smile wobbled. "I *miss* having you there, playing with me."

Vale smiled sadly. "I miss that too."

"There are good people online too, Vale. Friends who'll back you up no matter what."

"Yeah, but I know some pretty cool people in *real* life too. Friends who'd literally risk their lives to climb a mountain and get a message out to save us."

Ash smirked. "That friend of yours sounds pretty badass."

"Oh, he's the badass-est of all."

"Then you should keep hanging out with him. Maybe even game with him once in a while."

"Game, huh? Is this the same friend who's looking for another member of his Dungeons & Dragons party? 'Cause I'm pretty sure I've already talked to him about this."

"Yeah, that's him," Ash said. "And I've gotta tell you, if he's that badass about mountain climbing, I bet his gaming skills are pretty solid too."

"Unless orcs are involved," she teased.

Vale giggled, and Ash laughed, but it turned into a cough, and from there to wheezing gasps. Suddenly the lighthearted joking was gone, fear in its place. Ash groaned and fell back against the nest of pine branches.

"You okay?" Vale asked when he could breathe again.

"Not so much, actually. I feel like something's broken inside. Hurts to breathe."

Vale bit the inside of her lip to keep from crying. There was no more denying it. Ash was getting worse, not better. They needed help and fast. "We'll get you out of here. Promise."

He nodded, but didn't answer.

Vale watched Ash for a long time as sleep took hold of him once more. In the wake of the coughing fit, an unsettling rattling sound had started in his chest. Vale reached out to touch his forehead, then pulled her hand away like she'd been burned.

His fever was worse.

The night was misty and frigid. A bitter wind whistled through the valley, tossing the treetops and forcing icy fingers through the meager shelter of the lean-to's walls. Ash woke twice, shivering in the dark. *Why's it so cold tonight?* He struggled to pull the jackets and emergency blanket up, only to find that he'd pushed them off sometime earlier. His whole body shook as he reached down with his good hand, fumbling to find them.

"What's wrong?" a familiar voice whispered. "Are you sick?" *Vale.*

"N-not sick," he said through chattering teeth. "J-just knocked off the jackets."

"Are you cold?" Vale sat up and pulled the coats up from where they'd fallen between them. "Here," she said. "Let me cover you." Her hand brushed his forehead, then disappeared. "You stay here. I'll add some more firewood."

She tucked the coats around his shoulders, then crawled from the shelter. The hollow between the vapor barrier of the garbage bags atop the branches and the jackets was a welcome warmth.

Ash was relieved as the heat returned, then—a heartbeat later—frustrated that he'd needed to ask for her help at all. He watched her silhouette as Vale moved from place to place, backlit by the bonfire. She had a log as big around as Ash's leg burning, and she pushed the unburned end of it inward toward the fire. Flames leaped upward, a wave of heat expanding to reach the nearby shelter. This approach to keeping the fire going was smart. *Very smart.* And it was Vale. She'd come up with it with the ease that left him both annoyed and grateful. They didn't have an ax, but Vale had thought *around* that challenge.

No question. She's keeping us BOTH alive.

Ash's eyelids fluttered closed as another wave of shivering overtook him. Even with a raging fire, the chill air sucked the warmth from the air. There was no layer of snow to insulate the shelter as there'd been their first two nights. Yesterday—when Ash had stumbled back to camp—was a blur. But tonight he alternated between chattering teeth and raging fever.

Just want to go home, he thought as Vale crawled back into the shelter next to him. *Back at home . . . back in my bed . . . back under the covers, warm and safe . . .* Another bout of shivering racked his body despite the layers. When he'd headed into the hut, Vale had insisted he take the position nearest to the fire. He felt her carefully ease around him and lift the corner of the two jackets, crawling underneath. She lay behind *him* this time, trying to keep warm. Feeling her slide into place, Ash rolled over to face her spot rather than give her his back.

Ash opened his eyes. In the darkness, Vale's face was an onyx statue, the planes of her cheeks and forehead carved in tones of blue. She shivered and blew on her hands. It struck Ash that she'd just built up the fire without wearing a jacket. She'd left *him* the extra warmth, rather than take her coat. Guilt rose inside him as she snuggled into their shared burrow. *I should be helping her too.*

He opened his mouth to speak, then closed it again. All day he'd wanted to sleep, but now it felt more elusive than ever. *What do I say?* Vale's shivering finally stilled, and she let out a slow, even breath as she relaxed. Sensing her hovering on the edge of sleep, he reached out with his good hand and nudged her shoulder.

Vale's eyes flashed open at once. "What . . . ?"

"Hey," he said in a low voice.

She blinked. "Hey yourself, Ash." A second later, the worry line he'd noticed so often appeared between her narrow brows. "What's wrong?"

"Nothing. I . . . I just wanted to say I'm sorry."

"Sorry for what?"

"For walking off on you the other morning. For . . . for trying to climb that stupid mountain alone." The tickle in the bottom of his lung returned, and he turned his face away and coughed, groaning a second later. When he looked back, Vale was waiting. "I should have woken you up and told you I was going," he said.

"I wouldn't have let you go."

"I know that. I . . . also know we wouldn't be in this situation if you had."

Vale smiled. "It's okay. We're doing fine."

"We're *not* doing fine. We're totally fragged."

"Disagree." She smiled. In the near dark, her eyes looked like glass, the reflection of firelight dancing in the edges. "And I'm the leader of Survival Squad, right? I get to make that call."

"Well, if you're in command, then—" Ash moved, and his damaged arm shot a dagger of pain through his chest. He yelped.

"Your arm again?"

"Uh-huh." Ash settled carefully back into place. "Did I ever tell you about the guy who busted his left arm?"

Vale shook her head. "Must have missed that one."

"Doctors were worried about him at first . . . but he was all right."

Vale began to giggle, then Ash did too, but in seconds, his laughter turned into a fit of coughing. When he could breathe again, he wiped tears from the sides of his eyes. He took a rattling breath and slowly let it out. "Tomorrow we start walking out of here. Right?"

The line between Vale's brows grew deeper. "You think you're ready?"

"I don't think we have a choice anymore."

"But—"

"I *need* a doctor, Vale. You know it. So do I. If this was a game, my energy bar would be flashing red. I'm sick. *Really* sick." His voice hitched. "And I'm scared."

The wind rose around the hut, wheedling its way in through the pine boughs and reaching under the coats. Ash began to shiver.

"Hold still," Vale said. "I'll warm you up."

She pulled him against her chest and tucked the coats around him. She was soft and warm, and Ash let himself relax against her as waves of shivers ran through him. Tears prickled against his eyelids, and he was glad it was dark so she couldn't see them when they started to fall.

"I—I'm sorry," he said in a broken voice. "Sorry for everything."

"Shhh . . . ," she whispered. "You're going to be fine, Ash. Just sleep now."

And after a time, he did.

CHAPTER TWELVE

"Let's go. There's nothing to fear here."
"That's what scares me."
SATIPO AND INDIANA JONES, *RAIDERS OF THE LOST ARK*

VALE STARED DOWN at her panties in frustration. "Well, this is just *great*!"

It was barely light, but the bloody smear that announced the arrival of her period was unmistakable. She was annoyed, but not entirely surprised. Her period was due on Wednesday; today was Monday. With all the stress, it had arrived early.

Fuming, Vale pulled up her panties and jeans and walked back to the camp. Ash was dozing by the fire, but he glanced up as she arrived.

"You ready to go?"

"Just a second," she said. "I've got to . . . do something." Vale dug through the pack until she found the supplies. There were two pads left (the third had been used for Ash's bandage), plus six tampons.

She grabbed her second pair of panties, a sanitary pad, and a tampon, then headed back to the bushes where she'd been minutes earlier. The cramps that heralded her period's arrival were already making her uterus feel like she'd been punched in the gut. Walking today would be unpleasant.

"Not cool, body. Not cool."

Shivering, Vale undid her jeans. The first speckles of rain splattered the bare skin of her thighs. The storm she'd been waiting for was about to arrive, and Vale feared that at some point the rain would turn to snow. The air was already icy cold. With numbed fingers, Vale applied the pad to the fresh panties, grateful she'd brought them along. *Thank goodness the blood didn't soak through my jeans.* She inserted the tampon and tucked the plastic into her pocket, then headed back to the fire.

Cramps or not, it was time to leave.

"This sucks!" Ash grumbled.

Vale looked up from where she was wrapping the scarf around his ribs. "Did I make the binding too tight again?"

"No. The wrapping is just fine." He lifted his chin toward the slate gray sky. "It's just this. *All* of this! I mean, it's October, for God's sake. Feels like December this morning."

Vale shrugged. "True. But we're in the mountains. The higher you go, the worse the weather gets." She reached for his sweatshirt. "Lift up your hands—actually, make that *hand*—and I'll help you get your sweatshirt on."

Ash groaned as she pulled the fabric over his head "Feel like such a noob when you help me. Fricking *hate* that."

She smirked. "My, my . . . *You're* in a good mood this morning."

"I'm fine. Just . . . tired and achy."

The truth was, after another night on the cold hard ground, *everything hurt*. Pain had sharpened his temper, but he made a note to try to control it. *Vale doesn't need to worry more than she already is.* Ash felt worse than he'd felt yesterday, but he certainly wasn't going to say that to Vale. Not with her doing *everything* else. He waited as she tucked the floppy sleeve under his damaged arm and tethered it to the tape sling to hold it in place. She looked up at him and grinned. His frustration dropped a notch. *She's trying to help. I'm the one who is being a jerk about it.*

"See?" Vale said. "You're as good as new."

"Good as new?" Ash said with a laugh. "I'm never taking *you* shopping. This is a Salvation Army discount sling if I ever saw one."

Vale shook her head and laughed. "You *know* what I mean."

"I do." He coughed, then yelped as his ribs pulled. The wrapping helped, but didn't fix them. "So you ready to go?"

"Yeah. Just give me a minute. I'm going to grab some burning coals." She headed over to the fire.

"Coals?"

"Yeah. We're all out of gum wrappers. I want to try to move some of the embers to the next site so we can have a fire."

Ash stared at her. "How?"

She dug through the dying fire with the end of a green branch. "Well, I had this idea that I could maybe just put a bunch in the pack. Sure, some will go out, but not all of them. Right?"

"Your pack isn't gonna hold that."

Vale dropped the stick and looked up at him. "It might."

"No, it won't." Ash took a step, wanting to join her at the fire, but pain stopped him before he'd gone two steps. He hissed.

"Ash!" Vale sprinted back to his side. "Hold on. Let me help."

He breathed through a wave of nausea, then forced a weak smile. "Sorry," he said. "I . . . I should've waited for you to help me."

Vale slid her arm around his waist. "Hold on. I'll help." She looked up at him. "Back over to the fire?"

"Yeah. That'd be good."

Step by step, Vale helped him move to the other side of the campfire, then slowly let him slide to the ground. He let out a wheezing breath, seeing stars. Walking together was doable. If he was careful not to jar his ribs, and Vale braced his good side, he could make it. *Just think about the next few steps*, he thought. *Don't even worry about the rest of the day.*

"You okay now?"

He squinted up at her. "Yeah." He gestured to the backpack at her feet. "I was trying to tell you that you can't do it that way."

Vale frowned. "Why not?"

"Your pack will either burn up—and burn you too—or the fire will go out."

Vale stood up and dusted her hands off. "Maybe, but our prison lighter is done and our last attempt at starting a fire by rubbing sticks together didn't go so well."

Ash nodded to the larger branches. "How about we make a torch or something?"

"It's cold and damp. It'll be raining by nightfall. The torch isn't going to last as long as it'll take us to hike out of here. Even if Waterton *is* on the other side of that mountain, we're going to spend the night up there. We need something that'll keep the coals alive."

Ash glanced around the camp. There were so few items to choose from! Even the few days they'd been staying there had stripped the resources, and most of the dried brush had been burned away. His gaze lit on a piece of curled outer bark—too wet to burn—that lay amid the ashes.

"How about that thing?"

"What *thing*?"

"That wood. The bark."

Vale followed his pointed finger to where it lay at the edge of the fire. "What about it?" she asked.

"It's not burning, right?"

"Right."

"So let's put a bunch of coals into the curl of the bark," Ash said, "then put *that* into the pack. We take a bunch of embers together and kind of . . . carry them. You know? Isn't that what the First Nations peoples did when they moved camps?"

"I . . . honestly don't know."

"I think that's what I read last year in social studies. Anyhow, the bark isn't burning, so it shouldn't light anything on fire, and if we get enough coals, at least *some* of them should be left when we reach the next site."

"All right, then. Let's try that." Vale reached down for the curl of bark and set it aside. A moment later she took two unburned sticks and rolled a bright cinder of glowing coal into it. She carefully lifted it into the pack. Finished, she stood from the fire and brushed the ashes off on the sides of her pants. "Now, we should get walking, because I want to be out of this valley by nightfall."

"Lead the way, Commander."

"Stop," she laughed.

"What?" he scoffed. "It's a good thing." He gestured to the forest. "We're Survival Squad. You're leading us to victory!"

"You're so weird sometimes, Ash." She took her place at his side, wrapping her arm around him.

"Weird?"

"I mean weird in a *good* way."

He gave her a dubious look, and Vale giggled. "Seriously, Ash. I'm glad you're out here with me." Her smile faded. "Ready to stand?"

Ash nodded.

"One . . . two . . ." She heaved upward, and Ash let out a groan of pain. He wobbled in place, the urge to faint threatening to take him to his knees. "You okay, Ash? You're looking—"

"Fine," he lied, then forced a smile. (He hoped Vale bought it.) "You know, if we're handing out medals for 'weirdness,' then you and I are gonna tie for first prize."

"Okay, then we're *both* weird." Vale grinned. "Happy now?"

"Always." He gritted his teeth. "Now let's get walking." And with the first, grueling step, they began.

The first couple of kilometers were pure torture. Ash's body screamed with each step. He kept waiting for muscle memory to kick in, but every part of him was raw, demanding his attention. His nail-less fingers kept brushing his jeans. His broken ribs grated sickeningly. His lungs simply couldn't keep up for more than short stretches at a time. The biggest issue was the cold air. Every so often he was hit with a blast of it and that triggered a bout of coughing. It felt like he had something wet in the bottom of his lungs, and no matter how hard he hacked, it would not come free. As his breath returned to normal after a particularly rough fit, he discovered Vale watching him, her fingers pressed to her mouth.

"Wh-what?" he panted.

"You sound terrible."

He grimaced. "Thanks for the vote of confidence."

"It's not a judgment call. It's your lungs. They sound congested."

"They'll be fine." Ash stood up, wobbling as vertigo hit. "Just the ribs giving me trouble." He tried to move, then gasped as pain shot through him. His vision darkened. "I . . . I don't know if I can go on."

Vale jumped back to his side, catching hold of him as he swayed. "Yes, Ash. You can."

"My ribs *hurt.* They hurt bad!" Ash's voice cracked, but there was no way to stop it. His whole body felt like it was dying. "I . . . I can't do this hike. I can't—"

"Not alone, maybe, but *together* we can make it."

"Vale. Listen—"

"Hold on to me. Don't rush yourself." She tightened her arm around his waist and hooked her thumb in his belt loop. "See? Feels better already, doesn't it?"

Ash shook his head.

"Let me help you, Ash. Just . . . try. Okay?"

Ash's shoulders slumped. He wanted to be strong about this hike, but the short distance they'd gone had already proven he wasn't up to it. He swallowed against the lump in his throat. "O-okay."

"There, now . . . We're going to take it a step at a time." Vale took a step and Ash struggled to follow. "No rushing," she said. "Just take your time."

Ash nodded. Another fall would do more damage than he could handle. "Thanks, Vale. I—I owe you one."

"No you don't. Friends take care of their friends, right?"

Ash swallowed hard. "Right."

And arm in arm, they walked again.

They headed southwest, walking past the area where Ash had climbed and fallen, and into a dip between two mountain peaks. They couldn't go due south—or they'd end up climbing the same sheer cliff that had broken Ash's ribs—but they went as close as they could, only veering west when they absolutely had to. Ash wondered if they'd see the chain of Waterton Lakes as they reached the summit. Right now, that dip between the two peaks felt like an impossible challenge. He put his chin down and forced himself to keep moving. Twice, he stumbled and Vale caught him. The second time, he leaned against a nearby tree, panting.

"I . . . I can't . . . I can't walk anymore."

"Ash," Vale warned, "you're just tired. We'll take a little break, then keep moving."

"No. I mean I really *can't*."

Ash expected her to argue with him. (Vale *always* argued.) Instead, she was quiet for a long time. She checked the coals and the binding on his ribs. Ash's breathing returned to seminormal. Eventually, Vale reshouldered her bag and cleared her throat. "Ready to go?"

"I said I can't."

"I know what you said, but that's not a choice."

He glared at her.

"You know, Ash. If you want me to be part of your D&D group, then you'd better keep moving."

"Blackmail, huh?" Ash smiled despite himself, but it was a ghost of his usual grin. "Nice, Vale. Very nice."

"I'm going to do whatever it takes to get us through." She tightened her grip around his waist, and he winced. "We need to keep moving. We *can't* give up, Ash. That's not gonna happen."

"See? Now *that* sounds like a true gamer."

"Maybe," Vale said. "Don't think about the whole hike. Just this next bit. We've got to keep walking. You ready to go?"

He nodded. "Yeah."

One step after another took them away from the forest and the little lake where they'd spent the past two days. Every so often, Vale checked inside the pack. Crouching, she carefully pulled out the curled hollow of bark and blew on the embers. A thin line of smoke wafted to her nostrils. She leaned closer, adding bits of tinder to the glowing coals.

"Still burning?" Ash asked.

"Yeah. Just a bit, but it's there." Vale blew on the coal, and a tiny flicker of orange appeared. She looked up, catching Ash staring. "What?"

"Thanks."

"Thanks for . . . ?"

"For listening to my idea about the bark." He tried to shrug, but the pain in his right shoulder stopped him. "Just . . . thanks."

Vale shoved the items back into the pack. A bit of plastic tumbled out and blew away, but Ash didn't bother to tell her. (He was *not* going to search for it at this point.) Finished, Vale stood and took her position next to his good arm. "Carrying the coal inside the bark was a good idea, Ash. It really was."

"I know, but you didn't have to take it. So . . . thanks."

"You're welcome."

And then they were walking again, and Ash had to focus on that, and nothing else. The last of the snow had melted since he'd made the ill-fated attempt at the summit. Though colder, it almost looked like the same autumn day as when they'd left. Ash frowned as he counted back the days. They'd come out on a Thursday and gotten separated from the others. Friday they tried walking south, and had narrowly avoided the avalanche. They'd found the little lake and the valley that night. *And that night the elk came through the camp.* Saturday morning he'd taken off on Vale and tried to climb the rock face alone. Ash winced. *And I fell.* He remembered little of the rest of that day, but he'd made it back to the camp by the lake that night. Vale had fixed him up. The next day had been Sunday, but with Ash in rough shape, they'd been stuck in camp. Even now, Ash found himself struggling to keep up with Vale's pace, and he *knew* she was going slowly to accommodate his injuries. That made today—

"Monday," Ash said aloud.

Vale looked up. "What's that?"

"I was trying to figure out how long we've been here. It's been four days total, but it feels longer."

"That's 'cause it always feels like time slows down when things go wrong." She glanced up at him. "You ever been in a car accident?"

"Uh-huh. Once with my mom and Leo. Guy tried to drive across the highway right as we were coming past Coalhurst. Total wreck. Our car was trashed."

"You remember much about it?"

Ash frowned as he was drawn back into the memory. It had been the year Ash was in eighth grade, his brother in sixth. He'd been sitting in the passenger seat, Leo in the back, as his mother drove down the highway. Ash remembered seeing the truck slow down at the Coalhurst crossroads; he remembered seeing the man look toward them. Ash could recall his mother saying: *"Don't even think about it, buddy . . ."*

And the guy pulled out in front of them.

"Yeah. Guy drove straight out onto the highway without stopping," Ash said. "Right in front of us. Worst crash I've ever been in."

"How did it *feel* when it happened?"

"What do you mean?"

"That exact moment when the crash happened. What was it like? I bet you can remember lots about it."

"Oh, okay. Well . . ." Ash frowned as he brought the image back. His mother had slammed on the brakes; the car swerved but couldn't stop. The old beater truck pulled out farther, farther, until it was right in front of them. And there was the explosion of sound and movement. Everything came in flashes: The guy's face through the windshield. His mother's scream. Leo yelling. The searing pain as Ash was thrown against the seat belt. Flying glass and the roar of metal against metal. "It felt *slow*, I guess. Like everything was happening at once, but I had all this time to think about things. To remember."

Vale squeezed his waist gently. "That's what *this* is like. That's why it feels like forever since Thursday."

"But we're going so fricking slow today," Ash said with a weary laugh. "Sheesh! We can't be going more than five K an hour."

"Not walking speed. *Time.* The days we're here. They feel longer, because they *are* longer in a way. We've only been here a couple days, but with all the trouble, we . . ." Vale's words faded, and she pulled him to a stop. In the past few minutes, they'd wandered into an open patch, punctuated by lush bushes that varied in height from half a foot to well over six feet. "Do you smell something?"

Ash sniffed the air. "Uh . . . not really. No."

"You sure? Like, something kind of rotten . . . foul."

"You sure it isn't us?" He chuckled. "I haven't had a shower in like four d—"

Vale caught his arm. "Quiet!"

"What's going—?"

"Shhh!" she hissed. "We need to be quiet. I just found the source." She pointed out in front of them. "There. See?"

Ash followed the line of her finger to the hollow between two bushes. The second he caught sight of the ravaged carcass, adrenaline rushed through him. A dead elk lay, stiff-legged, across from them, the path where they were headed blocked. It looked so odd—legs outstretched—that for a second it seemed like a clipping error from a game. Then the stench wafted forward.

Ash's stomach turned. "Ugh. That's nasty."

"I'm betting the bear I saw killed it. And that means it's around here too," Vale said in a low voice. "We've got to get out of here, Ash. *Fast.*"

Ash turned to look behind them and wilted. "Do we go back? Retrace our steps to the lake?"

"We can't go back. We need out of the valley."

"Then let's keep walking. We can go around that . . ." He pointed to the dead elk. "And come around by those trees over there."

"Let's give it a try." Vale's arm tightened, his signal that she was ready to walk. They'd only gone three steps when Vale pulled him to a sudden stop. The abrupt movement caught him so unexpectedly that he let out a hiss of pain.

And then, strangely, *something hissed back at him.*

Ash gasped as a massive brindle-and-gray feline with black-tipped ears—four times the size of Vale's cat—stepped out from behind the carcass. And then another . . . and another. Three pairs of eyes turned at once, watching.

Ash's eyes widened. "What are *those*?"

"Shhh! They're lynx."

Seeing the three mountain cats standing only feet from them sent Ash's heart into overtime. The trio stood in a clearing full of bushes, the kill a stone's throw away from them. The bear who'd killed the elk was almost certainly in the valley too, and likely in the berries, which left Ash and Vale with no clear exit.

The first lynx hissed and lowered its head.

"Vale . . . ?"

"We should move," she said in a barely audible voice. "Let's just back away as quietly as we can." Vale pointed to an open patch. "There."

"Got it."

With jerking steps, the two of them crept toward it. "We need to be very, very careful," she said.

Ash shot her a worried look. "*Obviously*, but which way do we go?"

"South," she said. "Just keep walking."

They made it ten steps before they heard the bushes near the carcass rustle. Vale froze. Her gaze moved to Ash, wide-eyed and terrified. His hand tightened on her shoulder. *Keep going!* he mouthed.

Vale glanced back at the bushes, then shook her head. She pointed. "The lynx!"

Ash took another step, but Vale didn't move. He tugged her hand. *Come ON, Vale!* he mouthed. *We can't STAY here!* Eventually she took one step away. He pulled her again. They took two more steps. They backed up until they were ten feet from the source of the sound.

She shook her head again. "The lynx are right there."

"I don't care," Ash whispered. "We need to—"

The rustling of the leaves interrupted them as the largest of the lynx stepped directly out of the bushes in front of them, blocking their path. Long seconds passed. It bared its teeth and hissed, the fur on its shoulders puffing. "We're too close to their food," Vale whispered. "We can't stay here!"

"Then let's turn around."

The lynx growled low in its throat.

"But we need out of the valley!" she snapped.

If Ash wasn't so panicked, he would have laughed. They were trapped by a gigantic house cat. If that wasn't the stupidest way to die, he didn't know what was. He swore.

The lynx hissed again.

Suddenly, Vale turned to him, the speed of her movement making him dizzy. "You okay to stand on your own?"

"Yeah, but—"

Vale carefully lowered the pack with the embers on the ground next to him. "Hold on," she muttered. "Lynx are wild, but . . . they're still cats."

"What're you—?"

Vale was already in motion. She lunged toward the massive cat, her arms swinging wildly. "GO ON!" she screamed. "Go! Get OUT of here!"

The lynx stepped back and hissed, its ears flattening.

"Get out of the way!" Vale roared. "Go on! MOVE!" She kicked at the bushes nearby, and the lynx backed up two steps. "GET OUT OF HERE!" She swung her leg again, and one of the nearby lynx—still feeding—darted into the bushes.

Ash's eyes widened. *One down, two to go.*

Vale's voice rose. "MOVE IT! I MEAN IT!"

The second lynx disappeared into the shadows of the forest.

"GO!" Vale screamed. "You GET OUT OF HERE BEFORE I GET THE SPRAY BOTTLE!"

With one last hiss, the largest lynx spun and darted away.

Three for three.

Ash began to laugh. "Spray bottle, huh?"

Vale grinned. "Improvising."

"I like it."

The searchers reached the valley just as the rain hit. They were far past the Alberta/British Columbia border. The terrain was rugged and bare, a snapshot of Canada's not-so-distant past, when the First Nations peoples lived at one with the land and trappers had used this passage to move from the interior of BC to the trading hubs in Alberta. Today, the secret passages those first peoples had forged through these mountains were largely forgotten. It was a dangerous landscape. *Untamed.*

Grant McNealy, a Waterton park warden, slowed his steps before lifting a pair of binoculars to his eyes.

"You see something?" one of the volunteers asked him.

"Think so . . ." Grant frowned as he scanned the high alpine valley. The landmark he needed was a small lake, almost hidden by trees. That's what the helicopter pilot, Amanda, had described. He turned the other direction, searching. "There," he said, pointing west. "That little lake over there. A pilot reportedly saw what looked like the remains of a campsite."

Grant took his bearings and marked his coordinates in his satellite phone, then blazed a nearby tree with a hatchet and flashing tape. Done, he headed directly into the dense forest. The same volunteer—a woman in her thirties—jogged up to his side.

"What lake is this?" she asked.

Grant's gaze flicked up. He didn't know her name, but she was familiar—one of the Lethbridge folk who'd shown up to help when the kids went missing. Warden Banks had assigned the woman to Grant's group. "Doesn't have a name," he said. "Lots of 'em out here don't. Probably has a number on a map somewhere, nothing else."

"And you think that Ash and Vale are camped there?"

"That's what Amanda told me she figured."

"Amanda?"

"The helicopter pilot. She flew over the site this afternoon, but I won't know if it's a camp or not until I see the site myself." Grant glanced over at her as the group trudged through the forest. The woman looked worried. "You know one of the kids?"

"I know *both* of them, actually." She gave him a tired smile and offered her hand to shake. "I'm Janelle Holland. The kids were"—she winced—"*are* in my class. I volunteered to help find them."

"Ah . . . sorry about that." Grant nodded. So *that* was why Aya had assigned the woman to his team. "But signs are good. Amanda told me it looked like they had a fire going."

"I hope so," Janelle said, then fell back into line.

Ash's lungs were on fire, his vision spinning unnervingly when they stopped on the sloping ridge on the far side of the valley to catch their breath. He glanced back at the expanse of forest and the small lake twinkling in the distance. He frowned. It seemed impossible that they'd only come that far. *We're not even out of the fricking valley yet!*

"You okay, Ash?"

He turned, forcing a neutral expression. "Yeah. Fine."

"Your ribs any worse?"

"Uh . . ." They *were* worse, but there was no use bringing that up. "Not really. Hey! That was a pretty close call with the lynx."

"Yeah." Vale laughed. "Glad my crazy cat-lady vibe worked."

Ash laughed, then cringed. The grating felt like a blade caught in his side, turning at each breath. "That was cool how you chased them off," he panted. "You were totally badass."

Vale laughed tiredly. "Thanks."

A distant rumble echoed over her words. Ash flinched and peered upward. Heavy rain clouds the color of his bruises filled the sky as far as he could see. Lightning flickered deep within the clouds as a second growl of thunder rumbled in from the east. Rain splattered Ash's forehead and eyes.

He shook his head. "So tired of the rain."

"Me too." Vale sighed. "If you've caught your breath, we better start hiking again. The weather's going to be trouble."

"What do you mean?"

Vale pointed at the leaden sky. "That's the *start* of a storm, not the end of one. More rain is coming . . . Maybe snow too." Her arm around him tightened, and tears came to his eyes. "We have to move," she said. "'Cause we'll die if we're stuck out here in the open."

Ash hunched against the wind, tightened his grip, and forced his legs to move. "South it is."

The rain started in earnest as they left the protection of the trees. The southwestern slope was a treacherous climb, and Ash's vision seemed perpetually on the verge of winking out. Dark shadows crept in from his periphery, growing darker as the incline increased.

"Just a few more steps," Vale said. "We can do this."

Ash took another gulping breath—made hard by damaged ribs—and forced his body to comply. For what felt like hours, they walked, the weather growing worse by the minute. Every so often Ash glanced back the way they'd come. Their progress up the slope seemed comically slow compared to his first ascent of the southern ridge. He wanted to go faster, but his body didn't want to follow his orders. He stumbled as they reached a shale shoulder of the mountain, and he came down hard on his knees. Vale took most of his weight, but the sudden movement set off a wave of coughing.

"You okay?" Vale asked when he could breathe again.

"S-sort of," he said. "Having trouble catching my breath."

She held out her hand and pulled him back to his feet. "You want to take a break?"

"Maybe a little later." The truth was, Ash was afraid that if he sat down, he'd never be able to get himself up again. He smiled through the pain. "Let's keep going."

The two of them took a handful of steps before Ash began to wobble.

"Whoa. Hold on there," Vale said. "I got you." She tightened her arm around his waist. It sent a stabbing pain through him, but his balance returned. "That better?"

"Y-yeah. Good."

"You sure? We can stop for a bit. You're not looking so hot."

"You're not either, Vale." He snorted. "You fricking stink."

She giggled. "Nice one. And I'd be offended if *you* didn't smell ten times worse. Good to know your sense of humor's holding up."

"Always a good sign, right?"

"Right. But seriously, though . . . you okay, Ash?"

"Fine." He took slow breaths until the darkness clouding his vision faded. "Just . . . need . . . a minute." Ash glanced out at the valley, and his heart sank. Storm clouds filled the sky.

Ash turned back to Vale. "We should go," he said. "It's getting colder, and we're walking slow."

"We're already more than three days late," she said with a half smile. "Pretty sure another couple hours won't make any difference."

"Okay."

By late afternoon the rain was coming down in a steady hum. Vale kept pausing to check the coals—adding tinder every so often. Ash prayed he wouldn't fall each time she stepped away from him. The top of the ridge was a crumbling backbone of rock, leaving them scrambling over the boulders that marked the border between the valley they were in and the next one over. Ash leaned on Vale as they hit the top. His hunger was a physical ache in his gut, the urge to eat so intense he could hardly think. The spruce grouse and berries they'd eaten for dinner the night before were long gone.

Ash staggered, and Vale's arm tightened, grating his broken ribs together.

"We're almost to the trees," she said. "Just a few more steps. We can do this."

"And after the trees? Then what?"

"And then . . . we make a fire and find water, I guess."

Ash lifted his gaze from the ground and looked down into the unexplored valley. His heart sank. There were no Twin Lakes *here*, no long stretch of Upper and Lower Waterton Lakes either. His heart sank. "This isn't the Twin Lakes valley," he said.

"We're not going to worry about that yet. For now, we need shelter."

Ash shivered. The wind wasn't as bad on this side of the incline, but with the rain, the temperature was dropping. *We need protection.* Vale led them down the slope to a knot of trees and leaned him up against one.

"Just stand here," she said. "I need a bit more kindling for the coals." She looked up, frowning. "Ash? You okay?"

"Y-yeah. F-fine. Just cold."

She nodded. "Just . . . catch your breath. I'm going to find some dry wood." And before he could answer her, she headed into the trees. The wind whirled around him, tossing raindrops at his face and neck, chilling him to the bone. Damp settled into his limbs. He glanced over to where Vale crouched over her pack, blowing on the coals. He coughed.

Vale glanced up. "You still doing okay?"

Ash took a breath so he could answer her and was caught up in another bout of hacking.

This one didn't stop.

The unknown valley grew dark, and his vision blurred; blood rushed in his ears. He tried to breathe, but each cough made it worse. He heard Vale shout, but he couldn't understand her words. The ground abruptly tilted sideways and—

Vale dropped the smoldering ember in the curl of bark back into the bag and jumped up at the same moment Ash's body went limp.

"Ash, NO!"

Flame forgotten, she sprinted forward, but she wasn't fast enough. Ash tumbled to the ground next to the tree, his feet kicking out from under him. Vale skidded into place next to him. She put her hand on his chest. *Still breathing.* But when she looked at his face, her fear returned. He lay flat on his back, eyes rolled back in his head.

"Oh my God! Wake up, Ash!" Terrified, Vale shook him, but he didn't move. "Ash? Ash, can you hear me?" She shook harder. "Ash, wake UP!"

Still there was no response.

Tears blurred her vision. With the rain coming harder, Vale had been preoccupied with keeping the fire alive. Now Ash was unconscious. Frustration flared—bright and angry—inside her. They'd come so far! This couldn't be how it ended!

"No!" Vale screamed. "Not like this! Not now!" She crouched on the ground next to him and tried to pick him up. With a groan, she let go, and he slumped back down. "No, Ash!" she cried. "You can't just LEAVE me like this!" She tried to lift him a second time, but barely got his head and shoulders off the ground. Above the treetops, thunder rumbled and another wave of rain began, blurring with the tears on Vale's face. "No, Ash! This is NOT okay!" She shook his arm again, panic rising. "Listen to me! If you don't wake up, I'm going to have to drag you! And you're too HEAVY! Do you get that? I can't just—"

"Please, for the love of God, stop yelling at me," he groaned. "I give in."

Vale let out a sob and leaned forward, hugging him. The terror that had gripped her loosened slightly. "Oh my God, Ash! You're awake!"

"Yeah . . . feel like crap, but I'm awake. What're you—?"

"You passed out. I couldn't get you to answer me." She put her hand on his forehead. Her breath caught. "Oh my God! Your fever's back. We've got to get you someplace out of the rain."

"Rain?"

"Yes! It's raining." She looked up at the sky, which hung like wool over the mountain peaks. "Can't you feel that?"

"I . . . I guess so . . . I . . ." He laughed and then moaned. "It's never easy, is it?"

Vale let out a teary laugh. She leaned forward, blocking the rain as she checked Ash's vitals. *He can't give up. Not now! Not ever!* "No, Ash. It's not. But we're going to get through this."

He reached out for her hand. The gesture brought another wave of tears to Vale's eyes.

"You sure?" he whispered.

She nodded.

"Good." He groaned and rolled sideways. "'Cause if Vale Shumway says something's true, it's gotta be true. Survival Squad commander. Right?"

"That's right," she said brokenly. "I'm going to grab the pack. You rest here a second, and then we'll go. The rain's getting worse, and we need to move. I'm freezing."

"Me too."

Vale jogged back to the trees. She zipped up the open pack without checking the coals and slid it onto her shoulders. Ash lay, unmoving, but he looked up at her as she returned. "You ready?" she asked.

"Yeah. On three, right?"

"Uh-huh." She put her arms around him. "One . . . two . . ."

Ash cried out, and staggered like an old man, but eventually Vale was able to pull him to his feet. Arm in arm, the two of them took unsteady steps down into the valley. He took a breath and moaned in pain. Vale's heart ached, but she forced a smile.

"Go slow, Ash. You've got this."

"Keep calm and respawn."

Vale nodded. "Exactly. Now walk."

And with the rain at their backs, a dark bank of clouds looming over the horizon, and no food or water, they headed down into the unknown valley.

CHAPTER THIRTEEN

"As long as you can still grab a breath, you fight. You breathe . . . keep breathing."

HUGH GLASS, *THE REVENANT*

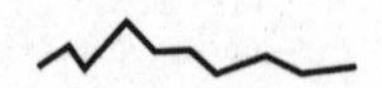

WITH THE RAIN falling harder, Vale tightened her grip on Ash's belt and guided them down the slippery incline. He had fallen silent in the past half hour—no longer bothering to joke about their predicament—and it had only grown worse since he'd coughed himself unconscious. His brooding silence worried her far more than his goofy behavior ever had. Quiet was decidedly *not* like Ash.

"You doing okay?" she asked.

"Yeah." His voice was barely a whisper.

Above them, the rain fell in heavy sheets, too intense to avoid. The garbage-bag rain slickers did little to keep the water out. Twice, Vale was certain she heard an engine humming somewhere in the distance, but the thunder was too loud to be sure. She frowned and kept marching. If there was an air search going on, they'd *never* see past the clouds that covered the valley.

They were just inside the tree line when something caught Vale's eye. "Do you see that?"

Ash turned. He was wheezing for breath, lips bluish. "Wh-what?"

"There," she said. "That dark area at the bottom of the rocks." She squinted. "You see? It's right above the tree line on that grassy slope. I think it might be a cave."

"M-maybe." His words were hollow. *Indifferent* even. Hearing them, Vale felt the band of anxiety tighten painfully around her chest.

She forced a smile. "I think we should check it out."

"B-but—"

"It's a cave," she said. "I'm almost certain of it; we're going to go there."

"W-wait . . . we are?" He coughed so hard he began to choke. It was cold enough now that his breath appeared in white clouds. Vale frowned. *The rain is going to change into snow soon, and we're both wet.* Even with the tattered garbage bags as rain gear, the downpour had soaked them through.

"Yes, Ash. C'mon. Let's go." She tugged his hand. "It's too slippery to make it all the way down the valley," she said. "I'm pretty sure we can make it to the cave, though. Let's check it out. All right?"

"T-too tired."

"Just a few steps, Ash." She grinned. "Think of it as a side quest."

He didn't laugh. Didn't even answer her. He just lowered his head and followed without arguing. Vale's stomach twisted uneasily. Ash never just agreed. He always had some oddball idea he was focused on, or some joke to make about—

He doesn't think we're going to make it.

The unexpected thought made her stumble. Ash shouted as she bumped his ribs, his fingers tightening painfully around her shoulder. "Ow!"

"Sorry!" Vale said. "Wasn't watching where I was going. I—I'm sorry."

He tried to say something, but with his teeth chattering, Vale couldn't make out what it was.

"I'll be more careful." She pointed up ahead. "See? We're halfway there."

He bowed his head, and the gesture made her want to cry.

"Just a little bit farther," she whispered. "Only a bit more. We can do this."

Ten minutes later they reached the cave. The small cavern had been hollowed into the mountainside, the result of erosion where two hard layers of rock sandwiched a softer one that had worn away. From a distance, it looked like a black half circle cut straight into the mountainside. Close up, it was an upside-down bowl with an opening along one side. Arriving, Vale lowered Ash to the ground against a nearby tree and headed to the cave to look. *Just in case . . .*, she told herself. This mountain wasn't her home, but it *was* home to animals. She needed to know if anyone else lived there.

Vale crouched down and peered inside the doorway. "Hello . . . ?" she called. She took a single, crouching half step inward and waited for her vision to adjust. Eventually she could see again, and she found an empty—though somewhat dirty—space. The entrance was too low to walk through, though the ceiling flared up and away, leaving the rocky floor dry. Piles of leaves—blown in by the autumn winds—

cluttered the corners, but it was otherwise bare. Vale set her pack down on the floor and rushed out to get Ash.

"All good," she called. "It's totally empty in . . ." Her voice faded as she saw Ash slumped over to one side next to the tree. "Ash?" She rushed to his side and grabbed his good hand. It felt like ice. "Ash! Can you hear me?" She tapped his cheek once, then harder. "Oh no, no, no, no!" She slapped his cheek with enough force that it stung the palm of her hand.

He opened his eyes at once. "What the hell, Vale?"

"Sorry, I—"

"You can't just punch someone!"

"I didn't punch you. I slapped you. I—" She let out a teary laugh. "I couldn't wake you up. You passed out again, I thought—"

"I'm *tired*, Vale. Sheesh!" He turned and began to hack. The sound rattled through him, leaving him gasping for air. When the fit ended, he closed his eyes.

Vale swallowed against a lump in her throat. "I'm sorry for hitting you," she said in a thick voice. "I really am. I . . . guess you did just climb a mountain with broken ribs." Vale rubbed the moisture away from her cheeks, glad for the cover of rain. "You ready to sit up?"

He groaned but didn't make any movement to comply.

"Come on, Ash. Just a few steps. I can't carry you."

"F-fine." He rolled sideways, and Vale wrapped her arms around him to help him sit up.

"One more boost should do it," she grunted as she got ready to lift. "Get your legs under you and one . . . two . . . THREE!"

Ash cried out and began to cough, but between the two of them they got him upright. "Sorry for pulling on you," Vale said. "It's just a couple more steps. Hold on . . . almost there."

Ash's teeth were chattering as they reached the entrance to the cave, and Vale helped him to his knees. He crawled forward on one hand, then collapsed on the dirt floor. Vale considered trying to get branches to make a softer bed, but the most pressing need was fire. She pulled a pile of the leaves from the corner—wrinkling her nose at the sour smell of them—and laid them in a pile near the entrance. She darted into the rain for kindling. The rain was coming down heavy now, angry peals of thunder rolling from one side of the valley to the other. Thunder wasn't unknown in the fall (though it was far more common in the spring), but it always spelled trouble. They were in for an unpleasant night.

She glanced over at Ash. He hadn't moved since she'd brought him inside, but his rattling breath was audible even over the howl of the wind.

"G-got some k-kindling," Vale said through chattering teeth. "J-just give me a bit, and I'll have us warm in n-no time." She grabbed her backpack and lifted out the curl of unburned wood. She hadn't checked it since Ash had fallen. (She couldn't risk letting go of him.) But the pack was still snug and dry. Smiling, Vale set the curl of wood down near the kindling. She took a twig and poked the ashes aside, searching for the burning ember of coal she'd tended all afternoon.

There was no resulting glow.

"Oh no . . ." Vale leaned in and blew directly on the blackened bit of wood. Ashes flew up and around her, but the ember remained a dull black. Outside the cave, the rain was a steady roar. "No way. Not now. This *can't* be happening." Vale blew again and again—panic arriving in time to her gasps—but to no avail. "N-no . . . It can't . . ."

She put her finger directly into the coals. The embers were hot, but not enough to burn. Tears filled Vale's eyes. *I let it go out.* One thing was certain: They were going to die here if she couldn't get the fire going. A second thought joined the first: There was no way to start a fire, because the ember she'd so carefully protected had completely burned out. In her panic to get Ash into the cave, she'd sentenced them both to death.

The terrain grew rockier the closer the searchers got to the valley with the lake. Grant scanned the tree line warily. This was high country . . . *grizzly country.* An encounter here—even with bear spray—would likely result in injuries.

He lifted his hand above his head, shouting out to the group that followed him: "Eyes up, everyone! Keep alert. Talk and keep talking. I don't want us running into any bears without them knowing we're coming."

Nervous chatter followed his command. Half an hour later, the trees thinned and the group found themselves standing near a small lake. A crude lean-to was built around the base of one tree. And a campfire—long gone cold—announced that someone had, quite recently, been in residence. Grant walked slowly around the camp as the searchers spread into the trees.

"Vale!"

"Ash!"

"Helloooo! Can you hear us?"

"Vale! Ash! You there?"

Grant crouched down to check the tracks and brushed away the autumn leaves that obscured them. One was smaller and lighter. *The girl, Vale.* The other was larger and heavier . . . but the right side didn't match the left. Grant frowned. The boy was favoring one side. *He's hurt.* In the trees, the voices of the searchers grew louder, then faded as they spread through the forest. Grant grimaced and stood up. The kids were gone. He wasn't sure *where*, since there were tracks throughout the forest, but it was clear they were no longer here. A cold wind needled under Grant's jacket, bits of sleet joining the rain, and he blew on his hands. Wherever the kids were, he hoped they were warm. Tonight was going to be nasty.

An hour after the search team had arrived, the drizzle turned to a steady downpour and Grant called them back together. Janelle Holland stood, pale and shivering, at the front of the team.

"They aren't here anymore," Grant announced. "But they *were* here in the past day or so." He pointed around the camp. "Tracks are still new. The rain hasn't even washed them away yet."

"So where *are* they?"

Grant looked up. It was Janelle again.

"Not sure," he said. "But I can tell you right now, the teams need to focus their attention in this valley, and they need to keep looking. These kids are in danger." He lifted his gaze toward the steely sky. "The storm's getting worse, and this one doesn't look like it's going to let up easy."

"So we stay?" another volunteer asked.

"We'll split up. Cover the entire valley, see if we can figure out where they went before nightfall. We'll set up camp here. Stay the night, if we don't find 'em. Most important thing right now is to locate their tracks and see if—" A crack of lightning appeared overhead, followed quickly by the boom of thunder, making the searchers jump. Grant waited until the echoes faded before he continued. "Once we find the tracks, we can follow them to wherever they went next."

"And if we can't find their tracks?" Janelle asked.

"Then those kids are gonna be in even *worse* trouble, 'cause if the forecast for tomorrow is right, this rain is going to turn to snow and then we won't have any tracks at all."

"Until it melts," a voice at the back offered.

"Nah," Grant said. "We're deep enough into the backcountry now that if they get a good, heavy snowfall, it's going to last for days, maybe weeks. Possibly *more* if the conditions are right."

"My God . . ."

"It's still light for another hour," Grant said. "Let's get looking while we can. These kids need our help." He peered up at the clouds. The late afternoon sky was already darkening. "And let's do it *fast*."

Oh my God! I let the fire go out!

Vale crawled to Ash's side, her throat aching. "Ash?"

He looked up groggily. "Y-yeah?"

"I . . . I need to tell you something." Her voice broke. "I'm sorry, but—" The words caught in her throat.

"Wh-what—" Ash tried to answer, but it set off a bout of coughing. It expanded until he was curled over—gasping for breath—and ended in rasping bellows. His face was flushed, cheeks sweaty.

Vale scooted to his side. "Shhh . . . Just breathe. It'll be okay." She put her hand on his forehead. The feverish heat under his skin felt like fire. "Hold on, I'll grab the pills." She pulled out her water canister and walked to the edge of the cave, finding a steady trickle of water that poured from the ledge. Outside, the rain came down in waves so heavy that the trees beyond seemed to shimmer and fade, before popping back in focus. When Vale had half a cup of water, she returned to the first aid kit and popped out the last two pills.

"Here," she said as she came back to Ash's side. "Take these."

He swallowed them without argument and handed back her canteen. "S-so cold. The fire . . . ?"

Vale felt tears fill her eyes. "The ember went out," she said in a broken voice. "I tried, Ash, but I couldn't—"

A flash of lightning—so near it filled the cave with pinkish light—blinded her, the crash of thunder booming half a second later. The smell of ozone filled the air. Ash had begun to cough again, and Vale crouched next to him.

"S-so fricking c-cold—" His coughing grew worse.

"Here. Take my coat for a while."

She slid the jacket off her shoulders and laid it on Ash's shoulders. She added the emergency blanket on top of that. Even here in the cave, completely out of the rain, the heat was sucked from her body in seconds. A damp chill gripped the mountain's hollow, and with the wind rising, it grew colder. Rain poured like water from a faucet over the lip of the entrance. Leaden clouds churned the sky and drowned out the light. Out in the valley, lightning clawed down from the sky, piercing the unnerving late afternoon darkness.

A tremor of fear ran through Vale, and she began to shake. They were cold and wet. They had no fire. They were *not* in Waterton Park anymore, as far as she could tell, but she had no idea where in the world they were. Somewhere in BC was her guess, but that was a massive area to search. *It might take weeks for searchers to find us.* Vale felt the first bubble of panic rise in her throat, and she swallowed it down. Lightning slashed through the sky, closer now. *Most people die of exposure long before they die of hunger or thirst . . .* Another bubble of panic rose, coming out as a sob, just as Ash was hit with another coughing fit. The sound tore at Vale. She put her head down against her knees and wrapped her arms around herself, letting the tears come. *Oh God . . . we're not getting out of this alive.*

"H-hey—" Ash coughed again. "V-Vale . . . ?" He choked back another cough.

"Y-yeah?"

Ash's face was sweaty, bits of mud stuck to his cheeks from when he'd lain down on the ground. "A-are y-you okay?"

"I—I'm—" At another time Vale might have laughed about how he looked, but at this moment she found herself drawn to the details. Face gaunt, his tangled hair stuck to his head, jaw stubbled with four days of growth. She wanted to remember this moment—*remember Ash!*—in case they didn't walk away from here. *He's hurt and sick, and I can't fix it.* The thought set off a wave of sobs.

"I screwed up!"

Vale felt the first hiccups of panicked sobbing break through the barrier of her throat, and she covered her mouth with her hands. Her fear had reached chain reaction, and there was no longer a way to stop it. She imagined the phone call to her parents. *I'm sorry, Mr. and Mrs. Shumway, but we have some bad news.* Her mother would be inconsolable, her father stoic but broken. Another sob broke free, then another and another, her self-control crumbling. She wanted to stop—to be strong for Ash—but the terror mixed with a sudden realization of what this moment would do to her family had destroyed any semblance of control.

"N-no. You didn't." Ash stared at her with a pained expression. "It's okay—" He broke off and coughed. "P-put your j-jacket on. I-it's freezing."

Vale's tears came harder.

"P-please." A hand bumped her arm, and she turned to discover Ash had crawled up to his knees.

"What are you doing?" she cried.

"Y-you're c-cold. Please. T-take your coat." Ash held out her jacket with his left hand. The gesture brought another wave of tears. Vale slid her coat on. She got the zipper started, but with her hands shaking, she couldn't make it go up the rest of the way. Defeated, she put her face back down on her knees and sobbed.

"H-here. Let me take a look." Ash reached down with his good hand and jiggled the zipper. It jerked once against the snag of fabric, then slid free. "I-it's okay. It was just stuck—" Another crack of lightning lit the dim cave. Vale's ears rang with the boom of thunder.

"I-it's not okay!" she cried. "There's no fire! I c-can't—"

"V-Vale. J-just calm down. It's okay. Y—" He let out a choking cough. "You're going to be okay."

"I'm not! This whole situation is awful!"

"S-stop crying, please." Ash reached out and patted her back. The motion had the same awkwardness Vale recognized from her father's attempts to console her. If she hadn't been so upset, she would have found it funny. (This was her buddy Ash, full-time gamer and the school slacker.) But right now, Vale couldn't even think beyond: *We're going to die here!*

He stopped patting and squeezed her shoulder. "B-better?"

She cried harder.

"P-please, Vale—" With a groan, Ash pulled her into a hug. "I-it's okay. Shhh . . . You're fine." The nervous patting stopped as his hand settled against her back. "W-we're okay. It's going to be okay."

"B-but it's raining, and there's no fire, and—"

"It's okay."

Any other time, she would have been horrifically embarrassed by her outburst, but Vale was upset enough it didn't even register. She was furious with herself for letting the ember go out. She was terrified by Ash's hacking. And her thoughts of her parents and home had completely broken her heart.

"Shhh . . . ," Ash whispered. "Y-you're okay." The thunderstorm clamored around them as Vale's choking gasps finally calmed. He let go of her and sat back on his heels. "You f-feel okay now?" he said.

"Yeah . . . a bit better." She gave a teary laugh. "Given the crappy situation."

He smiled, though the expression was anything but happy. "Th-that's the truth, isn't it?"

Vale waited for him to make a joke. Waited for the moment to end. *It didn't.* Instead, Ash reached out and squeezed her hand. He smiled, but the expression made Vale's heart hurt. "I-it's going to be okay," he said quietly, then let go of her fingers. "*You* are g-going to be okay."

"How do you know that?"

"N-no idea."

"But—"

"V-Vale, listen. Y-you're my friend. My *best friend*, and w-we're stuck here in this together." He shrugged. "A-at least w-we're not alone."

"But we're going to die!"

"N-not *both* of us," he said. "T-tomorrow I n-need you t-to leave me here and—"

"NO!"

A bolt of lightning pierced the sky directly above the cave at the same time Vale screamed. It sliced downward, cutting into a nearby tree, the pink-purple bolt burning an afterimage into Vale's vision. Thunder boomed. Pebbles rolled down from the wall, and the smell of smoke reached Vale's nostrils. When she could see again, she bolted away from Ash's side, banging her head on the ceiling.

"W-what's wrong?" he asked.

"The lightning!" she said, pointing. "It hit a tree. It's burning!" Vale whooped in excitement. "Fire!" she shouted. "We've got FIRE!"

Grant woke in the darkness to the sound of someone calling to him from outside the tent. "Warden McNealy?" the voice said. "You still awake?"

Amanda. He groaned and rolled over, fumbling for the lantern and flicking it on. *I'm awake now.*

"Yeah," he grumbled, then cleared his throat. "I'm awake. What's up?"

There was a long moment, filled with the sound of rain buzzing on the tent fly. "I just . . . I need to talk to you a second. There's an issue."

Grant fought the urge to swear. This whole search had been one problem after another, and their first solid clue—footprints leading to the southwest ridge—had arrived at nightfall, preventing the searchers from following them.

Grant unzipped the sleeping bag and shivered. It was getting colder by the hour. "A'right," he said. "Give me a second. I'll step out so we can talk." He pulled on his jacket, then unzipped the fly to crawl out. Rain soaked his hair and wet his face a moment later.

Amanda, the pilot who'd seen the empty campsite from the sky, gave a wary smile as he appeared. "Sorry for waking you, Grant," she said. "But it's important."

"What's up?"

"I used the spotlight. Buzzed the valley walls, like you asked me to," she said. "There was a bear on the southwestern side."

Grant frowned. The team of searchers had spent more than three full days searching the mountains, sleeping in a rough camp each night so they could head out at dawn the next morning. Just before nightfall, Grant had found the clue he'd been looking for: a dropped plastic baggie snagged on the branches of a cinquefoil bush. It was located in the same brush-covered area where the searchers had found the remains of an elk. The bag was a clear sign of the two lost students, a sign that they'd come this way, sometime recently. The southwestern side of the valley was where the kids' tracks went. That section of the mountain was their focus area tomorrow.

"Southwest?" Grant said. "You sure that's where the bear was?"

"Yeah. There's a number of game trails there. I saw the bear come out of the bushes as I was traversing the valley."

Grant sighed. A bear in the area would make it much more risky. "Was it a grizzly or black?"

"A grizzly," she said, her voice dropping. "And it was a big one." She flinched. "I . . . think the sound of the rotors spooked it. It took off running when I was checking the forest there. Headed up over the ridge into the next valley." She swallowed. "The ridge to the southwest."

"Goddamnit. That's where the kids' tracks were headed."

"I heard that."

He rubbed his hand over his face, fighting the urge to yell. It wasn't Amanda's fault. She was doing what he'd *told* her to do, but it made everything worse. Bears at this time of year were getting ready to hibernate. They were owlish, ready to defend their territory at all costs. And grizzlies could be deadly if interrupted while feeding. It troubled Grant that they'd found carrion in the berry patch not far from here.

Amanda cleared her throat. "Sorry, Grant. I truly am."

"It's fine," he said. "You did what you were asked to do. I'll just be careful when I head out tomorrow." He glanced into the darkness. "You see anything else while you were out there?"

"Sorry, no," she said. "Too rainy to see much of anything."

Grant frowned. "Prints aren't going to last long in this mess. And if it snows . . ." He left the thought hanging.

"Well, I should probably let you get a bit more sleep." Amanda gave a tired smile. "Dawn's coming. You've got to rest."

"You should get some sleep too."

"I'm going to head back to Waterton tonight, refuel the chopper, and catch a few hours of shut-eye." She touched his arm. "But I'll be back tomorrow. All right? And if you need me sooner, you just radio it in."

Grant nodded. "Thanks."

"We *are* going to find those kids. There's only so many places they can be, and if the boy's injured, the two of them will be walking slower. They can't be far."

"Yeah, I just hope we find them *sooner* rather than later."

"Me too." Amanda nodded. "G'night, Grant." And with a wave, she turned and walked away.

"G'night, Amanda."

Grant watched her until she disappeared between the lines of tents, then crouched down to crawl into his own. He set the wet rain slicker aside to dry and wiggled back into his sleeping bag. He shivered. The night air was cold, his body tensed as if waiting for a blow. Eventually his legs thawed, and then his feet, and finally his body was warm once more.

Still, sleep eluded him.

He lay in the dark, staring up into the shadows. *Got a bear in the valley*, he thought. *Need to tell the searchers to be careful . . . tell them to bring bear spray in case it comes back.* Another thought flickered in the back of his mind, and he frowned.

Just hope that grizzly doesn't run across those two kids before we get to them . . .

CHAPTER FOURTEEN

"Fear causes hesitation, and hesitation will cause your worst fears to come true."

BODHI, *POINT BREAK*

DAWN ARRIVED, cold and rainy.

Grant climbed out of his sleeping bag into the icy embrace of another rainy day. There was no more time to rest. They needed to find those kids . . . fast. If he could locate the path they'd taken the day before, there was a good chance they could find Vale and Ash—possibly even this morning. If he couldn't, then this afternoon's snow would cover it and the trail would go cold.

Grant grimaced. *Then we'll have a real issue.*

He dressed in the murky half light of the tent, anxious to begin. The *tick tick tick* on the tent flap announced worsening weather. *Rain is already turning to sleet.* Grant slid on his raincoat before gathering up his backpack with its survival gear, satellite phone, and signal flares. He and the other searchers were far outside the park now, but

Grant carried no firearm. (He never did.) Instead, he double-checked the safety on his canister of bear spray and attached it to his belt.

He'd seen the bear scat and elk carcass yesterday afternoon and Amanda's late night warning had confirmed it: They had a grizzly to contend with.

The rough camp had been made halfway up the slope; the ridge that led to the next valley a short jaunt beyond. Packed, Grant climbed out of the tent. Freezing rain soaked him immediately, and he began to shiver. *Poor kids had to do another night in the open. Sure hope they had a fire.* He raised his field glasses and squinted across the valley. It was light, but the clouds blocked any rays. Snow was starting to appear on the north side of the tree stumps and upper branches, rain sluicing across the ground. Each hour that passed scoured away the footprints that Grant was counting on to lead him to the lost teens. He wasn't sure *why* they'd left their campsite near the lake, though he feared it had something to do with the bear.

Grant knew what had to be done. Find the southwest trail. Follow it to them. If they were alive a day ago, they could easily be alive today. He stared out at the ring of mountains that surrounded the search camp. Only one question remained: *How far did they go?* Best way to answer that was to get up high and look for smoke.

"You heading out already?" a voice asked.

He turned to see the teacher, Janelle Holland, up with the night crew. It struck him that she hadn't slept.

"Yeah," he said. "Going out now."

"Can I come along too?"

Grant hesitated and then nodded. He could only imagine her

panic to find her students. "Yeah," he said. "But make sure you grab a bear spray before we go."

"Bear spray?"

He nodded. "The helicopter pilot flushed out a grizzly last night. It's headed the same direction we're going. We need to be prepared."

"Got it," Janelle said. "I'll be ready to go in ten minutes."

"Make it five if you can."

When Ash awoke, the world outside the cave was preternaturally calm. The torrential rains of the night before had eased into a steady patter, occasionally flecked by bits of sleet that caught on bushes and painted the forest floor white. He squinted into the gloomy morning half light and shivered.

Snow's starting.

Ash pushed his good arm under him and tried to sit up, but the myriad pains in his body left him panting. He bit the inside of his lip to stop himself from screaming and shoved harder. Gravity shifted, and he tilted upright. *Ow! Ouch! Not good!* His damaged ribs flared to life. He wobbled, but, after a few slow breaths, held steady. Ash frowned as he took a mental tally of aches and pains. He felt *worse* than last night, and there was an unnerving gurgle in the bottom of his lungs that scared him.

Need to walk out of here. Need to get to the hospital.

It was cold, but Vale slept on. Upright, Ash used his one good hand to add wood to the fire. With the flames growing, the cold that had leached into him overnight eased away. He glanced down at his friend, asleep a few feet away from him. She lay on her side, snoring, her breath slow and steady. *Vale got us through this. She knew what to do. She—*

In the bushes a stone's throw from the cave, a branch broke. Ash looked up. His breath caught. "Oh God!"

A blondish-brown grizzly stood near the trees. Seeing Ash, the bear swung its head and a thunderous roar boomed through the valley.

Vale jerked awake. "Ash," she mumbled. "What's going on?" She struggled upright, pushing tangled hair from her eyes and standing. The grizzly turned.

Vale was now its target.

Grant and Janelle reached the top of the pass just after dawn. It was blustery, and fluffy white snowflakes interspersed the sleet.

"Where next?" Janelle panted.

"Not sure . . ." Grant frowned as he surveyed the scene that lay below them. There was no lake in this valley, no obvious path to follow. He crouched and searched the ground. The footprints they'd seen on the lower slopes were all but gone now.

"They came this way yesterday afternoon, right?"

Grant nodded. "Uh-huh. Least that's my guess. Could have been earlier." He frowned as he scanned the horizon. *Just need a sign . . .*

"That was when that big thunderstorm hit. Wasn't it?"

"Uh-huh." He nodded, only half listening. *Only need one little hint of where they went. A bit of garbage like we found yesterday. Some scat or a bit of blood.*

"Vale's a smart girl. I bet she tried to get them someplace safe," Janelle said. "Someplace out of the rain, like a cave or—"

Grant turned, grabbing her arm. "That's it!"

"What's it?"

He pointed up ahead to where the harder rock met a thin layer of crumbling softer rock. "There are caves there. Let's check those."

Janelle turned and followed his finger to the distant ridge of rock. She lifted her field glasses to her eyes, then dropped them to her chest. "I see smoke!"

"You what?"

"Look! There," she said. "There's a grayish smudge, and . . ." She lifted the glasses again. "Yes! I think I see a fire!"

Grant lifted his binoculars to his eyes and scanned the slope. He laughed. There wasn't just smoke, but a campfire—a big one—burning near the open entrance of a cave. "Well, I'll be damned!" Grinning, he scrambled to take off his pack. "Hold on a second, I'm going to grab the satellite phone and call the main camp. Let Amanda know where we are."

"You go for it. I'm heading down!"

"I'll send a signal flare for the others! Just wait for me!"

"I can't!" she shouted, already sprinting down the slope.

"Why?"

Janelle's worried voice echoed back toward him. "I see a bear!"

There was no time for thought, no time for fear. Ash knew the worst possible thing he could do was confront a grizzly. Vale had told him this at least ten times in the last few days. But he had no time to come up with another plan! Before he'd even gotten to his knees, the bear lunged toward Vale, slamming into her chest with the force of a Mack truck.

Time slowed.

Vale tumbled away, grizzly charging after her. Terrified, Ash forced his legs under him and stood up as the bear bit Vale midthigh. It shook Vale the way a dog would shake a rag doll. She swung limply back and forth, head smacking against the ground.

"No!" Ash screamed.

The grizzly roared and picked Vale up a second time—farther up her thigh—and shook her again. Vale's limbs swung slack, blood darkening her jeans.

"STOP!" Ash screamed.

The bear dropped Vale and turned. It opened its mouth, showing yellow-stained carnivorous teeth as it roared. The sound was so loud it made Ash's ears crackle. Adrenaline surged through his body, pushing him into action despite the pain. There was no time for thought, just flashes of life-and-death decisions, split-second reactions. A single thought pushed Ash forward.

I have to save Vale!

Ash reached down with his good hand and grabbed the unburned end of a branch from the campfire. Orange embers scattered as he lifted it up over his head. The movement caught the bear's attention.

With an ear-splitting roar, it charged.

Time slowed as Ash and the bear made eye contact. Details jumped into focus. *The bear galloping toward him. Snowflakes in the air. Vale on the ground.* Ash lifted the stick up, the way you'd hold a baseball bat. It was left-handed and unstable, but he forced every bit of his remaining strength into the swing. The burning bat whistled through the air and smashed into the side of the bear's muzzle as it reached him.

He might as well have hit a rock wall.

The grizzly roared and gnashed its teeth. It stood on its back legs, looming over him . . . at least eight feet tall. Ash swung the burning stick a second time. The grizzly swatted it from his hand like a toy.

"No!" Ash stumbled backward. "Get away! GO—"

His words were cut off as the bear slammed straight into his chest. Pain ricocheted across his ribs, threatening to send him into oblivion. Ash curled instinctively. Momentum tossed him back toward the fire, and he spun end over end. Dazed, he rolled to a sitting position. He looked over at Vale. She hadn't moved. *Is she dead?* His throat tightened, heartbreak tearing his chest open.

"Thanks, Vale. I owe you one."

"After crawling into camp last night in the shape you did? You owe me more *than one, my friend. I'm going to have to start charging you for all the rescues."*

"Maybe you should start a tally . . ."

"I'm sorry, Vale!" Tears rolled down his face. "I tried—I—I—"

There was a deafening gunshot boom, and an orange arc of light and smoke crossed the sky. Dumbstruck, Ash lifted his gaze. "Lightning . . . ?" It made no sense. *Nothing did.* The lightning disappeared into the snowy sky. Another orange explosion—like a meteor—followed it. This one detonated at the feet of the bear. It roared and stumbled backward, then turned and ran.

A rescue flare, some objective part of Ash's mind announced. He could hardly see it for the tears in his eyes. He tried to get his feet under him, but stumbled and fell. Desperate, Ash pushed through the pain, rolled sideways and sat up.

Vale was down, unmoving. The grizzly was retreating back into the forest. The burning flare filled the clearing with light, so brilliant it hurt his eyes.

Confused, Ash turned to look back the other direction as two figures appeared at the edge of the fire. One of them was Ms. Holland, flare gun in hand. The other was a man wearing a warden's uniform.

"Ashton!" Ms. Holland shouted. "Vale! Are you okay?"

Gravity shifted and Ash wobbled, then fell onto his back. Pain and unexpected relief filled him as his eyelids fluttered closed.

Their rescue had arrived.

Ash woke an indeterminate time later.

"Wha . . . ?"

"You're okay, Ash," a woman's calm voice said. "Just relax."

He blinked, struggling to focus on her words.

"I've got you now. I'm going to give you some oxygen. Okay?" She wove a narrow plastic tube over his face and pressed it under his nose. The dry scent reached his nostrils. "This will help you breathe."

He took a breath and coughed, wincing at his broken ribs.

"There you go," the woman said. "Take slow breaths."

Ash struggled to put his thoughts in order, but too many snippets jumbled his mind. Vale had been at his side one moment, gone the

bloody bandages in its place. An IV line ran from a pole to her wrist. Covered in mud, blood, and bandages, she looked absolutely terrible. A sob caught in Ash's throat.

He'd never been so happy to see anyone in his life.

"Hey," she said.

"Hey yourself. That was quite a super combo back there." Ash cleared his throat. "Fire and rain and a bear to top it off."

Vale smiled weakly. "Boss fight. Right?"

"Right. How're you feeling?"

She winced. "Like I tried to fight a bear and I lost."

He laughed, then groaned as his broken ribs grated together. "Yeah. Me too."

"That was pretty badass what you did," Vale said. She grinned at him, and the sight of it made Ash want to weep. "Seriously, though. It was awesome."

"Yeah," he said. "We make a good team." His throat ached, and he could feel tears ready to fall. He hated the feeling. But Ash couldn't stop staring. *Vale Shumway.* She wasn't just a friend, she was the best friend he'd ever had. Ash would fight for her. He'd die for her. Not even a question.

"Thanks for—" Vale's voice cracked. "Thanks for everything."

"That's what friends do, right?"

"Yeah."

Ash knew he should say something else—something memorable to mark the occasion—but big speeches were Vale's thing, not his. Besides, right now, he was too tired to talk.

The doors to the helicopter slammed shut, and the rotors began turning. One of the medical techs placed large sets of headphones over Ash's and Vale's ears, and all sound faded. Suddenly they were moving, up, up, and away, the valley falling down below them. Ash watched Vale the whole time. As exhaustion hit critical levels and his lids began to droop, he reached his hand out toward her.

Vale caught hold of his fingers, squeezed once, then let go. "We're going to be okay," she said, though Ash read the words on her lips rather than heard them. "We won."

Ash nodded. A moment later, sleep overtook him and he began to dream. He stood in the gamescape of *Immortal Defenders*, Vale in armor at his side.

CHAPTER FIFTEEN

"Once more into the fray. Into the last good fight I'll ever know."

JOHN OTTWAY, *THE GREY*

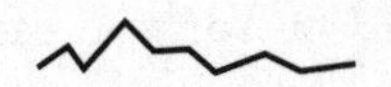

VALE STARED AT the clock, waiting for the alarm to ring.

6:29 a.m.

She blinked once . . . twice . . . and when she opened her eyes the third time, the digits changed.

6:30 a.m.

An upbeat song popped to life on the clock radio. On the bed, Mr. Bananas stood, stretched, then launched himself down to the floor. Vale heard the unlatched door jiggle, then open, as he padded down the hall.

With a yawn, Vale reached for the snooze button and clicked it off. She flopped back and stared at the ceiling, heart thudding in her chest. The day had arrived. With her leg healed and stitches out, it was time to return to regular classes.

Nothing to it but to do it.

She crawled from her bed and headed to the dresser to pull out jeans, a T-shirt, and then—with a sigh of annoyance—her gym clothes. She had just finished dressing and was pulling on her socks when Mr. Bananas reappeared in the doorway, Vale's mother close behind his flicking tail.

Debra stepped through the doorway and put her hands on her hips. "Get up, sleepyhead," she said. "It's time for . . ." Her words faded away as she caught sight of Vale dressed and sitting on her bed, gym clothes folded beside her. "Oh! You're already up."

"Uh-huh."

Her mother smiled, confusion mingling with joy. "Well, that's . . . that's *great*, Vale. Breakfast is on as soon as you're ready." She took a step toward the door, then turned back around. "Is everything okay, honey?"

"Everything's fine."

"You're up early today."

Vale shrugged. "It's my first day back. Didn't want to be late." The purring cat wound himself around Vale's legs, and she reached down to pet him. "Do you need something, Mom?"

"No, I just thought . . ." Her mother's narrow brows pulled together. "You sure you didn't have trouble sleeping? You're *never* up before your alarm."

"No trouble sleeping. No."

"You look a little pale."

"Do I?"

"Mm-hmm. You sure you're okay?" Debra laid a hand on Vale's forehead. "Do you feel warm? Is your fever back?"

"No, Mom. I just woke up before my alarm."

"Should I call Dr. Robbins? Check in with him?"

Vale squirmed away from her mother's hand. "Mom, stop. I don't think—"

"If you're in pain, Vale, then—"

"I'm fine," Vale said, though her mother's words carried on overtop of her.

"—we need to deal with it. I could try to get you an appointment today," Debra said. "I could call the Children's Hospital and see if—"

"Stop, Mom. Just . . . stop. I'm a little anxious about school. Nothing else. But it's fine."

"Anxious about what?"

Vale gave a tired laugh. "I don't know. About *everything*, I suppose. I just . . . I want to get today over with. Get back to normal." It surprised Vale to realize it was entirely true. While she'd once dreaded the thought of going to her first-period phys ed class, these days she hardly gave it a second thought. During her weeks at home, she'd finally made decisions on what she planned to do *after* high school too. A pile of college pamphlets sat on her bedside table along with her many books. Surviving in the Rocky Mountains with nothing but her wits to save her had given Vale a new perspective, a sense that she could survive, no matter *what* life threw at her.

She liked the feeling.

Vale's mother watched her for several seconds. "Ashton's already back at school, you know."

Vale turned her phone around to show her mother a long chain of texts. "I know that, Mom." She laughed. "He's texted me, like, five hundred times in the past two days." Vale and Ash had been best friends before they'd gotten lost in the woods. Surviving a bear attack had made them inseparable. "But even if Ash *wasn't* at school today, I'd be fine."

"Well, I'm glad you two have stayed in touch. You know what I heard?" Debra leaned toward her daughter and dropped her voice. "I heard he was pretty worried about you when you were in surgery."

Vale groaned. "Mom, don't start—"

"His mother told me he asked her every five minutes if there was news about you. Drove the nurses in the ward nuts."

"Mom, please stop—"

"I think he *likes* you, Vale." She tapped the phone's screen with her nail. "If he's texting you all the time, maybe there's *more* to it? I know you like him and—"

"It's not like that."

Debra had her mouth opened to say something else, but Vale lifted her hand and her mother closed it again. Vale was relieved. She'd had this discussion with her mother more than once in the past few years. She hoped at some point it would stick.

"Look, Mom, I'm *friends* with Ash, but nothing else. He's a nice guy. An amazing guy! And yes, we talk and text all the time. But I don't feel that way about him and I never will. I don't feel like that about . . . well, *anyone*." She shrugged. "So don't try to push the romance. Okay?"

"I . . . Okay."

Vale smiled. "Ash and I are friends. Really *good* friends and we have been forever. That's awesome on its own."

For a long time, her mother said nothing, and then she pulled Vale into a tight hug. "Yes, it is." She smiled as she let go. "I love you, Vale. You know that, right?"

"I do."

"You're tough. You're going to be fine today."

"I want to be *better* than fine, Mom. I want to be *happy* when I'm at school."

Her mother gave Vale a gentle smile. "Then go make that happen."

Vale nodded. "That's my plan."

Mike Reynolds was, of course, the first person Vale saw when she arrived at school. She rolled her eyes. *The universe has a really sick sense of humor.* Frustrated, she lifted her chin and headed through the doors.

"Yo! Valley Girl," Mike shouted as she neared. "Thought you were dead."

Screw you, Mike, Vale thought, and kept walking.

Mike followed.

"What?" He laughed. "You forget how to talk or something?" He stepped in front of her, and Vale skidded to a stop. Her hands were sweaty where they held on to her bag, but she wasn't scared. *Not anymore.* She wanted to get past.

"Get out of my way, Mike."

He laughed. "Ooooooh! Someone's in a bitchy mood this morning."

"I need to get to class. So do *you*." Vale took a step, and Mike moved to block her. She stepped the other way, and he did the same. Anger prickled under her calm. "Get *out* of my way, Mike."

"But I want to talk."

"I have literally zero interest in talking to you now or ever."

Mike's expression wobbled before he crossed his arms and grinned. "I heard that you were sleeping naked in a cave out there. Gone full Neanderth—"

"Move!" Vale snapped.

Again, she tried to get past, only to have Mike step back in front of her.

"Heard you and Hashbrown were doing the nasty when that helicopter—"

"I'm leaving." Vale put her chin down and started walking. "Move or I'm walking *through* you."

Mike stepped in her way, only this time Vale *didn't* stop, just slammed right into his shoulder and pushed past. Mike grunted and stumbled back against the wall. "What the . . . ?!"

She kept walking. *Not as heavy as a bear*, she thought. *Though he smells like one.*

"I'm not done talking!" he yelled.

Vale didn't slow down. Didn't turn back as he shouted: "Valley Girl!" She was done with Mike and the rest of the jerks who'd spent the past years taunting her. She wasn't backing down anymore. She didn't care. Didn't worry. Vale knew the truth.

She was tougher than the lot of them.

Ash was sitting on the bleachers in the gym, waiting for Ms. Holland to arrive, when he heard the whispers begin.

"Wondered if she was going to come back . . ."

". . . seems pretty late in the semester."

"Ash has been back for almost a week . . ."

He looked up from his new phone and followed the gaze of his classmates across the room to the doorway where Vale had just appeared. His breath caught. With her hair hanging in loose waves around her face and gym clothes on, she looked softer today. Less the tough-as-nails Vale he knew from the mountains and more the girl who was the last person chosen for every team, the target of relentless bullying.

The thought made his stomach hurt.

Ash stood and waved at her from the top of the bleachers, but Vale didn't see. She continued across the gym floor toward Ms. Holland. She held a piece of paper in one hand—a doctor's note, if Ash had to guess. Her chin was held high, jaw set.

A smile tugged the corner of Ash's mouth. *Such a badass.*

Ash stood from his seat and limped slowly down the bleachers. In the time since he'd returned to school, he had fallen back into the same place he'd been before. *Gamer, class clown, student voted most likely to live in his mother's basement until thirty . . . Ashton Hamid, everyone's friend.* Only Ash didn't know if any of that was *real* anymore. The mountains had changed something inside him, and the only person who understood this was Vale. She *got him* the way no one else did. Though texting was great, it was a relief to have her back at school again. His eyes followed her progress across the floor, but before he reached the bottom of the bleachers, another person reached Vale's side.

"Oh crap," Ash muttered. *Mike.* Seeing him, Ash's stride doubled.

For a few seconds, Mike and Vale spoke in tones too low to be heard. Suddenly Mike laughed, and his voice echoed forward: "Bet Ash could tell a story or two about that night, huh?"

People around them snickered.

"It wasn't like that," Vale said.

"Well, what *was* it like, huh?"

Ash broke into a jog.

"A bear came after us at the cave," Vale said. "Staying alive was kind of high on our priorities list."

Mike snorted. "I bet staying alive wasn't the *only* thing you two were doing."

Ash pushed himself into a sprint.

"We were literally trying not to die," Vale snapped. "Not that YOU would know a thing about survival."

Mike rolled his eyes. "Bet if I asked Ash about it, he'd tell me—"

Ash skidded to a stop at Vale's side. "Exactly the same thing as Vale did. So back off."

Mike laughed. "What's your problem, Hashbrown?"

"Vale and I are friends."

Mike smirked. "Friends with *benefits*. Am I right?"

"No," Ash growled. "We're *friends*, period. That's it. Not everything has to come down to sex, you know."

Mike laughed. "Only the *important* stuff."

"It. Isn't. Like. That!" Vale snapped.

Mike turned on her. "You know, Valley Girl, for such a stuck-up little know-it-all, you really—"

Ash's hands rolled into fists. "Stop!"

Mike turned. "Stop what?"

"You call her Valley Girl again," Ash said in a low voice, "and you're going to have to deal with me."

Mike's smile faltered. "What's that supposed to mean? I'll call her whatever I—"

"I'm not kidding, Mike."

"Jesus, Hashbrown. Don't be such a prissy little—"

"Try me!" Ash snapped.

At that moment, Ms. Holland arrived, the purple Tupperware container tucked under one arm. Ash knew he'd be suspended if he started a fight, but he didn't care. Vale had been his best friend for years. He owed her *this*, at least.

"Jesus!" Mike sneered. "Can't believe you're taking her side over—"

"Leave Vale ALONE!" Ash's voice boomed through the gym. Students paused midconversation to stare. On the far side of the gym, Ms. Holland abruptly switched directions, making a beeline toward them. "You're *always* going after Vale," Ash yelled. "Always messing with her. Just STOP!"

"So what? She's back, so you can't take a joke anymo—"

Ash stepped forward so fast, Mike's voice disappeared. Ashton Hamid was a foot taller than Mike, and today his happy face was flushed with anger. "Vale is my friend! All right? Leave her ALONE!"

"Or what?"

Ash stepped closer. "Or I'll MAKE you stop."

Mike smiled darkly. His stance widened. "Oh, you're gonna regret that. Nobody tells me what to—"

"Mike Reynolds!" Ms. Holland roared. "To the office NOW!" She stepped directly between the two boys. "Go NOW!"

Mike frowned. "But Ash was the one who—"

"GO!"

Swearing, Mike stormed away, heading out of the gym. Ms. Holland took two steps to follow him, then glanced back at Ash and Vale. "You okay?" she asked.

"Fine," Vale said.

"Yeah, I'm good," Ash added.

Ms. Holland nodded, then followed Mike out of the gym. The curious onlookers scattered, leaving the two friends standing alone in the center of the gym.

Vale turned to Ash and grinned. "Well, that escalated quickly."

Ash laughed. "Mike had it coming."

"Oh, he totally did." She bumped his shoulder. "Still pretty awesome, though."

Ash winked. "I try."

Vale giggled. "You succeed."

For a few minutes, they chatted about mindless day-to-day things—the homework they'd missed and the TV shows they were watching—only stopping when a whistle blew. Ms. Holland had returned to the gym. Mike had not.

"All right, everyone!" the teacher shouted. "New unit starts today. We're going to be doing paired fitness training. One person does the exercises, the other records times. Then you switch." Moans of disappointment followed her announcement. "You know the drill," Holland continued. She shook the box. "Toss your phones in the bin, then go find a partner. Doesn't matter who. We've got to get moving."

One by one, students dropped their phones into the box, then spread out as they fumbled to find partners. Ash set his phone into the purple container, his fingers twitchy without it warm in his palm. Vale did the same.

Ms. Holland paused next to them, and Ash's heart sank. *Am I getting sent to the office too?* But the teacher lowered her voice and said: "If Mike does anything like that again—if he *says* anything rude, or provokes you—I need you to tell me. Okay?"

Vale and Ash exchanged curious glances. "Uh . . . okay?" Ash said.

"You too, Vale," Ms. Holland added. "I'm serious here. That boy needs to stop. You tell me if he bothers you again. All right?"

Vale nodded. "I . . . I will."

"Good." And with a nod, Ms. Holland headed off.

Vale giggled.

"What?" Ash said.

"Only took her two months to notice."

Ash chuckled.

"So," Vale said. "Anything new? I mean, *besides* not dying in the woods."

Ash shrugged. "I've been doing a lot of gaming lately. Brian started a new D&D campaign. During our first adventure, I took command and—"

"You took my job?"

Ash stared. "Your . . . job?"

The corner of Vale's mouth twitched. "I thought we agreed I was going to be *commander*."

Ash's eyebrows rose. "But . . ."

"I've been waiting for you to tell me when the next Dungeons & Dragons campaign is happening."

"You have?"

"Of course I have. Thought I might try my hand at video games again too. So what's the plan? Are we taking on *Death Raiders* tonight, or *Immortal Defenders*, or both?"

A bright grin broke across Ash's face, and for the first time since he'd woken in the hospital, unbridled laughter overtook him. When he finally stopped, Vale was laughing too.

"Both would be fricking AMAZING!" he said.

"Then sign me up."

"I will, but . . . what changed your mind?"

"Well, you kept asking me about it, for one thing. And I had fun on the last D&D adventure . . . even if we *both* died." She laughed. "And I figured I ought to give video games a second chance. Got to level up somehow. Right?"

"Right," he said, then smiled. "You know, Vale: It's *really* good to have you back at school again."

She grinned. "Never thought I'd say it, but it really *is* good to be back."

ACKNOWLEDGMENTS

The writing of a book is a lengthy process, but I could not release *Switchback* without expressing my sincere gratitude to the many people who have shaped it along the way:

Thank you to my husband, my most enthusiastic collaborator, for reading every iteration of this project from beginning to end, so that I could make sure the language sounded "just right." You are the most patient human on Earth. Thank you also to my children for tolerating long periods when I couldn't play, as I wrote, rewrote, and rewrote again. A much-delayed thank-you to my late father for taking my siblings and me on any number of mountain "torture hikes" in a supposed attempt to build character. I think it worked.

A grateful shout-out to my fellow writers—far too many to name—who kept me going when my spark for writing was low. Thanks to Morty Mint, my agent, for his unwavering support and level-headed advice. An enthusiastic thank-you to Holly West, my editor, for her *Minority Report*–esque ability to see the larger structure of a story; she shaped this book into something worth reading. A heartfelt thank-you to the two sensitivity readers who went through each version of this book with an eye to details. My sincere gratitude and affection to the Swoon Reads publishing team, especially Emily Settle, Kelsey Marrujo, and Lauren Scobell, for their tireless efforts in bringing this project together. *Switchback* is yours as much as mine.

One final note of appreciation: For my grandfather, Frank Goble, who helped me to see the transcendent beauty of the mountains. In the 1930s and '40s, he trapped in the valley where Ash and Vale are lost. Frank never lived to see any of my books published, but I like to think he'd feel at home in this one.

Check out more books chosen for publication by readers like you.

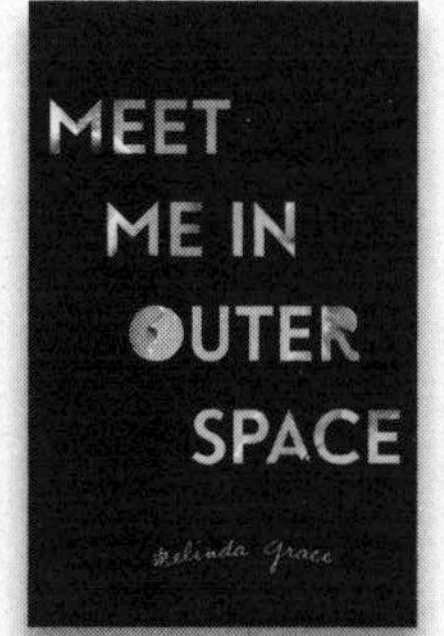